Ruskin Bond was born in Kasauli, Himachal Pradesh, in 1934, and grew up in Jamnagar (Gujarat), Dehradun and Shimla. In the course of a writing career spanning thirty-five years, he has written over a hundred short stories, essays, novels and more than thirty books for children. Three collections of the short stories, *The Night Train at Deoli*, *Time Stops at Shamli* and *Our Trees Still Grow in Dehra* have been published by Penguin India. He has also edited an anthology, *The Penguin Book of Indian Ghost Stories*.

The Room on the Roof was his first novel, written when he was seventeen, and it received the John Llewellyn Rhys Memorial Prize in 1957. *Vagrants in the Valley* was also written in his teens and picks up from where *The Room on the Roof* leaves off.

Ruskin Bond received the Sahitya Akademi Award for English writing in India for 1992, for *Our Trees Still Grow in Dehra*.

The Room on the Roof

✣

Vagrants in the Valley

two novels of adolescence

RUSKIN BOND

PENGUIN BOOKS

PENGUIN BOOKS
Published by the Penguin Group
Penguin Books India Pvt Ltd, 11 Community Centre, Panchsheel Park, New Delhi 110 017, India
Penguin Group (USA) Inc., 375 Hudson Street, New York, New York 10014, USA
Penguin Group (Canada), 10 Alcorn Avenue, Toronto, Ontario, Canada M4V 3B2 (a division of Pearson Penguin Canada Inc.)
Penguin Books Ltd, 80 Strand, London WC2R 0RL, England
Penguin Ireland, 25 St Stephen's Green, Dublin 2, Ireland (a division of Penguin Books Ltd)
Penguin Group (Australia), 250 Camberwell Road, Camberwell, Victoria 3124, Australia (a division of Pearson Australia Group Pty Ltd)
Penguin Group (NZ), cnr Airborne and Rosedale Road, Albany, Auckland 1310, New Zealand (a division of Pearson New Zealand Ltd)
Penguin Group (South Africa) (Pty) Ltd, 24 Sturdee Avenue, Rosebank, Johannesburg 2196, South Africa

Penguin Books Ltd, Registered Offices: 80 Strand, London WC2R 0RL, England

The Room on the Roof first published by André Deutsch 1956
Published by Penguin Books India 1987

Vagrants in the Valley first published by IBH Publishing Company, Bombay, as *The Young Vagrants* 1981

The Room on the Roof and *Vagrants in the Valley* first published in one volume by Penguin Books India 1993

Copyright © Ruskin Bond 1993

All rights reserved

10 9 8 7 6 5 4

Typeset in Palatino by Digital Technologies and Printing Solutions, New Delhi
Printed at Baba Barkhanath Printers, New Delhi

Contents

Introduction

These early works of fiction were written as separate novels, but they really belong together and to each other. *Vagrants in the Valley* carries on where *The Room on the Roof* leaves off, narrating the adolescent Rusty's further wanderings and adventures in search of an identity. Who was he, and where did he come from? Was he an Indian or an Anglo-Indian or an English boy born in India? I have since answered these questions for myself, certain that I am as Indian as the dust of the plains or the grass of a mountain meadow; but as a young man I had no such certainties, and to some extent Rusty represents the dilemma I faced. In *The Room* he 'discovers' the real India; in *Vagrants*, although he goes away, he knows he belongs here and that he will come back . . . .

The Room on the Roof was based on a journal I kept when I was seventeen, just out of school. When I went to England I turned it into a work of fiction, and after writing two drafts, found a sympathetic publisher in Andre Deutsch (and his partner, Diana Athill). It was not a best seller but it was kindly received by most critics (with the exception of John Wain, who said I wrote 'babu English'), and received the John Llewellyn Rhys Prize in 1957. This was an award given to a Commonwealth writer under thirty for 'an outstanding literary achievement'.

The Room has had a chequered publishing history, and is more widely read now than when it was first published. *Vagrants* has practically no publishing history.

Both books were serialized in *The Illustrated Weekly of India*, then edited by C. R. Mandy, who liked my work and published most of my early stories and novellas. *The Room*, illustrated by Mario, appeared in several issues of the *Weekly* in 1956; *Vagrants*, again illustrated by Mario, had its run in 1957. *The Room* had been written in England, when I was feeling very homesick for India; the boom of London's traffic was the boom of the Ganges, the naked elms and plane trees were mango trees laden with fruit . . . . But *Vagrants* was written the year after I had returned to India. It was not as successful, but I have always had a special affection for it, because it was written at a time when I was struggling to make a living as a freelance writer—no easy thing thirty-five years ago—living in a small rented flat above a ration shop on Dehra's Rajpur road, eating in a strange assortment of *dhabas*, and consorting with my fellow 'vagrants', some of whom are described in the book. It was a time of furious literary activity, when I wrote such stories as *The Night Train at Deoli* and *Time Stops at Shamli*, which are still favourites with many of my readers. Unlike the stories and unlike *The Room*, *Vagrants* remained unpublished (as a book) for many years. Although much of it is naïve, gauche and romantic (for I was all those things then), nevertheless it contained some of my best writing, and going through it again I find that it has lost none of its freshness. What was unique about both these novels was that they were portraits of adolescence written by an adolescent.

The other day I came across a letter from a boyhood friend, Jaishankar Kala, who came to see me shortly after I had left Dehra: 'You left Dehra rather mysteriously. Didn't leave a clue behind. Sometime after you left, I went to your room; your little plant wasn't there; I supposed that it must have died. Then I crept inside; your typewriter etc. wasn't there. Strange, I thought; everything in rather a domestic state; utensils, teapots, lipstick, powder. Perhaps Ruskin has got married, I thought. Thrill! I crept to the other room. A scream. A moan. A woman, three men! Protests, explanations. I managed to get out. Why did you run away from Dehra Dun?'

The main reason for running away was that I'd run out of money, and for two or three years I had to sit in an office in New Delhi, earning a monthly salary. Very little writing got done until, in the early 1960s, I made my great escape to the mountains.

When (in *Vagrants*), Sudheer the Lafunga borrows twenty rupees from his girlfriend, it may seem a trifling amount to the present-day reader. But in today's terms it was the equivalent of two or three hundred rupees. In 1957, freelancing from Dehra, I made three or four hundred rupees a month, just about enough to keep body and soul together. Isn't youth a wonderful thing? When we are young, we can put up with a great deal of discomfort in order to follow a dream. If, after thirty-five years, I'm still doing my own thing, it's because I haven't forgotten the dream.

Let no man take your dream away. It will sustain you to the end.

20 March 1993   *Ruskin Bond*

The Room on the Roof

Chapter I

THE light spring rain rode on the wind, into the trees, down the road; it brought an exhilarating freshness to the air, a smell of earth, a scent of flowers; it brought a smile to the eyes of the boy on the road.

The long road wound round the hills, rose and fell and twisted down to Dehra; the road came from the mountains and passed through the jungle and valley and, after passing through Dehra, ended somewhere in the bazaar. But just where it ended no one knew, for the bazaar was a baffling place, where roads were easily lost.

The boy was three miles out of Dehra. The further he could get from Dehra, the happier he was likely to be. Just now he was only three miles out of Dehra, so he was not very happy; and, what was worse, he was walking homewards.

He was a pale boy, with blue-grey eyes and fair hair; his face was rough and marked, and the lower lip hung loose and heavy. He had his hands in his pockets and his head down, which was the way he always walked, and which gave him a deceptively tired appearance. He was a lazy but not a tired person.

He liked the rain as it flecked his face, he liked the smell and the freshness; he did not look at his surroundings or notice them—his mind, as usual, was very far away—but he felt their atmosphere, and he smiled.

His mind was so very far away that it was a few minutes before he noticed the swish of bicycle wheels beside him. The cyclist did not pass the boy, but rode beside him, studying him, taking in every visible detail, the bare head, the open-necked shirt, the flannel trousers, the sandals, the thick hide belt round his waist. A European boy was no longer a common sight in Dehra, and Somi, the cyclist, was interested.

3

'Hullo,' said Somi, 'would you like me to ride you into town? If you are going to town?'

'No, I'm all right,' said the boy, without slackening his pace, 'I like to walk.'

'So do I, but it's raining.'

And to support Somi's argument, the rain fell harder.

'I like to walk in the rain,' said the boy. 'And I don't live in the town, I live outside it.'

Nice people didn't live *in* the town . . . .

'Well, I can pass your way,' persisted Somi, determined to help the stranger.

The boy looked again at Somi, who was dressed like him except for short pants and turban. Somi's legs were long and athletic, his colour was an unusually rich gold, his features were fine, his mouth broke easily into friendliness. It was impossible to resist the warmth of his nature.

The boy pulled himself up on the cross-bar, in front of Somi, and they moved off.

They rode slowly, gliding round the low hills, and soon the jungle on either side of the road began to give way to open fields and tea-gardens and then to orchards and one or two houses.

'Tell me when you reach your place,' said Somi. 'You stay with your parents?'

The boy considered the question too familiar for a stranger to ask, and made no reply.

'Do you like Dehra?' asked Somi.

'Not much,' said the boy with pleasure.

'Well, after England it must seem dull . . . . '

There was a pause and then the boy said: 'I haven't been to England. I was born here. I've never been anywhere else except Delhi.'

'Do you like Delhi?'

'Not much.'

They rode on in silence. The rain still fell, but the cycle moved smoothly over the wet road, making a soft, swishing sound.

Presently a man came in sight—no, it was not a man, it was a youth, but he had the appearance, the build of a man—walking towards town.

'Hey, Ranbir,' shouted Somi, as they neared the burly figure, 'want a lift?'

Ranbir ran into the road and slipped on to the carrier, behind Somi. The cycle wobbled a bit, but soon controlled itself and moved on, a little faster now.

Somi spoke into the boy's ear: 'Meet my friend Ranbir. He is the best wrestler in the bazaar.'

'Hullo, mister,' said Ranbir, before the boy could open his mouth.

'Hullo, mister,' said the boy.

Then Ranbir and Somi began a swift conversation in Punjabi, and the boy felt very lost; even, for some strange reason, jealous of the newcomer.

Now someone was standing in the middle of the road, frantically waving his arms and shouting incomprehensibly.

'It is Suri,' said Somi.

It was Suri.

Bespectacled and owlish to behold, Suri possessed an almost criminal cunning, and was both respected and despised by all who knew him. It was strange to find him out of town, for his interests were confined to people and their privacies; which privacies, when known to Suri, were soon made public.

He was a pale, bony, sickly boy, but he would probably live longer than Ranbir.

'Hey, give me a lift!' he shouted.

'Too many already,' said Somi.

'Oh, come on Somi, I'm nearly drowned.'

'It's stopped raining.'

'Oh, come on . . . .'

So Suri climbed on to the handlebar, which rather obscured Somi's view of the road and caused the cycle to wobble all over the place. Ranbir kept slipping on and off the carrier, and the boy found the cross-bar exceedingly uncomfortable. The cycle had barely been controlled when Suri started to complain.

'It hurts,' he whimpered.

'I haven't got a cushion,' said Somi.

'It is a cycle,' said Ranbir bitingly, 'not a Rolls Royce.'

Suddenly the road fell steeply, and the cycle gathered speed.

'Take it easy, now,' said Suri, 'or I'll fly off!'

'Hold tight,' warned Somi. 'It's downhill nearly all the way. We will have to go fast because the brakes aren't very good.'

'Oh, Mummy!' wailed Suri.

'Shut up!' said Ranbir.

The wind hit them with a sudden force, and their clothes blew up like balloons, almost tearing them from the machine. The boy forgot his discomfort and clung desperately to the cross-bar, too nervous to say a word. Suri howled and Ranbir kept telling him to shut up, but Somi was enjoying the ride. He laughed merrily, a clear, ringing laugh, a laugh that bore no malice and no derision but only enjoyment, fun . . . .

'It's all right for you to laugh,' said Suri, 'If anything happens, *I'll* get hurt!'

'If anything happens,' said Somi, 'we *all* get hurt!'

'That's right,' shouted Ranbir from behind.

The boy closed his eyes and put his trust in God and Somi—but mainly Somi . . . .

'Oh, Mummy!' wailed Suri.

'Shut up!' said Ranbir.

The road twisted and turned as much as it could, and rose a little only to fall more steeply the other side. But eventually it began to even out, for they were nearing the town and almost in the residential area.

'The run is over,' said Somi, a little regretfully.

'Oh, Mummy!'

'Shut up.'

The boy said: 'I must get off now, I live very near.' Somi skidded the cycle to a standstill, and Suri shot off the handlebar into a muddy side-track. The boy slipped off, but Somi and Ranbir remained on their seats, Ranbir steadying the cycle with his feet on the ground.

'Well, thank you,' said the boy.

Somi said: 'Why don't you come and have your meal with us, there is not much further to go.'

The boy's shyness would not fall away.

'I've got to go home,' he said. 'I'm expected. Thanks very much.'

'Well, come and see us some time,' said Somi. 'If you come to the chaat shop in the bazaar, you are sure to find one of us. You know the bazaar?'

'Well, I have passed through it—in a car.'

'Oh.'

The boy began walking away, his hands once more in his pockets.

'Hey!' shouted Somi. 'You didn't tell us your name!'

The boy turned and hesitated and then said, 'Rusty . . . . '

'See you soon, Rusty,' said Somi, and the cycle pushed off.

The boy watched the cycle receding down the road, and Suri's shrill voice came to him on the wind. It had stopped raining, but the boy was unaware of this; he was almost home, and that was a miserable thought. To his surprise and disgust, he found himself wishing he had gone into Dehra with Somi.

He stood in the side-track and stared down the empty road; and, to his surprise and disgust, he felt immeasurably lonely.

Chapter II

WHEN a large white butterfly settled on the missionary's wife's palatial bosom, she felt flattered, and allowed it to remain there. Her garden was beginning to burst into flower, giving her great pleasure—her husband gave her none—and such fellow-feeling as to make her tread gingerly among the caterpillars.

Mr John Harrison, the boy's guardian, felt only contempt for the good lady's buoyancy of spirit, but nevertheless gave her an ingratiating smile.

'I hope you'll put the boy to work while I'm away,' he said. 'Make some use of him. He dreams too much. Most unfortunate that he's finished with school, I don't know what to do with him.'

'He doesn't know what to do with himself,' said the missionary's wife. 'But I'll keep him occupied. He can do some weeding, or read to me in the afternoon. I'll keep an eye on him.'

'Good,' said the guardian. And, having cleared his conscience, he made quick his escape.

Over lunch he told the boy: 'I'm going to Delhi tomorrow. Business.'

It was the only thing he said during the meal. When he had finished eating, he lighted a cigarette and erected a curtain of smoke between himself and the boy. He was a heavy smoker, his fingers were stained a deep yellow.

'How long will you be gone, sir?' asked Rusty, trying to sound casual.

Mr Harrison did not reply. He seldom answered the boy's questions, and his own were stated, not asked; he probed and suggested, sharply, quickly, without ever encouraging loose conversation. He never talked about himself; he never argued: he would tolerate no argument.

He was a tall man, neat in appearance; and, though over forty, looked younger because he kept his hair short, shaving above the ears. He had a small ginger toothbrush moustache.

Rusty was afraid of his guardian.

Mr Harrison, who was really a cousin of the boy's father, had done a lot for Rusty, and that was why the boy was afraid of him. Since his parents had died, Rusty had been kept, fed and paid for, and sent to an expensive school in the hills that was run on 'exclusively European lines'. He had, in a way, been bought by Mr Harrison. And now he was owned by him. And he must do as his guardian wished.

Rusty was ready to do as his guardian wished: he had always obeyed him. But he was afraid of the man, afraid of his silence and of the ginger moustache and of the supple malacca cane that lay in the glass cupboard in the drawing-room.

Lunch over, the boy left his guardian giving the cook orders, and went to his room.

The window looked out on the garden path, and a sweeper boy moved up and down the path, a bucket clanging against his naked thighs. He wore only a loincloth, his body was bare and burnt a deep brown, and his head was shaved clean. He went to and from the water-tank, and every time he returned to it he bathed, so that his body continually glistened with moisture.

Apart from Rusty, the only boy in the European community of Dehra was this sweeper boy, the low-caste untouchable, the cleaner of pots. But the two seldom spoke to each other, one was a servant and the other a sahib and anyway, muttered Rusty to himself, playing with the sweeper boy would be unhygienic . . . .

The missionary's wife had said: 'Even if you were an Indian, my child, you would not be allowed to play with the sweeper boy.' So that Rusty often wondered: with whom, then, could the sweeper boy play?

The untouchable passed by the window and smiled, but Rusty looked away.

Over the tops of the cherry trees were mountains. Dehra lay in a valley in the foothills, and the small, diminishing European community had its abode on the outskirts of the town.

Mr John Harrison's house, and the other houses, were all built in an English style, with neat front gardens and name-plates on the gates. The surroundings on the whole were so English that the people often found it difficult to believe that they did live at the foot of the Himalayas, surrounded by India's thickest jungles. India started a mile away, where the bazaar began.

To Rusty, the bazaar sounded a fascinating place, and what he had seen of it from the window of his guardian's car had been enough to make his heart pound excitedly and his imagination soar; but it was a forbidden place—'full of thieves and germs' said the missionary's wife—and the boy never entered it save in his dreams.

For Mr Harrison, the missionaries, and their neighbours, this country district of blossoming cherry trees was India. They knew there was a bazaar and a real India not far away, but they did not speak of such places, they chose not to think about them.

The community consisted mostly of elderly people, the others had left soon after independence. These few stayed because they were too old to start life again in another country, where there would be no servants and very little sunlight; and, though they complained of their lot and criticized the government, they knew their money could buy them their comforts: servants, good food, whisky, almost anything—except the dignity they cherished most . . . .

But the boy's guardian, though he enjoyed the same comforts, remained in the country for different reasons. He did not care who were the rulers so long as they didn't take away his business; he had shares in a number of small tea-estates and owned some land—forested land—where, for instance, he hunted deer and wild pig.

Rusty, being the only young person in the community, was the centre of everyone's attention, particularly the ladies'.

He was also very lonely.

Every day he walked aimlessly along the road, over the hill-side; brooding on the future, or dreaming of sudden and perfect companionship, romance and heroics; hardly ever conscious of the present. When an opportunity for friendship did present itself, as it had the previous day, he shied away, preferring his own company.

His idle hours were crowded with memories, snatches of childhood. He could not remember what his parents were like, but in his mind there were pictures of sandy beaches covered with sea-shells of every description. They had lived on the west coast, in the Gulf of Kutch; there had been a gramophone that played records of Gracie Fields and Harry Lauder, and a captain of a cargo-ship who gave the child bars of chocolate and piles of comics—*The Dandy, Beano, Tiger Tim*—and spoke of the wonderful countries he had visited. But the boy's guardian seldom spoke of Rusty's childhood, or his parents, and this secrecy lent mystery to the vague, undefined memories that hovered in the boy's mind like hesitant ghosts.

Rusty spent much of his time studying himself in the dressing-table mirror; he was able to ignore his pimples and see a grown man, worldly and attractive. Though only sixteen, he felt much older.

He was white. His guardian was pink, and the missionary's wife a bright red, but Rusty was white. With his thick lower lip and prominent cheek-bones, he looked slightly Mongolian, especially in a half-light. He often wondered why no one else in the community had the same features.

*

Mr John Harrison was going to Delhi.

Rusty intended making the most of his guardian's absence: he would squeeze all the freedom he could out of the next few days; explore, get lost, wander afar; even if it were only to find new places to dream in. So he threw himself on the bed and visualized the morrow . . . where should he go—into the hills again, into the forest? Or should he listen to the devil in his heart and go into the bazaar? Tomorrow he would know, tomorrow . . . .

Chapter III

I T was a cold morning, sharp and fresh. It was quiet until the sun came shooting over the hills, lifting the mist from the valley and clearing the blood-shot from the sky. The ground was wet with dew.

On the maidan, a broad stretch of grassland, Ranbir and another youth wrestled each other, their muscles rippling, their well-oiled limbs catching the first rays of the sun as it climbed the horizon. Somi sat on his veranda steps; his long hair loose, resting of his knees, drying in the morning sun. Suri was still dead to the world, lost in blanket; he cared not for the morning or the sun.

Rusty stood at the gate until his guardian was comfortably seated behind the wheel of the car, and did not move until it had disappeared round the bend in the road.

The missionary's wife, that large cauliflower-like lady, rose unexpectedly from behind a hedge and called: 'Good morning, dear! If you aren't very busy this morning, would you like to give me a hand pruning this hedge?'

The missionary's wife was fond of putting Rusty to work in her garden: if it wasn't cutting the hedge, it was weeding the flower-beds and watering the plants, or clearing the garden path of stones, or hunting beetles and ladybirds and dropping them over the wall.

'Oh, good morning,' stammered Rusty. 'Actually, I was going for a walk. Can I help you when I come back, I won't be long . . . . '

The missionary's wife was rather taken aback, for Rusty seldom said no; and before she could make another sally the boy was on his way. He had a dreadful feeling she would call him back; she was a kind woman, but talkative and boring, and Rusty knew what would follow the garden work: weak tea or lemonade, and then a game of cards, probably beggar-my-neighbour.

12

But to his relief she called after him: 'All right, dear, come back soon. And be good!'

He waved to her and walked rapidly down the road. And the direction he took was different to the one in which he usually wandered.

Far down this road was the bazaar. First Rusty must pass the rows of neat cottages, arriving at a commercial area—Dehra's Westernized shopping centre—where Europeans, rich Indians, and American tourists *en route* for Mussoorie, could eat at smart restaurants and drink prohibited alcohol. But the boy was afraid and distrustful of anything smart and sophisticated, and he hurried past the shopping centre.

He came to the Clock Tower, which was a tower without a clock. It had been built from public subscriptions but not enough money had been gathered for the addition of a clock. It had been lifeless five years but served as a good landmark. On the other side of the Clock Tower lay the bazaar, and in the bazaar lay India. On the other side of the Clock Tower began life itself. And all three—the bazaar and India and life itself—were forbidden.

Rusty's heart was beating fast as he reached the Clock Tower. He was about to defy the law of his guardian and of his community. He stood at the Clock Tower, nervous, hesitant, biting his nails. He was afraid of discovery and punishment, but hungering curiosity impelled him forward.

The bazaar and India and life itself all began with a rush of noise and confusion.

The boy plunged into the throng of bustling people; the road was hot and close, alive with the cries of vendors and the smell of cattle and ripening dung. Children played hopscotch in alleyways or gambled with coins, scuffling in the gutter for a lost anna. And the cows moved leisurely through the crowd, nosing around for paper and stale, discarded vegetables; the more daring cows helping themselves at open stalls. And above the uneven tempo of the noise came the blare of a loudspeaker playing a popular piece of music.

Rusty moved along with the crowd, fascinated by the sight of beggars lying on the roadside: naked and emaciated half-humans, some skeletons, some covered with sores; old men dying, children dying, mothers with sucking babies, living and dying. But, strangely enough, the boy could feel nothing for these people; perhaps it was because they were no longer recognizable as humans or because he could not see himself in the same circumstances. And no one else in the bazaar seemed to feel for them. Like the cows and the loudspeaker, the beggars were a natural growth in the bazaar, and only the well-to-do—sacrificing a few annas to placate their consciences—were aware of the beggars' presence.

Every little shop was different from the one next to it. After the vegetable stand, green and wet, came the fruit stall; and, after the fruit stall, the tea and betel-leaf shop; then the astrologer's platform (Manmohan Mukuldev, B.Astr., foreign degree), and after the astrologer's the toy shop, selling trinkets of gay colours. And then, after the toy shop, another from whose doors poured clouds of smoke.

Out of curiosity Rusty turned to the shop from which the smoke was coming. But he was not the only person making for it. Approaching from the opposite direction was Somi on his bicycle.

Somi, who had not seen Rusty, seemed determined on riding right into the smoky shop on his bicycle, unfortunately his way was blocked by Maharani, the queen of the bazaar cows, who moved aside for no one. But the cycle did not lose speed.

Rusty, seeing the cycle but not recognizing the rider, felt sorry for the cow, it was sure to be hurt. But, with the devil in his heart or in the wheels of his machine, Somi swung clear of Maharani and collided with Rusty and knocked him into the gutter.

Accustomed as Rusty was to the delicate scents of the missionary's wife's sweet-peas and the occasional smell of bathroom disinfectant, he was nevertheless overpowered by the odour of bad vegetables and kitchen water that rose from the gutter.

'What the hell do you think you're doing?' he cried, choking and spluttering.

'Hullo,' said Somi, gripping Rusty by the arm and helping him up, 'so sorry, not my fault. Anyway, we meet again!'

Rusty felt for injuries and, finding none, exclaimed: 'Look at the filthy mess I'm in!'

14

Somi could not help laughing at the other's unhappy condition. 'Oh, that is not filth, it is only cabbage water! Do not worry, the clothes will dry . . . .'

His laugh rang out merrily, and there was something about the laugh, some music in it perhaps, that touched a chord of gaiety in Rusty's own heart. Somi was smiling, and on his mouth the smile was friendly and in his soft brown eyes it was mocking.

'Well, I am sorry,' said Somi, extending his hand.

Rusty did not take the hand but, looking the other up and down, from turban to slippers, forced himself to say: 'Get out of my way, please.'

'You are a snob,' said Somi without moving. 'You are a very funny one too.'

'I am not a snob,' said Rusty involuntarily.

'Then why not forget an accident?'

'You could have missed me, but you didn't try.'

'But if I had missed you, I would have hit the cow! You don't know Maharani, if you hurt her she goes mad and smashes half the bazaar! Also, the bicycle might have been spoilt . . . . Now please come and have chaat with me.'

Rusty had no idea what was meant by the word chaat, but before he could refuse the invitation Somi had bundled him into the shop from which the smoke still poured.

At first nothing could be made out; then gradually the smoke seemed to clear and there in front of the boys, like some shining god, sat a man enveloped in rolls of glistening, oily flesh. In front of him, on a coal fire, was a massive pan in which sizzled a sea of fat; and with deft, practised fingers, he moulded and flipped potato cakes in and out of the pan.

The shop was crowded; but so thick was the screen of smoke and steam, that it was only the murmur of conversation which made known the presence of many people. A plate made of banana leaves was thrust into Rusty's hands, and two fried cakes suddenly appeared in it.

'Eat!' said Somi, pressing the novice down until they were both seated on the floor, their backs to the wall.

'They are tikkees,' explained Somi, 'tell me if you like them.'

15

Rusty tasted a bit. It was hot. He waited a minute, then tasted another bit. It was still hot but in a different way; now it was lively, interesting; it had a different taste to anything he had eaten before. Suspicious but inquisitive, he finished the tikkee and waited to see if anything would happen.

'Have you had before?' asked Somi.

'No,' said Rusty anxiously, 'what will it do?'

'It might worry your stomach a little at first, but you will get used to it the more often you eat. So finish the other one too.'

Rusty had not realized the extent of his submission to the other's wishes. At one moment he had been angry, ill-mannered; but, since the laugh, he had obeyed Somi without demur.

Somi wore a cotton tunic and shorts, and sat cross-legged, his feet pressed against his thighs. His skin was a golden brown, dark on his legs and arms but fair, very fair, where his shirt lay open. His hands were dirty; but eloquent. His eyes, deep brown and dreamy, had depth and roundness.

He said: 'My name is Somi, please tell me what is yours, I have forgotten.'

'Rusty . . . .'

'How do you do,' said Somi, 'I am very pleased to meet you, haven't we met before?'

Rusty mumbled to himself in an effort to sulk.

'That was a long time ago,' said Somi, 'now we are friends, yes, best favourite friends!'

Rusty continued to mumble under his breath, but he took the warm muddy hand that Somi gave him, and shook it. He finished the tikkee on his leaf, and accepted another. Then he said: 'How do you do, Somi, I am very pleased to meet you.'

Chapter IV

THE missionary's wife's head projected itself over the garden wall and broke into a beam of welcome. Rusty hurriedly returned the smile.

'Where have you been, dear?' asked his garrulous neighbour. 'I was expecting you for lunch. You've never been away so long, I've finished all my work now, you know . . . . Was it a nice walk? I know you're thirsty, come in and have a nice cool lemonade, there's nothing like iced lemonade to refresh one after a long walk. I remember when I was a girl, having to walk down to Dehra from Mussoorie, I filled my thermos with lemonade . . . .'

But Rusty had gone. He did not wish to hurt the missionary's wife's feelings by refusing the lemonade but, after experiencing the chaat shop, the very idea of a lemonade offended him. But he decided that this Sunday he would contribute an extra four annas to the missionary's fund for upkeep of church, wife and garden; and, with this good thought in mind, went to his room.

The sweeper boy passed by the window, his buckets clanging, his feet going slip-slop in the watery path.

Rusty threw himself on his bed. And now his imagination began building dreams on a new-found reality, for he had agreed to meet Somi again.

And so, the next day, his steps took him to the chaat shop in the bazaar; past the Clock Tower, past the smart shops, down the road, far from the guardian's house.

The fleshy god of the tikkees smiled at Rusty in a manner that seemed to signify that the boy was now likely to become a Regular Customer. The banana plate was ready, the tikkees in it flavoured with spiced sauces.

'Hallo, best favourite friend,' said Somi, appearing out of the

17

surrounding vapour, his slippers loose, chup-chup-chup; loose, open slippers that hung on to the toes by a strap and slapped against the heels as he walked. 'I am glad you come again. After tikkees you must have something else, chaat or gol-guppas, all right?'

Somi removed his slippers and joined Rusty, who had somehow managed to sit cross-legged on the ground in the proper fashion.

Somi said, 'Tell me something about yourself. By what misfortune are you an Englishman? How is it that you have been here all your life and never been to a chaat shop before?'

'Well, my guardian is very strict,' said Rusty. 'He wanted to bring me up in English ways, and he has succeeded . . . .'

'Till now,' said Somi, and laughed, the laugh rippling up in his throat, breaking out and forcing its way through the smoke.

Then a large figure loomed in front of the boys, and Rusty recognized him as Ranbir, the youth he had met on the bicycle.

'Another best favourite friend,' said Somi.

Ranbir did not smile, but opened his mouth a little, gaped at Rusty, and nodded his head. When he nodded, hair fell untidily across his forehead; thick black bushy hair, wild and uncontrollable. He wore a long white cotton tunic hanging out over his baggy pyjamas; his feet were bare and dirty; big feet, strong.

'Hullo, mister,' said Ranbir, in a gruff voice that disguised his shyness. He said no more for a while, but joined them in their meal.

They ate chaat, a spicy salad of potato, guava and orange; and then gol-guppas, baked flour-cups filled with burning syrups. Rusty felt at ease and began to talk, telling his companions about his school in the hills, the house of his guardian, Mr Harrison himself, and the supple malacca cane. The story was listened to with some amusement: apparently Rusty's life had been very dull to date, and Somi and Ranbir pitied him for it.

'Tomorrow is Holi,' said Ranbir, 'you must play with me, then you will be my friend.'

'What is Holi?' asked Rusty.

Ranbir looked at him in amazement. 'You do not know about Holi! It is the Hindu Festival of Colour! It is the day on which we celebrate the coming of spring, when we throw colour on each other and shout and sing and forget our misery, for the colours mean the rebirth of spring and a new life in our hearts . . . . You do not know of it!'

Rusty was somewhat bewildered by Ranbir's sudden eloquence, and began to have doubts about this game; it seemed to him a primitive sort of pastime, this throwing of paint about the place.

'I might get into trouble,' he said. 'I'm not supposed to come here, anyway, and my guardian might return any day . . . . '

'Don't tell him about it,' said Ranbir.

'Oh, he has ways of finding out. I'll get a thrashing.'

'Huh!' said Ranbir, a disappointed and somewhat disgusted expression on his mobile face. 'You are afraid to spoil your clothes, mister, that is it. You are just a snob.'

Somi laughed. 'That's what I told him yesterday, and only then did he join me in the chaat shop. I think we should call him a snob whenever he makes excuses.'

Rusty was enjoying the chaat. He ate gol-guppa after gol-guppa, until his throat was almost aflame and his stomach burning itself out. He was not very concerned about Holi. He was content with the present, content to enjoy the new-found pleasures of the chaat shop, and said: 'Well, I'll see . . . If my guardian doesn't come back tomorrow, I'll play Holi with you, all right?'

Ranbir was pleased. He said, 'I will be waiting in the jungle behind your house. When you hear the drum-beat in the jungle, then it is me. Then come.'

'Will you be there too, Somi?' asked Rusty. Somehow, he felt safe in Somi's presence.

'I do not play Holi,' said Somi. 'You see, I am different to Ranbir. I wear a turban and he does not, also there is a bangle on my wrist, which means that I am a Sikh. We don't play it. But I will see you the day after, here in the chaat shop.'

Somi left the shop, and was swallowed up by smoke and steam, but the chup-chup of his loose slippers could be heard for some time, until their sound was lost in the greater sound of the bazaar outside.

In the bazaar, people haggled over counters, children played in the spring sunshine, dogs courted one another, and Ranbir and Rusty continued eating gol-guppas.

*

The afternoon was warm and lazy, unusually so for spring; very quiet, as though resting in the interval between the spring and the coming winter. There was no sign of the missionary's wife or the sweeper boy when Rusty returned, but Mr Harrison's car stood in the driveway of the house.

At sight of the car, Rusty felt a little weak and frightened; he had not expected his guardian to return so soon and had, in fact, almost forgotten his existence. But now he forgot all about the chaat shop and Somi and Ranbir, and ran up the veranda steps in a panic.

Mr Harrison was at the top of the veranda steps, standing behind the potted palms.

The boy said, 'Oh, hullo, sir, you're back!' He knew of nothing else to say, but tried to make his little piece sound enthusiastic.

'Where have you been all day?' asked Mr Harrison, without looking once at the startled boy. 'Our neighbours haven't seen much of you lately.'

'I've been for a walk, sir.'

'You have been to the bazaar.'

The boy hesitated before making a denial; the man's eyes were on him now, and to lie Rusty would have had to lower his eyes—and this he could not do . . . .

'Yes, sir, I went to the bazaar.'

'May I ask why?'

'Because I had nothing to do.'

'If you had nothing to do, you could have visited our neighbours. The bazaar is not the place for you. You know that.'

'But nothing happened to me . . . .'

'That is not the point,' said Mr Harrison, and now his normally dry voice took on a faint shrill note of excitement, and he spoke rapidly. 'The point is, I have told you never to visit the bazaar. You belong here, to this house, this road, these people. Don't go where you don't belong.'

Rusty wanted to argue, longed to rebel, but fear of Mr Harrison held him back. He wanted to resist the man's authority, but he was conscious of the supple malacca cane in the glass cupboard.

'I'm sorry, sir . . . . '

But his cowardice did him no good. The guardian went over to the glass cupboard, brought out the cane, flexed it in his hands. He said: 'It is not enough to say you are sorry, you must be made to feel sorry. Bend over the sofa.'

The boy bent over the sofa, clenched his teeth and dug his fingers into the cushions. The cane swished through the air, landing on his bottom with a slap, knocking the dust from his pants. Rusty felt no pain. But his guardian waited, allowing the cut to sink in, then he administered the second stroke, and this time it hurt, it stung into the boy's buttocks, burning up the flesh, conditioning it for the remaining cuts.

At the sixth stroke of the supple malacca cane, which was usually the last, Rusty let out a wild whoop, leapt over the sofa and charged from the room.

He lay groaning on his bed until the pain had eased.

But the flesh was so sore that he could not touch the place where the cane had fallen. Wriggling out of his pants, he examined his back-side in the mirror. Mr Harrison had been most accurate: a thick purple welt stretched across both cheeks, and a little blood trickled down the boy's thigh. The blood had a cool, almost soothing effect, but the sight of it made Rusty feel faint.

He lay down and moaned for pleasure. He pitied himself enough to want to cry, but he knew the futility of tears. But the pain and the sense of injustice he felt were both real.

A shadow fell across the bed. Someone was at the window, and Rusty looked up.

The sweeper boy showed his teeth.

'What do you want?' asked Rusty gruffly.

'You hurt, Chotta Sahib?'

The sweeper boy's sympathies provoked only suspicion in Rusty.

'You told Mr Harrison where I went!' said Rusty.

But the sweeper boy cocked his head to one side, and asked innocently, 'Where you went, Chotta Sahib?'

'Oh, never mind. Go away.'

'But you hurt?'

'Get out!' shouted Rusty.

The smile vanished, leaving only a sad frightened look in the sweeper boy's eyes.

Rusty hated hurting people's feelings, but he was not accustomed to familiarity with servants; and yet, only a few minutes ago, he had been beaten for visiting the bazaar where there were so many like the sweeper boy.

The sweeper boy turned from the window, leaving wet finger-marks on the sill; then lifted his buckets from the ground and, with his knees bent to take the weight, walked away. His feet splashed a little in the water he had spilt, and the soft red mud flew up and flecked his legs.

Angry with his guardian and with the servant and most of all with himself, Rusty buried his head in his pillow and tried to shut out reality; he forced a dream, in which he was thrashing Mr Harrison until the guardian begged for mercy.

Chapter V

IN the early morning, when it was still dark, Ranbir stopped in
the jungle behind Mr Harrison's house, and slapped his drum.
His thick mass of hair was covered with red dust and his body,
naked but for a cloth round his waist, was smeared green; he
looked like a painted god, a green god. After a minute he slapped
the drum again, then sat down on his heels and waited.

Rusty woke to the sound of the second drum-beat, and lay in
bed and listened; it was repeated, travelling over the still air and
in through the bedroom window. Dhum! . . . a double-beat now,
one deep, one high, insistent, questioning . . . . Rusty remembered
his promise, that he would play Holi with Ranbir, meet him in the
jungle when he beat the drum. But he had made the promise on
the condition that his guardian did not return; he could not
possibly keep it now, not after the thrashing he had received.

Dhum-dhum, spoke the drum in the forest; dhum-dhum,
impatient and getting annoyed . . . .

'Why can't he shut up,' muttered Rusty, 'does he want to wake
Mr Harrison . . . . '

Holi, the Festival of Colours, the arrival of spring, the rebirth
of the new year, the awakening of love, what were these things to
him, they did not concern his life, he could not start a new life, not
for one day . . . and besides, it all sounded very primitive, this
throwing of colour and beating of drums . . . .

Dhum-dhum!

The boy sat up in bed.

The sky had grown lighter.

From the distant bazaar came a new music, many drums and
voices, faint but steady, growing in rhythm and excitement. The
sound conveyed something to Rusty, something wild and
emotional, something that belonged to his dream-world, and on a

23

sudden impulse he sprang out of bed.

He went to the door and listened; the house was quiet, he bolted the door. The colours of Holi, he knew, would stain his clothes, so he did not remove his pyjamas. In an old pair of flattened rubber-soled tennis shoes, he climbed out of the window and ran over the dew-wet grass, down the path behind the house, over the hill and into the jungle.

When Ranbir saw the boy approach, he rose from the ground. The long hand-drum, the dholak, hung at his waist. As he rose, the sun rose. But the sun did not look as fiery as Ranbir who, in Rusty's eyes, appeared as a painted demon, rather than as a god.

'You are late, mister,' said Ranbir, 'I thought you were not coming.'

He had both his fists closed, but when he walked towards Rusty he opened them, smiling widely, a white smile in a green face. In his right hand was the red dust and in his left hand the green dust. And with his right hand he rubbed the red dust on Rusty's left cheek, and then with the other hand he put the green dust on the boy's right cheek; then he stood back and looked at Rusty and laughed. Then, according to the custom, he embraced the bewildered boy. It was a wrestler's hug, and Rusty winced breathlessly.

'Come,' said Ranbir, 'let us go and make the town a rainbow.'

*

And truly, that day there was an outbreak of spring.

The sun came up, and the bazaar woke up. The walls of the houses were suddenly patched with splashes of colour, and just as suddenly the trees seemed to have burst into flower; for in the forest there were armies of rhododendrons, and by the river the poinsettias danced; the cherry and the plum were in blossom; the snow in the mountains had melted, and the streams were rushing torrents; the new leaves on the trees were full of sweetness, and the young grass held both dew and sun, and made an emerald of every dew-drop.

The infection of spring spread simultaneously through the world of man and the world of nature, and made them one.

Ranbir and Rusty moved round the hill, keeping in the fringe of the jungle until they had skirted not only the European community but also the smart shopping centre. They came down dirty little side-streets where the walls of houses, stained with the wear and tear of many years of meagre habitation, were now stained again with the vivid colours of Holi. They came to the Clock Tower.

At the Clock Tower, spring had really been declared open. Clouds of coloured dust rose in the air and spread, and jets of water—green and orange and purple, all rich emotional colours—burst out everywhere.

Children formed groups. They were armed mainly with bicycle pumps, or pumps fashioned from bamboo stems, from which was squirted liquid colour. And the children paraded the main road, chanting shrilly and clapping their hands. The men and women preferred the dust to the water. They too sang, but their chanting held a significance, their hands and fingers drummed the rhythms of spring, the same rhythms, the same songs that belonged to this day every year of their lives.

Ranbir was met by some friends and greeted with great hilarity. A bicycle pump was directed at Rusty and a jet of sooty black water squirted into his face.

Blinded for a moment, Rusty blundered about in great confusion. A horde of children bore down on him, and he was subjected to a pumping from all sides. His shirt and pyjamas, drenched through, stuck to his skin; then someone gripped the end of his shirt and tugged at it until it tore and came away. Dust was thrown on the boy, on his face and body, roughly and with full force, and his tender, under-exposed skin smarted beneath the onslaught.

Then his eyes cleared. He blinked and looked wildly round at the group of boys and girls who cheered and danced in front of him. His body was running mostly with sooty black, streaked with red, and his mouth seemed full of it too, and he began to spit.

Then, one by one, Ranbir's friends approached Rusty.

Gently, they rubbed dust on the boy's cheeks, and embraced him; they were so like many flaming demons that Rusty could not distinguish one from the other. But this gentle greeting, coming so

25

soon after the stormy bicycle pump attack, bewildered Rusty even more.

Ranbir said: 'Now you are one of us, come,' and Rusty went with him and the others.

'Suri is hiding,' cried someone. 'He has locked himself in his house and won't play Holi!'

'Well, he will have to play,' said Ranbir, 'even if we break the house down.'

Suri, who dreaded Holi, had decided to spend the day in a state of siege; and had set up camp in his mother's kitchen, where there were provisions enough for the whole day. He listened to his playmates calling to him from the courtyard, and ignored their invitations, jeers, and threats; the door was strong and well-barricaded. He settled himself beneath a table, and turned the pages of the English nudists' journal, which he bought every month chiefly for its photographic value.

But the youths outside, intoxicated by the drumming and shouting and high spirits, were not going to be done out of the pleasure of discomfiting Suri. So they acquired a ladder and made their entry into the kitchen by the skylight.

Suri squealed with fright. The door was opened and he was bundled out, and his spectacles were trampled.

'My glasses!' he screamed. 'You've broken them!'

'You can afford a dozen pairs!' jeered one of his antagonists.

'But I can't see, you fools, I can't see!'

'He can't see!' cried someone in scorn. 'For once in his life, Suri can't see what's going on! Now, whenever he spies, we'll smash his glasses!'

Not knowing Suri very well, Rusty could not help pitying the frantic boy.

'Why don't you let him go,' he asked Ranbir. 'Don't force him if he doesn't want to play.'

'But this is the only chance we have of repaying him for all his dirty tricks. It is the only day on which no one is afraid of him!'

Rusty could not imagine how anyone could possibly be afraid of the pale, struggling, spindly-legged boy who was almost being torn apart, and was glad when the others had finished their sport with him.

All day Rusty roamed the town and countryside with Ranbir and his friends, and Suri was soon forgotten. For one day, Ranbir and his friends forgot their homes and their work and the problem of the next meal, and danced down the roads, out of the town and into the forest. And, for one day, Rusty forgot his guardian and the missionary's wife and the supple malacca cane, and ran with the others through the town and into the forest.

The crisp, sunny morning ripened into afternoon.

In the forest, in the cool dark silence of the jungle, they stopped singing and shouting, suddenly exhausted. They lay down in the shade of many trees, and the grass was soft and comfortable, and very soon everyone except Rusty was fast asleep.

Rusty was tired. He was hungry. He had lost his shirt and shoes, his feet were bruised, his body sore. It was only now, resting, that he noticed these things, for he had been caught up in the excitement of the colour game, overcome by an exhilaration he had never known. His fair hair was tousled and streaked with colour, and his eyes were wide with wonder.

He was exhausted now, but he was happy.

He wanted this to go on for ever, this day of feverish emotion, this life in another world. He did not want to leave the forest; it was safe, its earth soothed him, gathered him in, so that the pain of his body became a pleasure . . . .

He did not want to go home.

Chapter VI

MR Harrison stood at the top of the veranda steps. The house was in darkness, but his cigarette glowed more brightly for it. A road lamp trapped the returning boy as he opened the gate, and Rusty knew he had been seen, but he didn't care much; if he had known that Mr Harrison had not recognized him, he would have turned back instead of walking resignedly up the garden path.

Mr Harrison did not move, nor did he appear to notice the boy's approach. It was only when Rusty climbed the veranda steps that his guardian moved and said: 'Who's that?'

Still he had not recognized the boy; and in that instant Rusty become aware of his own condition, for his body was a patchwork of paint. Wearing only torn pyjamas he could, in the half-light, have easily been mistaken for the sweeper boy or someone else's servant. It must have been a newly-acquired bazaar-instinct that made the boy think of escape. He turned about.

But Mr Harrison shouted, 'Come here, you!' and the tone of his voice—the tone reserved for the sweeper boy—made Rusty stop.

'Come up here!' repeated Mr Harrison.

Rusty returned to the veranda, and his guardian switched on a light; but even now there was no recognition.

'Good evening, sir,' said Rusty.

Mr Harrison received a shock. He felt a wave of anger, and then a wave of pain: was this the boy he had trained and educated—this wild, ragged, ungrateful wretch, who did not know the difference between what was proper and what was improper, what was civilized and what was barbaric, what was decent and what was shameful—and had the years of training come to nothing? Mr Harrison came out of the shadows and cursed. He brought his hand down on the back of Rusty's neck, propelled him into the drawing-room, and pushed him across the room so violently that the boy lost his balance, collided with a table and rolled over on to the ground.

Rusty looked up from the floor to find his guardian standing over him, and in the man's right hand was the supple malacca cane, and the cane was twitching.

Mr Harrison's face was twitching too, it was full of fire. His lips were stitched together, sealed up with the ginger moustache, and he looked at the boy with narrowed, unblinking eyes.

'Filth!' he said, almost spitting the words in the boy's face. 'My God, what filth!'

Rusty stared fascinated at the deep yellow nicotine stains on the fingers of his guardian's raised hand. Then the wrist moved suddenly and the cane cut across the boy's face like a knife, stabbing and burning into his cheek.

Rusty cried out and cowered back against the wall; he could feel the blood trickling across his mouth. He looked round desperately for a means of escape, but the man was in front of him, over him, and the wall was behind.

Mr Harrison broke into a torrent of words. 'How can you call yourself an Englishman, how can you come back to this house in such a condition? In what gutter, in what brothel have you been! Have you seen yourself? Do you know what you look like?'

'No,' said Rusty, and for the first time he did not address his guardian as 'sir'. 'I don't care what I look like.'

'You don't . . . well, I'll tell you what you look like! You look like the mongrel that you are!'

'That's a lie!' exclaimed Rusty.

'It's the truth. I've tried to bring you up as an Englishman, as your father would have wished. But, as you won't have it our way, I'm telling you that he was about the only thing English about you. You're no better than the sweeper boy!'

Rusty flared into a temper, showing some spirit for the first time in his life. 'I'm no better than the sweeper boy, but I'm as good as him! I'm as good as you! I'm as good as anyone!' And, instead of cringing to take the cut from the cane, he flung himself at his guardian's legs. The cane swished through the air, grazing the boy's back. Rusty wrapped his arms round his guardian's legs and pulled on them with all his strength.

Mr Harrison went over, falling flat on his back.

The suddenness of the fall must have knocked the breath from his body, because for a moment he did not move.

Rusty sprang to his feet. The cut across his face had stung him to madness, to an unreasoning hate, and he did what previously he would only have dreamt of doing. Lifting a vase of the missionary's wife's best sweet-peas off the glass cupboard, he flung it at his guardian's face. It hit him on the chest, but the water and flowers flopped out over his face. He tried to get up; but he was speechless.

The look of alarm on Mr Harrison's face gave Rusty greater courage. Before the man could recover his feet and his balance, Rusty gripped him by the collar and pushed him backwards, until they both fell over on to the floor. With one hand still twisting the collar, the boy slapped his guardian's face. Mad with the pain in his own face, Rusty hit the man again and again, wildly and awkwardly, but with the giddy thrill of knowing he could do it: he was a child no longer, he was nearly seventeen, he was a man. He could inflict pain, that was a wonderful discovery; there was a power in his body—a devil or a god—and he gained confidence in his power; and he was a man!

'Stop that, stop it!'

The shout of a hysterical woman brought Rusty to his senses. He still held his guardian by the throat, but he stopped hitting him. Mr Harrison's face was very red.

The missionary's wife stood in the doorway, her face white with fear. She was under the impression that Mr Harrison was being attacked by a servant or some bazaar hooligan. Rusty did not wait until she found her tongue but, with a new-found speed and agility, darted out of the drawing-room.

He made his escape from the bedroom window. From the gate he could see the missionary's wife silhouetted against the drawing-room light. He laughed out loud. The woman swivelled round and came forward a few steps. And Rusty laughed again and began running down the road to the bazaar.

*

It was late. The smart shops and restaurants were closed. In the bazaar, oil lamps hung outside each doorway; people were asleep on the steps and platforms of shopfronts, some huddled in blankets, others rolled tight into themselves. The road, which during the day was a busy, noisy crush of people and animals, was quiet and deserted. Only a lean dog still sniffed in the gutter. A woman sang in a room high above the street—a plaintive, tremulous song—and in the far distance a jackal cried to the moon. But the empty, lifeless street was very deceptive; if the roofs could have been removed from but a handful of buildings, it would be seen that life had not really stopped but, beautiful and ugly, persisted through the night.

It was past midnight, though the Clock Tower had no way of saying it. Rusty was in the empty street, and the chaat shop was closed, a sheet of tarpaulin draped across the front. He looked up and down the road, hoping to meet someone he knew; the chaat-wallah, he felt sure, would give him a blanket for the night and a place to sleep; and the next day when Somi came to meet him, he would tell his friend of his predicament, that he had run away from his guardian's house and did not intend returning. But he would have to wait till morning: the chaat shop was shuttered, barred and bolted.

He sat down on the steps; but the stone was cold and his thin cotton pyjamas offered no protection. He folded his arms and huddled up in a corner, but still he shivered. His feet were becoming numb, lifeless.

Rusty had not fully realized the hazards of the situation. He was still mad with anger and rebellion and, though the blood on his cheek had dried, his face was still smarting. He could not think clearly: the present was confusing and unreal and he could not see beyond it; what worried him was the cold and the discomfort and the pain.

The singing stopped in the high window. Rusty looked up and saw a beckoning hand. As no one else in the street showed any

31

signs of life, Rusty got up and walked across the road until he was under the window. The woman pointed to a stairway, and he mounted it, glad of the hospitality he was being offered.

The stairway seemed to go to the stars, but it turned suddenly to lead into the woman's room. The door was slightly ajar, and he knocked and a voice said, 'Come . . . .'

The room was filled with perfume and burning incense. A musical instrument lay in one corner. The woman reclined on a bed, her hair scattered about the pillow; she had a round, pretty face, but she was losing her youth, and the fat showed in rolls at her exposed waist. She smiled at the boy, and beckoned again.

'Thank you,' said Rusty, closing the door. 'Can I sleep here?'

'Where else?' said the woman.

'Just for tonight.'

She smiled, and waited. Rusty stood in front of her, his hands behind his back.

'Sit down,' she said, and patted the bedclothes beside her.

Reverently, and as respectfully as he could, Rusty sat down. The woman ran little fair fingers over his body, and drew his head to hers; their lips were very close, almost touching, and their breathing sounded terribly loud to Rusty, but he only said: 'I am hungry.'

A poet, thought the woman, and kissed him full on the lips; but the boy drew away in embarrassment, unsure of himself, liking the woman on the bed and yet afraid of her . . . .

'What is wrong?' she asked.

'I'm tired,' he said.

The woman's friendly smile turned to a look of scorn; but she saw that he was only a boy whose eyes were full of unhappiness, and she could not help pitying him.

'You can sleep here,' she said, 'until you have lost your tiredness.'

But he shook his head. 'I will come some other time,' he said, not wishing to hurt the woman's feelings. They were both pitying each other, liking each other, but not enough to make them understand each other.

Rusty left the room. Mechanically, he descended the staircase, and walked up the bazaar road, past the silent sleeping forms, until he reached the Clock Tower. To the right of the Clock Tower was a broad stretch of grassland where, during the day, cattle grazed and children played and young men like Ranbir wrestled and kicked footballs. But now, at night, it was a vast empty space.

But the grass was soft, like the grass in the forest, and Rusty walked the length of the maidan. He found a bench and sat down, warmer for the walk. A light breeze was blowing across the maidan, pleasant and refreshing, playing with his hair. Around him everything was dark and silent and lonely. He had got away from the bazaar, which held the misery of beggars and homeless children and starving dogs, and could now concentrate on his own misery; for there was nothing like loneliness for making Rusty conscious of his unhappy state. Madness and freedom and violence were new to him: loneliness was familiar, something he understood.

Rusty was alone. Until tomorrow, he was alone for the rest of his life.

If tomorrow there was no Somi at the chaat shop, no Ranbir, then what would he do? This question badgered him persistently, making him an unwilling slave to reality. He did not know where his friends lived, he had no money, he could not ask the chaat-wallah for credit on the strength of two visits. Perhaps he should return to the amorous lady in the bazaar; perhaps . . . but no, one thing was certain, he would never return to his guardian . . . .

The moon had been hidden by clouds, and presently there was a drizzle. Rusty did not mind the rain, it refreshed him and made the colour run from his body; but, when it began to fall harder, he started shivering again. He felt sick. He got up, rolled his ragged pyjamas up to the thighs and crawled under the bench.

There was a hollow under the bench, and at first Rusty found it quite comfortable. But there was no grass and gradually the earth began to soften: soon he was on his hands and knees in a pool of muddy water, with the slush oozing up through his fingers and toes. Crouching there, wet and cold and muddy, he was overcome by a feeling of helplessness and self-pity: everyone and everything seemed to have turned against him; not only his people but also

33

the bazaar and the chaat shop and even the elements. He admitted to himself that he had been too impulsive in rebelling and running away from home; perhaps there was still time to return and beg Mr Harrison's forgiveness. But could his behaviour be forgiven? Might he not be clapped into irons for attempted murder? Most certainly he would be given another beating: not six strokes this time, but nine.

His only hope was Somi. If not Somi, then Ranbir. If not Ranbir . . . well, it was no use thinking further, there was no one else to think of.

The rain had ceased. Rusty crawled out from under the bench, and stretched his cramped limbs. The moon came out from a cloud, and played with his wet, glistening body, and showed him the vast, naked loneliness of the maidan and his own insignificance. He longed now for the presence of people, be they beggars or women, and he broke into a trot, and the trot became a run, a frightened run, and he did not stop until he reached the Clock Tower.

Chapter VII

THEY who sleep last, wake first. Hunger and pain lengthen the night, and so the beggars and dogs are the last to see the stars; hunger and pain hasten the awakening, and beggars and dogs are the first to see the sun. Rusty knew hunger and pain, but his weariness was even greater, and he was asleep on the steps of the chaat shop long after the sun had come striding down the road, knocking on nearly every door and window.

Somi bathed at the common water-tank. He stood under the tap and slapped his body into life and spluttered with the shock of mountain water.

At the tank were many people: children shrieking with delight—or discomfort—as their ayahs slapped them about roughly and affectionately; the ayahs themselves, strong, healthy hill-women, with heavy bracelets on their ankles; the *bhisti*—the water-carrier—with his skin bag; and the cook with his pots and pans. The ayahs sat on their haunches, bathing the children, their saris rolled up to the thighs; every time they moved their feet, the bells on their ankles jingled; so that there was a continuous shrieking and jingling and slapping of buttocks. The cook smeared his utensils with ash and washed them, and filled an earthen *chatty* with water; the *bhisti* hoisted the water-bag over his shoulder and left, dripping; a piedog lapped at water rolling off the stone platform; and a baleful-looking cow nibbled at wet grass.

It was with these people that Somi spent his mornings, laughing and talking and bathing with them. When he had finished his ablutions, dried his hair in the sun, dressed and tied his turban, he mounted his bicycle and rode out of the compound.

At this advanced hour of the morning Mr Harrison still slept. In the half empty church, his absence was noted: he seldom missed Sunday morning services; and the missionary's wife was impatiently waiting for the end of the sermon, for she had so much to talk about.

Outside the chaat shop Somi said, 'Hey, Rusty, get up, what has happened? Where is Ranbir? Holi finished yesterday, you know!'

He shook Rusty by the shoulders, shouting into his ear; and the pale boy lying on the stone steps opened his eyes and blinked in the morning sunshine; his eyes roamed about in bewilderment, he could not remember how he came to be lying in the sunshine in the bazaar.

'Hey,' said Somi, 'your guardian will be very angry!'

Rusty sat up with a start. He was wide awake now, sweeping up his scattered thoughts and sorting them out. It was difficult for him to be straightforward; but he forced himself to look Somi straight in the eyes and, very simply and without preamble, say: 'I've run away from home.'

Somi showed no surprise. He did not take his eyes off Rusty's; nor did his expression alter. A half-smile on his lips, he said: 'Good. Now you can come and stay with me.'

Somi took Rusty home on the bicycle. Rusty felt weak in the legs, but his mind was relieved and he no longer felt alone: once again, Somi gave him a feeling of confidence.

'Do you think I can get a job?' asked Rusty.

'Don't worry about that yet, you have only just run away.'

'Do you think I can get a job,' persisted Rusty.

'Why not? But don't worry, you are going to stay with me.'

'I'll stay with you only until I find a job. Any kind of job, there must be something.'

'Of course, don't worry,' said Somi, and pressed harder on the pedals.

They came to a canal; it was noisy with the rush of mountain water, for the snow had begun to melt. The road, which ran parallel to the canal, was flooded in some parts, but Somi steered a steady course. Then the canal turned left and the road kept straight, and presently the sound of water was but a murmur, and the road quiet and shady; there were trees at the road-sides covered in pink and white blossoms, and behind them more trees, thicker and greener; and in amongst the trees were houses.

A boy swung on a creaking wooden gate. He whistled out, and Somi waved back; that was all.

'Who's that?' asked Rusty.

'Son of his parents.'

'What do you mean?'

'His father is rich. So Kishen is somebody. He has money, and it is as powerful as Suri's tongue.'

'Is he Suri's friend or yours?'

'When it suits him, he is our friend. When it suits him, he is Suri's friend.'

'Then he's clever as well as rich,' deduced Rusty.

'The brains are his mother's.'

'And the money his father's?'

'Yes, but there isn't much left now. Mr Kapoor is finished . . . . He looks like his father too, his mother is beautiful. Well, here we are!'

Somi rode the bicycle in amongst the trees and along a snaky path that dodged this way and that, and then they reached the house.

It was a small flat house, covered completely by a crimson bougainvillaea creeper. The garden was a mass of marigolds, which had sprung up everywhere, even in the cracks at the sides of the veranda steps. No one was at home. Somi's father was in Delhi, and his mother was out for the morning, buying the week's vegetables.

'Have you any brothers?' asked Rusty, as he entered the front room.

'No. But I've got two sisters. But they're married. Come on, let's see if my clothes will fit you.'

Rusty laughed, for he was older and bigger than his friend; but he was thinking in terms of shirts and trousers, the kind of garments he was used to wearing. He sat down on a sofa in the front room, whilst Somi went for the clothes.

The room was cool and spacious, and had very little furniture. But on the walls were many pictures, and in the centre a large one of Guru Nanak, the founder of the Sikh religion: his body bare, the saint sat with his legs crossed and the palms of his hands touching in prayer, and on his face there was a serene expression: the serenity of Nanak's countenance seemed to communicate itself to the room. There was a serenity about Somi too; maybe because of the smile that always hovered near his mouth.

Rusty concluded that Somi's family were middle class people; that is, they were neither rich nor beggars, but managed to live all the same.

Somi came back with the clothes.

'They are mine,' he said, 'so maybe they will be a little small for you. Anyway, the warm weather is coming and it will not matter what you wear—better nothing at all!'

Rusty put on a long white shirt which, to his surprise, hung loose; it had a high collar and broad sleeves.

'It is loose,' he said, 'how can it be yours?'

'It is made loose,' said Somi.

Rusty pulled on a pair of white pyjamas, and they were definitely small for him, ending a few inches above the ankle. The sandals would not buckle; and, when he walked, they behaved like Somi's and slapped against his heels.

'There!' exclaimed Somi in satisfaction. 'Now everything is settled, chaat in your stomach, clean clothes on your body, and in a few days we find a job! Now is there anything else?'

Rusty knew Somi well enough now to know that it wasn't necessary to thank him for anything; gratitude was taken for granted; in true friendship there are no formalities and no obligations. Rusty did not even ask if Somi had consulted his mother about taking in guests; perhaps she was used to this sort of thing.

'Is there anything else?' repeated Somi.

Rusty yawned. 'Can I go to sleep now, please?'

Chapter VIII

USTY had never slept well in his guardian's house, because he had never been tired enough; also his imagination would disturb him. And, since running away, he had slept very badly, because he had been cold and hungry and afraid. But in Somi's house he felt safe and a little happy, and so he slept; he slept the remainder of the day and through the night.

In the morning Somi tipped Rusty out of bed and dragged him to the water-tank. Rusty watched Somi strip and stand under the jet of tap water, and shuddered at the prospect of having to do the same.

Before removing his shirt, Rusty looked around in embarrassment; no one paid much attention to him, though one of the ayahs, the girl with the bangles, gave him a sly smile; he looked away from the women, threw his shirt on a bush and advanced cautiously to the bathing place.

Somi pulled him under the tap. The water was icy cold and Rusty gasped with the shock. As soon as he was wet, he sprang off the platform, much to the amusement of Somi and the ayahs.

There was no towel with which to dry himself; he stood on the grass, shivering with cold, wondering whether he should dash back to the house or shiver in the open until the sun dried him. But the girl with the bangles was beside him holding a towel; her eyes were full of mockery, but her smile was friendly.

At the midday meal, which consisted of curry and curds and chapattis, Rusty met Somi's mother, and liked her.

She was a woman of about thirty-five; she had a few grey hairs at the temples, and her skin—unlike Somi's—was rough and dry. She dressed simply, in a plain white sari. Her life had been difficult. After the partition of the country, when hate made religion its own, Somi's family had to leave their home in the Punjab and trek southwards; they had walked hundreds of miles and the mother had carried Somi, who was then six, on her back. Life in India had to be started again right from the beginning, for they had lost most of their property: the father found work in Delhi, the sisters were married off, and Somi and his mother settled down in Dehra, where the boy attended school.

The mother said: 'Mister Rusty, you must give Somi a few lessons in spelling and arithmetic. Always, he comes last in class.'

'Oh, that's good!' exclaimed Somi. 'We'll have fun, Rusty!' Then he thumped the table. 'I have an idea! I know, I think I have a job for you! Remember Kishen, the boy we passed yesterday? Well, his father wants someone to give him private lessons in English.'

'Teach Kishen?'

'Yes, it will be easy. I'll go and see Mr Kapoor and tell him I've found a professor of English or something like that, and then you can come, and see him. Brother, it is a first-class idea, you are going to be a teacher!'

Rusty felt very dubious about the proposal; he was not sure he could teach English or anything else to the wilful son of a rich man; but he was not in a position to pick and choose. Somi mounted his bicycle and rode off to see Mr Kapoor to secure for Rusty the post of Professor of English. When he returned he seemed pleased with himself, and Rusty's heart sank with the knowledge that he had got a job.

'You are to come and see him this evening,' announced Somi, 'he will tell you all about it. They want a teacher for Kishen, especially if they don't have to pay.'

'What kind of a job without pay?' complained Rusty. 'No pay,' said Somi, 'but everything else. Food—and no cooking is better than Punjabi cooking; water—'

'I should hope so,' said Rusty.

'And a room, sir!'

'Oh, even a room,' said Rusty ungratefully, 'that will be nice.'

'Anyway,' said Somi, 'come and see him, you don't have to accept.'

*

The house the Kapoors lived in was very near the canal; it was a squat, comfortable-looking bungalow, surrounded by uncut hedges, and shaded by banana and papaya trees. It was late evening when Somi and Rusty arrived, and the moon was up, and the shaggy branches of the banana trees shook their heavy shadows out over the gravel path.

In an open space in front of the house a log fire was burning; the Kapoors appeared to be giving a party. Somi and Rusty joined the people who were grouped round the fire, and Rusty wondered if he had been invited to the party. The fire lent a friendly warmth to the chilly night, and the flames leapt up, casting the glow of roses on people's faces.

Somi pointed out different people: various shopkeepers, one or two Big Men, the sickly looking Suri (who was never absent from a social occasion such as this) and a few total strangers who had invited themselves to the party just for the fun of the thing and a free meal. Kishen, the Kapoors' son, was not present; he hated parties, preferring the company of certain wild friends in the bazaar.

Mr Kapoor was once a Big Man himself, and everyone knew this; but he had fallen from the heights; and, until he gave up the bottle, was not likely to reach them again. Everyone felt sorry for his wife, including herself.

Presently Kapoor tottered out of the front door arm-in-arm with a glass and a bottle of whisky. He wore a green dressing-gown and a week's beard; his hair, or what was left of it, stood up on end; and he dribbled slightly. An awkward silence fell on the company; but Kapoor, who was a friendly, gentle sort of drunkard, looked round benevolently, and said: 'Everybody here? Fine, fine, they are all here, all of them . . . . Throw some more wood on the fire!'

The fire was doing very well indeed, but not well enough for Kapoor; every now and then he would throw a log on the flames until it was feared the blaze would reach the house. Meena, Kapoor's wife, did not look flustered, only irritated; she was a capable person, still young, a charming hostess; and, in her red sari and white silk jacket, her hair plaited and scented with jasmine, she looked beautiful. Rusty gazed admiringly at her; he wanted to compliment her, to say, 'Mrs Kapoor, you are beautiful'; but he had no need to tell her, she was fully conscious of the fact.

Meena made her way over to one of the Big Men, and whispered something in his ear, and then she went to a Little Shopkeeper and whispered something in his ear, and then both the Big Man and the Little Shopkeeper advanced stealthily towards the spot where Mr Kapoor was holding forth, and made a gentle attempt to convey him indoors.

But Kapoor was having none of it. He pushed the men aside and roared: 'Keep the fire burning! Keep it burning, don't let it go out, throw some more wood on it!'

And, before he could be restrained, he had thrown a pot of the most delicious sweetmeats on to the flames.

To Rusty this was sacrilege. 'Oh, Mr Kapoor . . . ' he cried, but there was some confusion in the rear, and his words were drowned in a series of explosions.

Suri and one or two others had begun letting off fireworks: fountains, rockets, and explosives. The fountains gushed forth in green and red and silver lights, and the rockets struck through the night with crimson tails; but it was the explosives that caused the confusion. The guests did not know whether to press forward into the fires, or retreat amongst the fireworks; neither prospect was pleasing, and the women began to show signs of hysterics. Then Suri burnt his finger and began screaming, and this was all the women had been waiting for; headed by Suri's mother, they rushed the boy and smothered him with attention; whilst the men, who were in a minority, looked on sheepishly and wished the accident had been of a more serious nature.

Something rough brushed against Rusty's cheek.

It was Kapoor's beard. Somi had brought his host to Rusty, and the bemused man put his face close to Rusty's and placed his hands on the boy's shoulders in order to steady himself. Kapoor nodded his head, his eyes red and watery.

'Rusty. . . so you are Mister Rusty . . . . I hear you are going to be my schoolteacher.'

'Your son's sir,' said Rusty, 'but that is for you to decide.'

'Do not call me "Sir",' he said, wagging his finger in Rusty's face, 'call me by my name. So you are going to England, eh?'

'No, I'm going to be your schoolteacher.' Rusty had to put his arm round Kapoor's waist to avoid being dragged to the ground; Kapoor leant heavily on the boy's shoulders.

'Good, good. Tell me after you have gone, I want to give you some addresses of people I know. You must go to Monte Carlo, you've seen nothing until you've seen Monte Carlo, it's the only place with a future . . . . Who built Monte Carlo, do you know?'

It was impossible for Rusty to make any sense of the conversation or discuss his appointment as Professor in English to Kishen Kapoor. Kapoor began to slip from his arms, and the boy took the opportunity of changing his own position for a more comfortable one, before levering his host up again. The amused smiles of the company rested on this little scene.

Rusty said: 'No, Mr Kapoor, who built Monte Carlo?'

'I did. I built Monte Carlo!'

'Oh yes, of course.'

'Yes, I built this house, I'm a genius, there's no doubt of it! I have a high opinion of my own opinion, what is yours?'

'Oh, I don't know, but I'm sure you're right.'

'Of course I am. But speak up, don't be afraid to say what you think. Stand up for your rights, even if you're wrong! Throw some more wood on the fire, keep it burning.'

Kapoor leapt from Rusty's arms and stumbled towards the fire. The boy cried a warning and, catching hold of the end of the green dressing-gown, dragged his host back to safety. Meena ran to them and, without so much as a glance at Rusty, took her husband by the arm and propelled him indoors.

Rusty stared after Meena Kapoor, and continued to stare even when she had disappeared. The guests chattered pleasantly, pretending nothing had happened, keeping the gossip for the next morning; but the children giggled amongst themselves, and the devil Suri shouted: 'Throw some more wood on the fire, keep it burning!'

Somi returned to his friend's side. 'What did Mr Kapoor have to say?'

'He said he built Monte Carlo.'

Somi slapped his forehead. *'Toba!* Now we'll have to come again tomorrow evening. And then, if he's drunk, we'll have to discuss with his wife, she's the only one with any sense.'

They walked away from the party, out of the circle of fire-light, into the shadows of the banana trees. The voices of the guests became a distant murmur: Suri's high-pitched shout came to them on the clear, still air.

Somi said: 'We must go to the chaat shop tomorrow morning, Ranbir is asking for you.'

Rusty had almost forgotten Ranbir: he felt ashamed for not having asked about him before this. Ranbir was an important person, he had changed the course of Rusty's life with nothing but a little colour, red and green, and the touch of his hand.

Chapter IX

AGAINST his parents' wishes, Kishen Kapoor spent most of his time in the bazaar; he loved it because it was forbidden, because it was unhealthy, dangerous and full of germs to carry home.

Ranbir loved the bazaar because he was born in it; he had known few other places. Since the age of ten he had looked after his uncle's buffaloes grazing them on the maidan and taking them down to the river to wallow in mud and water; and in the evening he took them home, riding on the back of the strongest and fastest animal. When he grew older, he was allowed to help in his father's cloth shop, but he was always glad to get back to the buffaloes.

Kishen did not like animals, particularly cows and buffaloes. His greatest enemy was Maharani, the Queen of the Bazaar; who, like Kishen was spoilt and pampered and fond of having her own way. Unlike other cows, she did not feed at dustbins and rubbish-heaps, but lived on the benevolence of the bazaar people.

But Kishen had no time for religion; to him a cow was just a cow, nothing sacred; and he saw no reason why he should get off the pavement in order to make way for one, or offer no protest when it stole from under his nose. One day, he tied an empty tin to Maharani's tail and looked on in great enjoyment as the cow pranced madly and dangerously about the road, the tin clattering behind her. Lacking in dignity, Kishen found some pleasure in observing others lose theirs. But a few days later Kishen received Maharani's nose in his pants, and had to pick himself up from the gutter.

Kishen and Ranbir ate mostly at the chaat shop; if they had no money they went to work in Ranbir's uncle's sugar-cane fields and earned a rupee for the day; but Kishen did not like work, and Ranbir had enough of his own to do, so there was never much money for chaat; which meant living on their wits—or, rather, Kishen's wits, for it was his duty to pocket any spare money that might be lying about in his father's house—and sometimes helping themselves at the fruit and vegetable stalls when no one was looking.

Ranbir wrestled. That was why he was so good at riding buffaloes. He was the best wrestler in the bazaar; not very clever, but powerful; he was like a great tree, and no amount of shaking could move him from whatever spot he chose to plant his big feet. But he was gentle by nature. The women always gave him their babies to look after when they were busy, and he would cradle the babies in his open hands, and sing to them, and be happy for hours.

Ranbir had a certain innocence which was not likely to leave him. He had seen and experienced life to the full, and life had bruised and scarred him, but it had not crippled him. One night he strayed unwittingly into the intoxicating arms of a local temple dancing-girl; but he acted with instinct, his pleasure was unpremeditated, and the adventure was soon forgotten—by Ranbir. But Suri, the scourge of the bazaar, uncovered a few facts and threatened to inform Ranbir's family of the incident; and so Ranbir found himself in the power of the cunning Suri, and was forced to please him from time to time; though, at times such as the Holi festival, that power was scorned.

On the morning after the Kapoors' party Ranbir, Somi, and Rusty were seated in the chaat shop, discussing Rusty's situation. Ranbir looked miserable; his hair fell sadly over his forehead, and he would not look at Rusty.

'I have got you into trouble,' he apologized gruffly, 'I am too ashamed.'

Rusty laughed, licking sauce from his fingers and crumpling up his empty leaf bowl.

'Silly fellow,' he said, 'for what are you sorry? For making me happy? For taking me away from my guardian? Well, I am not sorry, you can be sure of that.'

'You are not angry?' asked Ranbir in wonder.

'No, but you will make me angry in this way.'

Ranbir's face lit up, and he slapped Somi and Rusty on their backs with such sudden enthusiasm that Somi dropped his bowl of allu chole.

'Come on, misters,' he said, 'I am going to make you sick with gol-guppas so that you will not be able to eat any more until I return from Mussoorie!'

'Mussoorie?' Somi looked puzzled. 'You are going to Mussoorie?'

'To school!'

'That's right,' said a voice from the door, a voice hidden in smoke. 'Now we've had it . . . . '

Somi said, 'It's that monkey-millionaire Kishen come to make a nuisance of himself.' Then, louder: 'Come over here, Kishen, come and join us in gol-guppas!'

Kishen appeared from the mist of vapour, walking with an affected swagger, his hands in his pockets; he was the only one present wearing pants instead of pyjamas.

'Hey!' exclaimed Somi, 'who has given you a black eye?'

Kishen did not answer immediately, but sat down opposite Rusty. His shirt hung over his pants, and his pants hung over his knees; he had bushy eyebrows and hair, and a drooping, disagreeable mouth; the sulky expression on his face had become a permanent one, not a mood of the moment. Kishen's swagger, money, unattractive face and qualities made him—for Rusty, anyway—curiously attractive . . . .

He prodded his nose with his forefinger, as he always did when a trifle excited. 'Those damn wrestlers, they piled on to me.'

'Why?' said Ranbir, sitting up instantly.

'I was making a badminton-court on the maidan, and these fellows came along and said they had reserved the place for a wrestling ground.'

'So then?'

Kishen's affected American twang became more pronounced. 'I told them to go to hell!'

Ranbir laughed. 'So they all started wrestling you?'

'Yeah, but I didn't know they would hit me too. I bet if you fellows were there, they wouldn't have tried anything. Isn't that so, Ranbir?'

Ranbir smiled; he knew it was so, but did not care to speak of his physical prowess. Kishen took notice of the newcomer.

'Are you Mister Rusty?' he asked.

'Yes, I am,' said the boy. 'Are you Mister Kishen?'

'I am Mister Kishen. You know how to box, Rusty?'

'Well,' said the boy, unwilling to become involved in a local feud, 'I've never boxed wrestlers.'

Somi changed the subject. 'Rusty's coming to see your father this evening. You must try and persuade your pop to give him the job of teaching you English.'

Kishen prodded his nose, and gave Rusty a sly wink.

'Yes, Daddy told me about you, he says you are a professor. You can be my teacher on the condition that we don't work too hard, and you support me when I tell them lies, and that you tell them I am working hard. Sure, you can be my teacher, sure . . . better you than a real one.'

'I'll try to please everyone,' said Rusty.

'You're a clever person if you can. But I think you are clever.'

'Yes,' agreed Rusty, and was inwardly amazed at the way he spoke.

*

As Rusty had now met Kishen, Somi suggested that the two should go to the Kapoors' house together; so that evening, Rusty met Kishen in the bazaar and walked home with him.

There was a crowd in front of the bazaar's only cinema, and it was getting restive and demonstrative.

One had to fight to get into this particular cinema, as there was no organized queuing or booking.

'Is anything wrong?' asked Rusty.

'Oh, no,' said Kishen, 'it is just Laurel and Hardy today, they are very popular. Whenever a popular film is shown, there is usually a riot. But I know of a way in through the roof, I'll show you some time.'

'Sounds crazy.'

'Yeah, the roof leaks, so people usually bring their umbrellas. Also their food, because when the projector breaks down or the electricity fails, we have to wait a long time. Sometimes, when it is a long wait, the chaat-wallah comes in and does some business.'

'Sounds crazy,' repeated Rusty.

'You'll get used to it. Have a chewing-gum.'

Kishen's jaws had been working incessantly on a lump of gum that had been increasing in size over the last three days; he started on a fresh stick every hour or so, without throwing away the old ones. Rusty was used to seeing Indians chew paan, the betel-leaf preparation which stained the mouth with red juices, but Kishen wasn't like any of the Indians Rusty had met so far. He accepted a stick of gum, and the pair walked home in silent concentration, their jaws moving rhythmically, and Kishen's tongue making sudden sucking sounds.

As they entered the front room, Meena Kapoor pounced on Kishen.

'Ah! So you have decided to come home at last! And what do you mean by asking Daddy for money without letting me know? What have you done with it, Kishen bhaiya? Where is it?'

Kishen sauntered across the room and deposited himself on the couch. 'I've spent it.'

Meena's hands went to her hips. 'What do you mean, you've spent it!'

'I mean I've eaten it.'

He got two resounding slaps across his face, and his flesh went white where his mother's fingers left their mark. Rusty backed towards the door; it was embarrassing to be present at this intimate family scene.

'Don't go, Rusty,' shouted Kishen, 'or she won't stop slapping me!'

Kapoor, still wearing his green dressing-gown and beard, came in from the adjoining room, and his wife turned on him.

'Why do you give the child so much money?' she demanded. 'You know he spends it on nothing but bazaar food and makes himself sick.'

Rusty seized at the opportunity of pleasing the whole family; of saving Mr Kapoor's skin, pacifying his wife, and gaining the affection and regard of Kishen.

'It is all my fault,' he said, 'I took Kishen to the chaat shop. I'm very sorry.'

Meena Kapoor became quiet and her eyes softened; but Rusty resented her kindly expression because he knew it was prompted by pity—pity for him—and a satisfied pride. Meena was proud because she thought her son had shared his money with one who apparently hadn't any.

'I did not see you come in,' she said.

'I only wanted to explain about the money.'

'Come in, don't be shy.'

Meena's smile was full of kindness, but Rusty was not looking for kindness; for no apparent reason, he felt lonely; he missed Somi, felt lost without him, helpless and clumsy.

'There is another thing,' he said, remembering the post of Professor in English.

'But come in, Mister Rusty . . . .'

It was the first time she had used his name, and the gesture immediately placed them on equal terms. She was a graceful woman, much younger than Kapoor; her features had a clear, classic beauty, and her voice was gentle but firm. Her hair was tied in a neat bun and laced with a string of jasmine flowers.

'Come in . . . .'

'About teaching Kishen,' mumbled Rusty.

'Come and play carom,' said Kishen from the couch. 'We are none of us any good. Come and sit down, pardner.'

'He fancies himself as an American,' said Meena. 'If ever you see him in the cinema, drag him out.'

The carom board was brought in from the next room, and it was arranged that Rusty partner Mr Kapoor. They began play, but the game didn't progress very fast because Kapoor kept leaving the table in order to disappear behind a screen, from the direction of which came a tinkle of bottles and glasses. Rusty was afraid of Kapoor getting drunk before he could be approached about the job of teaching Kishen.

'My wife,' said Kapoor in a loud whisper to Rusty, 'does not let me drink in public any more, so I have to do it in a cupboard.'

He looked sad; there were tear-stains on his cheeks; the tears were caused not by Meena's scolding, which he ignored, but by his own self-pity; he often cried for himself, usually in his sleep.

Whenever Rusty pocketed one of the carom men, Kapoor exclaimed: 'Ah, nice shot, nice shot!' as though it were a cricket match they were playing. 'But hit it slowly, slowly . . . .' And when it was his turn, he gave the striker a feeble push, moving it a bare inch from his finger.

'Play properly,' murmured Meena, who was intent on winning the game; but Kapoor would be up from his seat again, and the company would sit back and wait for the tune of clinking glass.

It was a very irritating game. Kapoor insisted on showing Rusty how to strike the men; and whenever Rusty made a mistake, Meena said 'thank you' in an amused and conceited manner that angered the boy. When she and Kishen had cleared the board of whites, Kapoor and Rusty were left with eight blacks.

'Thank you,' said Meena sweetly.

'We are too good for you,' scoffed Kishen, busily arranging the board for another game.

Kapoor took sudden interest in the proceedings: 'Who won, I say, who won?'

Much to Rusty's disgust, they began another game, and with the same partners; but they had just started when Kapoor flopped forward and knocked the carom board off the table. He had fallen asleep. Rusty took him by the shoulders, eased him back into the chair. Kapoor's breathing was heavy; saliva had collected at the sides of his mouth, and he snorted a little.

Rusty thought it was time he left. Rising from the table, he said, 'I will have to ask another time about the job . . . .'

'Hasn't he told you as yet?' said Meena.

'What?'

'That you can have the job.'

'Can I!' exclaimed Rusty.

Meena gave a little laugh. 'But of course! Certainly there is no one else who would take it on, Kishen is not easy to teach. There is no fixed pay, but we will give you anything you need. You are not our servant. You will be doing us a favour by giving Kishen some of your knowledge and conversation and company, and in return we will be giving you our hospitality. You will have a room of your own, and your food you will have with us. What do you think?'

'Oh, it is wonderful!' said Rusty.

And it was wonderful, and he felt gay and light-headed, and all the troubles in the world scurried away: he even felt successful: he had a profession. And Meena Kapoor was smiling at him, and looking more beautiful than she really was, and Kishen was saying: 'Tomorrow you must stay till twelve o'clock, all right, even if Daddy goes to sleep. Promise me?'

Rusty promised.

An unaffected enthusiasm was bubbling up in Kishen; it was quite different to the sulkiness of his usual manner. Rusty had liked him in spite of the younger boy's unattractive qualities, and now liked him more; for Kishen had taken Rusty into his home and confidence without knowing him very well and without asking any questions. Kishen was a scoundrel, a monkey—crude and well-spoilt—but, for him to have taken a liking to Rusty (and Rusty held himself in high esteem), he must have some virtues . . . or so Rusty reasoned.

His mind, while he walked back to Somi's house, dwelt on his relationship with Kishen; but his tongue, when he loosened it in Somi's presence, dwelt on Meena Kapoor. And when he lay down to sleep, he saw her in his mind's eye, and for the first time took conscious note of her beauty, of her warmth and softness; and made up his mind that he would fall in love with her.

Chapter X

MR Harrison was back to normal in a few days, and telling everyone of Rusty's barbaric behaviour.

'If he wants to live like an animal, he can. He left my house of his own free will, and I feel no responsibility for him. It's his own fault if he starves to death.'

The missionary's wife said: 'But I do hope you will forgive him if he returns.'

'I will, madam. I have to. I'm his legal guardian. And I hope he doesn't return.'

'Oh, Mr Harrison, he's only a boy. . . .'

'That's what you think.'

'I'm sure he'll come back.'

Mr Harrison shrugged indifferently.

*

Rusty's thoughts were far from his guardian. He was listening to Meena Kapoor tell him about his room, and he gazed into her eyes all the time she talked.

'It is a very nice room,' she said, 'but of course there is no water or electricity or lavatory.'

Rusty was bathing in the brown pools of her eyes.

She said: 'You will have to collect your water at the big tank, and for the rest, you will have to do it in the jungle . . . .'

Rusty thought he saw his own gaze reflected in her eyes.

'Yes?' he said.

'You can give Kishen his lessons in the morning until twelve o'clock. Then no more, then you have your food.'

'Then?'

He watched the movement of her lips.

'Then nothing, you do what you like, go out with Kishen or Somi or any of your friends.'

'Where do I teach Kishen?'

'On the roof, of course.'

Rusty retrieved his gaze, and scratched his head. The roof seemed a strange place for setting up school.

'Why the roof?'

'Because your room is on the roof.'

*

Meena led the boy round the house until they came to a flight of steps, unsheltered, that went up to the roof. They had to hop over a narrow drain before climbing the steps.

'This drain,' warned Meena, 'is very easy to cross. But when you are coming downstairs be sure not to take too big a step because then you might bump the wall on the other side or fall over the stove which is usually there . . . .'

'I'll be careful,' said Rusty.

They began climbing, Meena in the lead. Rusty watched Meena's long, slender feet. The slippers she wore consisted only of two straps that passed between her toes, and the backs of the slippers slapped against her heels like Somi's, only the music—like the feet—was different . . . .

'Another thing about these steps,' continued Meena, 'there are twenty-two of them. No, don't count, I have already done so . . . . But remember, if you are coming home in the dark, be sure you take only twenty-two steps, because if you don't, then'—and she snapped her fingers in the air—'you will be finished! After twenty-two steps you turn right and you find the door, here it is. If you do not turn right and you take *twenty-three* steps, you will go over the edge of the roof!'

They both laughed, and suddenly Meena took Rusty's hand and led him into the room.

It was a small room, but this did not matter much as there was very little in it: only a string bed, a table, a shelf and a few nails in the wall. In comparison to Rusty's room in his guardian's house, it wasn't even a room: it was four walls, a door and a window.

The door looked out on the roof, and Meena pointed through it, at the big round water-tank.

'That is where you bathe and get your water,' she said.

'I know, I went with Somi.'

There was a big mango tree behind the tank, and Kishen was sitting in its branches, watching them. Surrounding the house were a number of litchee trees, and in the summer they and the mango would bear fruit.

Meena and Rusty stood by the window in silence, hand in hand. Rusty was prepared to stand there, holding hands for ever. Meena felt a sisterly affection for him; but he was stumbling into love.

From the window they could see many things. In the distance, towering over the other trees, was the Flame of the Forest, its flowers glowing red-hot against the blue of the sky. Through the window came a shoot of pink bougainvillaea creeper; and Rusty knew he would never cut it; and so he knew he would never be able to shut the window.

Meena said, 'If you do not like it, we will find another . . . . '

Rusty squeezed her hand, and smiled into her eyes, and said: 'But I like it. This is the room I want to live in. And do you know why, Meena? Because it isn't a real room, that's why!'

*

The afternoon was warm, and Rusty sat beneath the big banyan tree that grew behind the house, a tree that was almost a house in itself; its spreading branches drooped to the ground and took new root, forming a maze of pillared passages. The tree sheltered scores of birds and squirrels.

A squirrel stood in front of Rusty. It looked at him from between its legs, its tail in the air, back arched gracefully and nose quivering excitedly.

'Hallo,' said Rusty.

The squirrel brushed its nose with its forepaw, winked at the boy, hopped over his leg, and ran up a pillar of the banyan tree.

Rusty leant back against the broad trunk of the banyan, and

listened to the lazy drone of the bees, the squeaking of the squirrels and the incessant bird talk.

He thought of Meena and of Kishen, and felt miserably happy; and then he remembered Somi and the chaat shop. The chaat-wallah, that god of the tikkees, handed Rusty a leaf bowl, and prepared allu chole: first sliced potatoes, then peas, then red and gold chilli powders, then a sprinkling of juices, then he shook it all up and down in the leaf bowl and, in a simplicity, the allu chole was ready.

Somi removed his slippers, crossed his legs, and looked a question.

'It's fine,' said Rusty.

'You are sure?'

There was concern in Somi's voice, and his eyes seemed to hesitate a little before smiling with the mouth.

'It's fine,' said Rusty. 'I'll soon get used to the room.'

There was a silence. Rusty concentrated on the allu chole, feeling guilty and ungrateful.

'Ranbir has gone,' said Somi.

'Oh, he didn't even say good bye!'

'He has not gone for ever. And anyway, what would be the use of saying good-bye . . . .'

He sounded depressed. He finished his allu chole and said: 'Rusty, best favourite friend, if you don't want this job I'll find you another.'

'But I like it, Somi, I want it, really I do. You are trying to do too much for me. Mrs Kapoor is wonderful, and Mr Kapoor is good fun, and Kishen is not so bad, you know . . . . Come on to the house and see the room. It's the kind of room in which you write poetry or create music.'

They walked home in the evening. The evening was full of sounds. Rusty noticed the sounds, because he was happy, and a happy person notices things.

Carriages passed them on the road, creaking and rattling, wheels squeaking, hoofs resounding on the ground; and the whip-cracks above the horse's ear, and the driver shouts, and round go the wheels, squeaking and creaking, and the hoofs go clippety-clippety, clip-clop-clop . . . .

A bicycle came swishing through the puddles, the wheels purring and humming smoothly, the bell tinkling . . . . In the bushes there was the chatter of sparrows and seven-sisters, but Rusty could not see them no matter how hard he looked.

And there were footsteps . . . .

Their own footsteps, quiet and thoughtful; and ahead of them an old man, with a dhoti round his legs and a black umbrella in his hand, walking at a clockwork pace. At each alternate step he tapped with his umbrella on the pavement; he wore noisy shoes, and his footsteps echoed off the pavement to the beat of the umbrella. Rusty and Somi quickened their own steps, passed him by, and let the endless tapping die on the wind.

They sat on the roof for an hour, watching the sun set; and Somi sang.

Somi had a beautiful voice, clear and mellow, matching the serenity of his face. And when he sang, his eyes wandered into the night, and he was lost to the world and to Rusty; for when he sang of the stars he was of the stars, and when he sang of a river he was a river. He communicated his mood to Rusty, as he could not have done in plain language; and, when the song ended, the silence returned and all the world fell asleep.

Chapter XI

RUSTY watched the dawn blossom into light.

At first everything was dark, then gradually objects began to take shape—the desk and chair, the walls of the room—and the darkness lifted like the raising of a veil, and over the tree-tops the sky was streaked with crimson. It was like this for some time, while everything became clearer and more distinguishable; and then, when nature was ready, the sun reached up over the trees and hills, and sent one tentative beam of warm light through the window. Along the wall crept the sun, across to the bed, and up the boy's bare legs, until it was caressing his entire body and whispering to him to get up, get up, it is time to get up . . . .

Rusty blinked. He sat up and rubbed his eyes and looked around. It was his first morning in the room, and perched on the window-sill was a small brown and yellow bird, a maina, looking at him with its head cocked to one side. The maina was a common sight, but this one was unusual: it was bald: all the feathers had been knocked off its head in a series of fights.

Rusty wondered if he should get up and bathe, or wait for someone to arrive. But he didn't wait long. Something bumped him from under the bed.

He stiffened with apprehension. Something was moving beneath him, the mattress rose gently and fell. Could it be a jackal or a wolf that had stolen in through the open door during the night? Rusty trembled, but did not move . . . . It might be something even more dangerous, the house was close to the jungle . . . . or it might be a thief . . . but what was there to steal?

Unable to bear the suspense, Rusty brought his fists down on the uneven lump in the quilt, and Kishen sprang out with a cry of pain and astonishment.

58

He sat on his bottom and cursed Rusty.

'Sorry,' said Rusty, 'but you frightened me.'

'I'm glad, because you hurt me, mister.'

'Your fault. What's the time?'

'Time to get up. I've brought you some milk, and you can have mine too, I hate it, it spoils the flavour of my chewing-gum.'

Kishen accompanied Rusty to the water-tank, where they met Somi. After they had bathed and filled their *sohrais* with drinking-water, they went back to the room for the first lesson.

Kishen and Rusty sat cross-legged on the bed, facing each other. Rusty fingered his chin, and Kishen played with his toes.

'What do you want to learn today?' asked Rusty.

'How should I know? That's your problem, pardner.'

'As it's the first day, you can make a choice.'

'Let's play noughts and crosses.'

'Be serious. Tell me, bhaiya, what books have you read?'

Kishen turned his eyes up to the ceiling. 'I've read so many I can't remember the names.'

'Well, you can tell me what they were about.'

Kishen looked disconcerted. 'Oh, sure . . . sure . . . let me see now . . . what about the one in which everyone went down a rabbit-hole?'

'What about it?'

'Called *Treasure Island*.'

'Hell!' said Rusty.

'Which ones have you read?' asked Kishen, warming to the discussion.

'*Treasure Island* and the one about the rabbit-hole, and you haven't read either. What do you want to be when you grow up, Kishen? A businessman, an officer, an engineer?'

'Don't want to be anything. What about you?'

'You're not supposed to be asking me. But if you want to know, I'm going to be a writer. I'll write books. You'll read them.'

'You'll be a great writer, Rusty, you'll be great . . . .'

'Maybe, who knows.'

'I know,' said Kishen, quite sincerely, 'you'll be a terrific writer. You'll be famous. You'll be a king.'

'Shut up. . . .'

*

The Kapoors liked Rusty. They didn't admire him, but they liked him. Kishen liked him for his company, Kapoor liked him for his flattering conversation, and Meena liked him because—well, because he liked her . . . .

The Kapoors were glad to have him in their house.

Meena had been betrothed to Kapoor since childhood, before they knew each other, and despite the fact that there was a difference of nearly twenty years between their ages. Kapoor was a promising young man, intelligent and beginning to make money; and Meena, at thirteen, possessed the freshness and promise of spring. After they were married, they fell in love.

They toured Europe, and Kapoor returned a connoisseur of wine. Kishen was born, looking just like his father. Kapoor never stopped loving his wife, but his passion for her was never so great as when the warmth of old wine filled him with poetry. Meena had a noble nose and forehead ('Aristocratic,' said Kapoor; 'she has blue blood') and long raven-black hair ('Like seaweed,' said Kapoor, dizzy with possessive glory). She was tall, strong, perfectly formed, and she had grace and charm and a quick wit.

Kapoor lived in his beard and green dressing-gown, something of an outcast. The self-made man likes to boast of humble origins and initial poverty, and his rise from rags can be turned to effective publicity; the man who has lost much recalls past exploits and the good name of his family, and the failure at least publicizes these things. But Kapoor had gone full cycle: he could no longer harp on the rise from rags, because he was fast becoming ragged; and he had no background except the one which he himself created and destroyed; he had nothing but a dwindling bank balance, a wife and a son. And the wife was his best asset.

But on the evening of Rusty's second day in the room, no one would have guessed at the family's plight. Rusty sat with them in the front room, and Kapoor extolled the virtues of chewing-gum, much to Kishen's delight and Meena's disgust.

'Chewing-gum,' declared Kapoor, waving a finger in the air,

'is the secret of youth. Have you observed the Americans, how young they look, and the English, how haggard? It has nothing to do with responsibilities, it is chewing-gum. By chewing, you exercise your jaws and the muscles of your face. This improves your complexion and strengthens the tissues of your skin.'

'You're very clever, Daddy,' said Kishen.

'I'm a genius,' said Kapoor, 'I'm a genius.'

'The fool!' whispered Meena, so that only Rusty could hear.

Rusty said, 'I have an idea, let's form a club.'

'Good idea!' exclaimed Kishen. 'What do we call it?'

'Before we call it anything, we must decide what sort of club it should be. We must have rules, we must have a president, a secretary . . . .'

'All right, all right,' interrupted Kishen, who was sprawling on the floor, 'you can be all those things if you like. But what I say is, the most important thing in a club is name. Without a good name what's the use of a club?'

'The Fools' Club,' suggested Meena.

'Inappropriate,' said Kapoor, 'inappropriate . . . .'

'Everyone shut up,' ordered Kishen, prodding at his nose, 'I'm trying to think.'

They all shut up and tried to think.

This thinking was a very complicated process, and it soon became obvious that no one had been thinking of the club; for Rusty was looking at Meena thinking, and Meena was wondering if Kishen knew how to think, and Kishen was really thinking about the benefits of chewing-gum, and Kapoor was smelling the whisky bottles behind the screen and thinking of them.

At last Kapoor observed: 'My wife is a devil, a beautiful, beautiful devil!'

This seemed an interesting line of conversation, and Rusty was about to follow it up with a compliment of his own, when Kishen burst out brilliantly: 'I know! The Devil's Club? How's that?'

'Ah, ha!' exclaimed Kapoor, 'The Devil's Club, we've got it! I'm a genius.'

They got down to the business of planning the club's activities. Kishen proposed carom and Meena seconded, and Rusty looked dismayed. Kapoor proposed literary and political discussions and Rusty, just to spite the others, seconded the proposal. Then they elected officers of the club. Meena was given the title of Our Lady and Patroness, Kapoor was elected President, Rusty the Secretary, and Kishen the Chief Whip. Somi, Ranbir and Suri, though absent, were accepted as Honorary Members.

'Carom and discussions are not enough,' complained Kishen, 'we must have adventures.'

'What kind?' asked Rusty.

'Climb mountains or something.'

'A picnic,' proposed Meena.

'A picnic!' seconded Kishen, 'and Somi and the others can come too.'

'Let's drink to it,' said Kapoor, rising from his chair, 'let's celebrate.'

'Good idea,' said Kishen, foiling his father's plan of action, 'we'll go to the chaat shop!'

As far as Meena was concerned, the chaat shop was the lesser of the two evils, so Kapoor was bundled into the old car and taken to the bazaar.

'To the chaat shop!' he cried, falling across the steering-wheel. 'We will bring it home!'

The chaat shop was so tightly crowded that people were breathing each other's breath.

The chaat-wallah was very pleased with Rusty for bringing in so many new customers—a whole family—and beamed on the party, rubbing his hands and greasing the frying-pan with enthusiasm.

'Everything!' ordered Kapoor. 'We will have something of everything.'

So the chaat-wallah patted his cakes into shape and flipped them into the sizzling grease; and fashioned his gol-guppas over the fire, filling them with the juice of the devil.

Meena sat curled up on a chair, facing Rusty. The boy stared at her: she looked quaint, sitting in this unfamiliar posture. Her eyes encountered Rusty's stare, mocking it. In hot confusion, Rusty moved his eyes upward, up the wall, on to the ceiling, until they could go no further.

'What are you looking at?' asked Kishen.

Rusty brought his eyes to the ground, and pretended not to have heard. He turned to Kapoor and said, 'What about politics?'

The chaat-wallah handed out four big banana leaves.

But Kapoor wouldn't eat. Instead, he cried: 'Take the chaat shop to the house. Put it in the car, we must have it! We must have it, we must have it!'

The chaat-wallah, who was used to displays of drunkenness in one form or another, humoured Kapoor. 'It is all yours, lallaji, but take me with you too, or who will run the shop?'

'We will!' shouted Kishen, infected by his father's enthusiasm. 'Buy it, Daddy. Mummy can make the tikkees and I'll sell them and Rusty can do the accounts!'

Kapoor threw his banana leaf of the floor and wrapped his arms round Kishen. 'Yes, we will run it! Take it to the house!' And, making a lunge at a bowl of chaat, fell to his knees.

Rusty helped Kapoor get up, then looked to Meena for guidance. She said nothing, but gave him a nod, and the boy found he understood the nod.

He said, 'It's a wonderful idea, Mr Kapoor, just put me in charge of everything. You and Meena go home and get a spare room ready for the supplies, and Kishen and I will make all the arrangements with the chaat-wallah.'

Kapoor clung to Rusty, the spittle dribbling down his cheeks. 'Good boy, good boy . . . we will make lots of money together, you and I . . . . ' He turned to his wife and waved his arm grandiloquently: 'We will be rich again, Meena, what do you say?'

Meena, as usual, said nothing; but took Kapoor by the arm and bundled him out of the shop and into the car.

'Be quick with the chaat shop!' cried Kapoor.

'I will have it in the house in five minutes,' called Rusty. 'Get everything ready!'

He returned to Kishen, who was stuffing himself with chaat; his father's behaviour did not appear to have affected him, he was unconscious of its ridiculous aspect and felt no shame; he was unconscious too of the considerate manner of the chaat-wallah, who felt sorry for the neglected child. The chaat-wallah did not know that Kishen enjoyed being neglected.

Rusty said, 'Come, let's go . . . .'

'What's the hurry, Rusty? Sit down and eat, there's plenty of dough tonight. At least give Mummy time to put the sleeping-tablets in the whisky.'

So they sat and ate their fill, and listened to other people's gossip; then Kishen suggested that they explore the bazaar.

The oil lamps were lit, and the main road bright and crowded; but Kishen and Rusty went down an alleyway, where the smells were more complicated and the noise intermittent; two women spoke to each other from their windows on either side of the road, a baby cried monotonously, a cheap gramophone blared. Kishen and Rusty walked aimlessly through the maze of alleyways.

'Why are you white like Suri?' asked Kishen.

'Why is Suri white?'

'He is Kashmiri; they are fair.'

'Well, I am English . . . .'

'English?' said Kishen disbelievingly. 'You? But you do not look like one.'

Rusty hesitated: he did not feel there was any point in raking up a past that was as much a mystery to him as it was to Kishen.

'I don't know,' he said. 'I never saw my parents. And I don't care what they were and I don't care what I am, and I'm not very interested . . . .'

But he couldn't help wondering, and Kishen couldn't help wondering, so they walked on in silence, wondering . . . . They reached the railway station, which was the end of the bazaar; the gates were closed, but they peered through the railings at the goods wagons. A pleasure house did business near the station.

'If you want to have fun,' said Kishen, 'let's climb that roof. From the skylight you can see everything.'

'No fun in just watching,' said Rusty.

'Have you ever watched?'

'Of course,' lied Rusty, turning homewards; he walked with a distracted air.

'What are you thinking of?' asked Kishen.

'Nothing.'

'You must be in love.'

'That's right.'

'Who is it, eh?'

'If I told you,' said Rusty, 'you'd be jealous.'

'But I'm not in love with anybody. Come on, tell me, I'm your friend.'

'Would you be angry if I said I loved your mother?'

'Mummy!' exclaimed Kishen. 'But she's old! She's married. Hell, who would think of falling in love with Mummy? Don't joke, mister.'

'I'm sorry,' said Rusty.

They walked on in silence and crossed the maidan, leaving the bazaar behind. It was dark on the maidan, they could hardly see each other's faces; Kishen put his hand on Rusty's shoulder.

'If you love her,' he said, 'I'm not jealous. But it sounds funny . . . . '

Chapter XII

IN his room, Rusty was a king. His domain was the sky and everything he could see. His subjects were the people who passed below, but they were his subjects only while they were below and he was on the roof; and he spied on them through the branches of the banyan tree. His close confidants were the inhabitants of the banyan tree; which, of course, included Kishen.

It was the day of the picnic, and Rusty had just finished bathing at the water-tank. He had become used to the people at the tank and had made friends with the ayahs and their charges. He had come to like their bangles and bracelets and ankle-bells. He liked to watch one of them at the tap, squatting on her haunches, scrubbing her feet, and making much music with the bells and bangles; she would roll her sari up to the knees to give her legs greater freedom, and crouch forward so that her jacket revealed a modest expanse of waist.

It was the day of the picnic, and Rusty had bathed, and now he sat on a disused chimney, drying himself in the sun.

Summer was coming. The litchees were almost ready to eat, the mangoes ripened under Kishen's greedy eye. In the afternoons the sleepy sunlight stole through the branches of the banyan tree, and made a patchwork of arched shadows on the walls of the house. The inhabitants of the trees knew that summer was coming; Somi's slippers knew it, and slapped lazily against his heels; and Kishen grumbled and became more untidy, and even Suri seemed to be taking a rest from his private investigations. Yes, summer was coming.

And it was the day of the picnic.

The car had been inspected, and the two bottles that Kapoor had hidden in the dickey had been found and removed; Kapoor was put into khaki drill trousers and a bush-shirt and pronounced fit to drive; a basket of food and a gramophone were in the dickey. Suri had a camera slung over his shoulders; Kishen was sporting a Gurkha hat; and Rusty had on a thick leather belt reinforced with steel knobs. Meena had dressed in a hurry, and looked the better for it. And for once, Somi had tied his turban to perfection.

'Everyone present?' said Meena. 'If so, get into the car.'

'I'm waiting for my dog,' said Suri, and he had hardly made the announcement when from around the corner came a yapping mongrel.

'He's called Prickly Heat,' said Suri. 'We'll put him in the back seat.'

'He'll go in the dickey,' said Kishen. 'I can see the lice from here.'

Prickly Heat wasn't any particular kind of dog, just a kind of dog; he hadn't even the stump of a tail. But he had sharp, pointed ears that wagged as well as any tail, and they were working furiously this morning.

Suri and the dog were both deposited in the dickey; Somi, Kishen and Rusty made themselves comfortable in the back seat, and Meena sat next to her husband in the front. The car belched and lurched forward, and stirred up great clouds of dust; then, accelerating, sped out of the compound and across the narrow wooden bridge that spanned the canal.

The sun rose over the forest, and a spiral of smoke from a panting train was caught by a slanting ray and spangled with gold. The air was fresh and exciting. It was ten miles to the river and the sulphur springs, ten miles of intermittent grumbling and gaiety, with Prickly Heat yapping in the dickey and Kapoor whistling at the wheel and Kishen letting fly from the window with a catapult.

Somi said: 'Rusty, your pimples will leave you if you bathe in the sulphur springs.'

'I would rather have pimples than pneumonia,' replied Rusty.

'But it's not cold,' and Kishen. 'I would bathe myself, but I don't feel very well.'

'Then you shouldn't have come,' said Meena from the front.

'I didn't want to disappoint you all,' said Kishen.

Before reaching the springs, the car had to cross one or two river-beds, usually dry at this time of the year. But the mountains had tricked the party, for there was a good deal of water to be seen, and the current was strong.

'It's not very deep,' said Kapoor, at the first river-bed, 'I think we can drive through easily.'

The car dipped forward, rolled down the bank, and entered the current with a great splash. In the dickey, Suri got a soaking.

'Got to go fast,' said Mr Kapoor, 'or we'll stick.'

He accelerated, and a great spray of water rose on both sides of the car. Kishen cried out for sheer joy, but at the back Suri was having a fit of hysterics.

'I think the dog's fallen out,' said Meena.

'Good,' said Somi.

'I think Suri's fallen out,' said Rusty.

'Good,' said Somi.

Suddenly the engines spluttered and choked, and the car came to a standstill.

'We have stuck,' said Kapoor.

'That,' said Meena bitingly, 'is obvious. Now I suppose you want us all to get out and push?'

'Yes, that's a good idea.'

'You're a genius.'

Kishen had his shoes off in a flash, and was leaping about in the water with great abandon. The water reached up to his knees and, as he hadn't been swept off his feet, the others followed his example.

Meena rolled her sari up to the thighs, and stepped gingerly into the current. Her legs, so seldom exposed, were very fair in contrast to her feet and arms, but they were strong and nimble, and she held herself erect. Rusty stumbled to her side, intending to aid her; but ended by clinging to her dress for support. Suri was not to be seen anywhere.

'Where is Suri?' said Meena.

'Here,' said a muffled voice from the floor of the dickey. 'I've got sick. I can't push.'

'All right,' said Meena. 'But you'll clean up the mess yourself.'

Somi and Kishen were looking for fish. Kapoor tootled the horn.

'Are you all going to push?' he said, 'or are we going to have the picnic in the middle of the river?'

Rusty was surprised at Kapoor's unusual display of common sense; when sober, Mr Kapoor did sometimes have moments of sanity.

Everyone put their weight against the car, and pushed with all their strength; and, as the car moved slowly forward, Rusty felt a thrill of health and pleasure run through his body. In front of him, Meena pushed silently, the muscles of her thighs trembling with the strain. They all pushed silently, with determination; the sweat ran down Somi's face and neck, and Kishen's jaws worked desperately on his chewing-gum. But Kapoor sat in comfort behind the wheel, pressing and pulling knobs, and saying 'harder, push harder', and Suri began to be sick again. Prickly Heat was strangely quiet, and it was assumed that the dog was sick too.

With one last final heave, the car was moved up the opposite bank and on to the straight. Everyone groaned and flopped to the ground. Meena's hands were trembling.

'You shouldn't have pushed,' said Rusty.

'I enjoyed it,' she said, smiling at him. 'Help me to get up.'

He rose and, taking her hand, pulled her to her feet. They stood together, holding hands. Kapoor fiddled around with starters and chokes and things.

'It won't go,' he said. 'I'll have to look at the engine. We might as well have the picnic here.'

So out came the food and lemonade bottles and, miraculously enough, out came Suri and Prickly Heat, looking as fit as ever.

'Hey,' said Kishen, 'we thought you were sick. I suppose you were just making room for lunch.'

'Before he eats anything,' said Somi, 'he's going to get wet. Let's take him for a swim.'

Somi, Kishen and Rusty caught hold of Suri and dragged him along the river-bank to a spot downstream where the current was mild and the water warm and waist-high. They unrobed Suri, took off their own clothes, and ran down the sandy slope to the water's edge; feet splashed ankle-deep, calves thrust into the current, and then the ground suddenly disappeared beneath their feet.

Somi was a fine swimmer; his supple limbs cut through the water and, when he went under, he was almost as powerful; the chequered colours of his body could be seen first here and then there, twisting and turning, diving and disappearing for what seemed like several minutes, and then coming up under someone's feet.

Rusty and Kishen were amateurs. When they tried swimming underwater, their bottoms remained on the surface, having all the appearance of floating buoys. Suri couldn't swim at all but, though he was often out of his depth and frequently ducked, managed to avoid his death by drowning.

They heard Meena calling them for food, and scrambled up the bank, the dog yapping at their heels. They ate in the shade of a poinsettia tree, whose red long-fingered flowers dropped sensually to the running water; and when they had eaten, lay down to sleep or drowse the afternoon away.

When Rusty awoke, it was evening, and Kapoor was tinkering about with the car, muttering to himself, a little cross because he hadn't had a drink since the previous night. Somi and Kishen were back in the river, splashing away, and this time they had Prickly Heat for company. Suri wasn't in sight. Meena stood in a clearing at the edge of the forest.

Rusty went to Meena, but she wandered into the thicket. The boy followed. She must have expected him, for she showed no surprise at his appearance.

'Listen to the jungle,' she said.

'I can't hear anything.'

'That's what I mean. Listen to nothing.'

They were surrounded by silence; a dark, pensive silence, heavy, scented with magnolia and jasmine.

It was shattered by a piercing shriek, a cry that rose on all sides, echoing against the vibrating air; and, instinctively, Rusty put his arm round Meena—whether to protect her or to protect himself, he did not really know—and held her tight.

'It is only a bird,' she said, 'of what are you afraid?'

But he was unable to release his hold, and she made no effort to free herself. She laughed into his face, and her eyes danced in the shadows. But he stifled her laugh with his lips.

It was a clumsy, awkward kiss, but fiercely passionate, and Meena responded, tightening the embrace, returning the fervour of the kiss. They stood together in the shadows, Rusty intoxicated with beauty and sweetness, Meena with freedom and the comfort of being loved.

A monkey chattered shrilly in a branch above them, and the spell was broken.

'Oh, Meena . . . .'

'Shh . . . you spoil these things by saying them.'

'Oh, Meena . . . .'

They kissed again, but the monkey set up such a racket that they feared it would bring Kapoor and the others to the spot. So they walked through the trees, holding hands.

They were barefooted, but they did not notice the thorns and brambles that pricked their feet; they walked through heavy foliage, nettles and long grass, until they came to a clearing and a stream.

Rusty was conscious of a wild urge, a desire to escape from the town and its people, and live in the forest with Meena, with no one but Meena . . . .

As though conscious of his thoughts, she said: 'This is where we drink. In the trees we eat and sleep, and here we drink.'

She laughed, but Rusty had a dream in his heart. The pebbles on the bed of the stream were round and smooth, taking the flow of water without resistance. Only weed and rock could resist water: only weed or rock could resist life.

'It would be nice to stay in the jungle,' said Meena.

'Let us stay. . . .'

'We will be found. We cannot escape—from—others . . . .'

'Even the world is too small. Maybe there is more freedom in your little room than in all the jungle and all the world.'

Rusty pointed to the stream and whispered, 'Look!'

Meena looked, and at the same time a deer looked up. They looked at each other with startled, fascinated eyes, the deer and Meena. It was a spotted cheetal, a small animal with delicate, quivering limbs and muscles, and young green antlers.

Rusty and Meena did not move; nor did the deer; they might

71

have gone on staring at each other all night if somewhere a twig hadn't snapped sharply.

At the snap of the twig, the deer jerked its head up with a start, lifted one foot pensively, sniffed the air; then leapt the stream and, in a single bound, disappeared into the forest.

The spell was broken, the magic lost. Only the water ran on and life ran on.

'Let's go back,' said Meena.

They walked back through the dappled sunlight, swinging their clasped hands like two children who had only just discovered love.

Their hands parted as they reached the river-bed.

Miraculously enough, Kapoor had started the car, and was waving his arms and shouting to everyone to come home. Everyone was ready to start back except for Suri and Prickly Heat, who were nowhere to be seen. Nothing, thought Meena, would have been better than for Suri to disappear for ever, but unfortunately she had taken full responsibility for his well-being, and did not relish the thought of facing his strangely affectionate mother. So she asked Rusty to shout for him.

Rusty shouted, and Meena shouted, and Somi shouted, and then they all shouted together, only Suri didn't shout.

'He's up to his tricks,' said Kishen. 'We shouldn't have brought him. Let's pretend we're leaving, then he'll be scared.'

So Kapoor started the engine, and everyone got in, and it was only then that Suri came running from the forest, the dog at his heels, his shirt-tails flapping in the breeze, his hair wedged between his eyes and his spectacles.

'Hey, wait for us!' he cried. 'Do you want me to die?'

Kishen mumbled in the affirmative, and swore quietly.

'We thought you were in the dickey,' said Rusty.

Suri and Prickly Heat climbed into the dickey, and at the same time the car entered the river with a determined splashing and churning of wheels, to emerge the victor.

Everyone cheered, and Somi gave Kapoor such an enthusiastic slap on the back that the pleased recipient nearly caught his head in the steering-wheel.

It was dark now, and all that could be seen of the countryside was what the headlights showed. Rusty had hopes of seeing a panther or tiger, for this was their territory, but only a few goats blocked the road. However, for the benefit of Suri, Somi told a story of a party that had gone for an outing in a car and, on returning home, had found a panther in the dickey.

Kishen fell asleep just before they reached the outskirts of Dehra, his fuzzy head resting on Rusty's shoulder. Rusty felt protectively towards the boy, for a bond of genuine affection had grown between the two. Somi was Rusty's best friend, in the same way that Ranbir was a friend, and their friendship was on a high emotional plane. But Kishen was a brother more than a friend. He loved Rusty, but without knowing or thinking or saying it, and that is the love of a brother.

Somi began singing. Then the town came in sight, the bazaar lights twinkling defiance at the starry night.

Chapter XIII

Rusty and Mr Harrison met in front of the town's main grocery store, the 'wine and general merchant's'; it was part of the smart shopping centre, alien to the bazaar but far from the European community—and thus neutral ground for Rusty and Mr Harrison.

'Hallo, Mr Harrison,' said Rusty, confident of himself and deliberately omitting the customary 'sir'.

Mr Harrison tried to ignore the boy, but found him blocking the way to the car. Not wishing to lose his dignity, he decided to be pleasant.

'This is a surprise,' he said, 'I never thought I'd see you again.'

'I found a job,' said Rusty, taking the opportunity of showing his independence. 'I meant to come and see you, but didn't get the time.'

'You're always welcome. The missionary's wife often speaks of you, she'd be glad to see you. By the way, what's your job?'

Rusty hesitated; he did not know how his guardian would take the truth—probably with a laugh or a sneer ('you're *teaching*!')—and decided to be mysterious about his activities.

'Baby-sitting,' he replied, with a disarming smile. 'Anyway, I'm not starving. And I've got many friends.'

Mr Harrison's face darkened, and the corners of his mouth twitched; but he remembered that times had changed, and that Rusty was older and also free, and that he wasn't in his own house; and he controlled his temper.

'I can get you a job,' he said. 'On a tea estate. Or, if you like to go abroad, I have friends in Guiana . . . .'

'I like baby-sitting,' said Rusty.

Mr Harrison smiled, got into the car, and lit a cigarette before starting the engine. 'Well, as I said, you're always welcome in the house.'

'Thanks,' said Rusty. 'Give my regards to the sweeper boy.'

The atmosphere was getting tense.

'Why don't you come and see him some time?' said Mr Harrison, as softly and as malevolently as he could.

It was just as well the engine had started.

'I will,' said Rusty.'

'I kicked him out,' said Mr Harrison, putting his foot down on the accelerator and leaving Rusty in a cloud of dust.

But Rusty's rage turned to pleasure when the car almost collided with a stationary bullock-cart, and a uniformed policeman brought it to a halt. With the feeling that he had been the master of the situation, Rusty walked homewards.

The litchee trees were covered with their pink-skinned fruit, and the mangoes were almost ripe. The mango is a passionate fruit, its inner gold sensuous to the lips and tongue. The grass had not yet made up its mind to remain yellow or turn green, and would probably keep its dirty colour until the monsoon rains arrived.

Meena met Rusty under the banana trees.

'I am bored,' she said, 'so I am going to give you a haircut. Do you mind?'

'I will do anything to please you. But don't take it all off.'

'Don't you trust me?'

'I love you.'

Rusty was wrapped up in a sheet and placed on a chair. He looked up at Meena, and their eyes met, laughing, blue and brown.

Meena cut silently, and the fair hair fell quickly, softly, lightly to the ground. Rusty enjoyed the snip of the scissors, and the sensation of lightness; it was as though his mind was being given more room in which to explore.

Kishen came loafing around the corner of the house, still wearing his pyjamas, which were rolled up to the knees. When he saw what was going on, he burst into laughter.

'And what is so funny?' said Rusty.

'You!' spluttered Kishen. 'Where is your hair, your beautiful golden hair? Has Mummy made you become a monk? Or have you got ringworm? Or fleas? Look at the ground, all that beautiful hair!'

'Don't be funny, Kishen bhaiya,' said Meena, 'or you will get the same treatment.'

'Is it so bad?' asked Rusty anxiously.

'Don't you trust me?' said Meena.

'I love you.'

Meena glanced swiftly at Kishen to see if he had heard the last remark, but he was still laughing at Rusty's haircut and prodding his nose for all he was worth.

'Rusty, I have a favour to ask you,' said Meena. 'Mr Kapoor and I may be going to Delhi for a few weeks, as there is a chance of him getting a good job. We are not taking Kishen bhaiya, as he is only nuisance value, so will you look after him and keep him out of mischief? I will leave some money with you. About how much will you need for two weeks?'

'When are you going?' asked Rusty, already in the depths of despair.

'How much will you need?'

'Oh, fifty rupees . . . but when—'

'A hundred rupees!' interrupted Kishen. 'Oh boy, Rusty, we'll have fun!'

'Seventy-five,' said Meena, as though driving a bargain, 'and I'll send more after two weeks. But we should be back by then. There, Rusty, your haircut is complete.'

But Rusty wasn't interested in the result of the haircut; he felt like sulking; he wanted to have some say in Meena's plans, he felt he had a right to a little power.

That evening, in the front room, he didn't talk much. Nobody spoke. Kishen lay on the ground, stroking his stomach, his toes tracing imaginary patterns on the wall. Meena looked tired; wisps of hair had fallen across her face, and she did not bother to brush them back. She took Kishen's foot and gave it a pull.

'Go to bed,' she said.

'Not tired.'

'Go to bed, or you'll get a slap.'

Kishen laughed defiantly, but got up from the floor and ambled out of the room.

'And don't wake Daddy,' she said.

Kapoor had been put to bed early, as Meena wanted him to be fresh and sober for his journey to Delhi and his interviews there. But every now and then he would wake up and call out for something—something unnecessary, so that after a while no one paid any attention to his requests. He was like an irritable invalid, to be humoured and tolerated.

'Are you not feeling well, Meena?' asked Rusty. 'If you like, I'll also go.'

'I am only tired, don't go . . . .'

She went to the window and drew the curtains and put out the light. Only the table lamp burned. The lampshade was decorated with dragons and butterflies—it was a Chinese lampshade—and, as Rusty sat gazing at the light, the dragons began to move and the butterflies flutter. He couldn't see Meena, but felt her presence across the room.

She turned from the window; and silently, with hardly a rustle, slipped to the ground. Her back against the couch, her head resting against the cushion, she looked up at the ceiling. Neither of them spoke.

From the next room came sounds of Kishen preparing for the night, one or two thumps and a muttered imprecation. Kapoor snored quietly to himself, and the rest was silence.

Rusty's gaze left the revolving dragons and prancing butterflies to settle on Meena, who sat still and tired, her feet lifeless against the table legs, her slippers fallen to the ground. In the lamplight, her feet were like jade.

A moth began to fly round the lamp, and it went round and round and closer, till—with a sudden plop—it hit the lampshade and fell to the ground. But Rusty and Meena were still silent, their breathing the only conversation.

Chapter XIV

URING the day, flies circled the room with feverish buzzing, and at night the mosquitoes came singing in one's ears; summer days were hot and sticky, the nights breathless.

Rusty covered his body in citronella oil, which had been given him by Somi's mother; its smell, while pleasant to his own senses, was repugnant to mosquitoes.

When Rusty rubbed the oil on his limbs he noticed the change in his physique. He had lost his puppy fat, and there was more muscle to his body; his complexion was a healthier colour, and his pimples had almost disappeared. Nearly everyone had advised him about his pimples: drink *dhai*, said Somi's mother, don't eat fat; eat carrots, said Somi; plenty of fruit; mangoes! said Kishen; not at all, oranges; see a doctor, said Meena; have a whisky, said Kapoor: but the pimples disappeared without any of these remedies, and Rusty put it down to his falling in love.

The bougainvillaea creeper had advanced further into the room, and was now in flower; and watching Rusty oil himself, was the bald maina bird; it had been in so many fights that the feathers on its head never got a chance to grow.

Suri entered the room without warning and, wiping his spectacles on the bed-sheet, said: 'I have written an essay, Mister Rusty, for which I am going to be marked in school. Correct it, if you please.'

'Let me finish with this oil . . . . It would be cheating, you know.'

'No, it won't. It has to be corrected some time, so you will save the master some trouble. Anyway, I'm leaving this rotten school soon. I'm going to Mussoorie.'

'To the same place as Ranbir? He'll be glad to see you.'

Suri handed Rusty the copy-book. On the cover was a pencil

78

sketch of a rather over-developed nude.

'Don't tell me this is your school book!' exclaimed Rusty.

'No, only rough work.'

'You drew the picture?'

'Of course, don't you like it?'

'Did you copy it, or imagine it, or did someone pose for you?'

Suri winked. 'Someone posed.'

'You're a liar. And a pig.'

'Oh, look who's talking! You're not such a saint yourself, Mister Rusty.'

'Just what do you mean,' said Rusty, getting between Suri and the door.

'I mean, how is Mrs Kapoor, eh?'

'She is fine.'

'You get on well with her, eh?'

'We get on fine.'

'Like at the picnic?'

Suri rubbed his hands together, and smiled beatifically. Rusty was momentarily alarmed.

'What do you mean, the picnic?'

'What did you do together, Mister Rusty, you and Mrs Kapoor? What happened in the bushes?'

Rusty leant against the wall, and returned Suri's smile, and said: 'I'll tell you what we did, my friend. There's nothing to hide between friends, is there? Well, Mrs Kapoor and I spent all our time making love. We did nothing but love each other. All the time. And Mr Kapoor only a hundred yards away, and you in the next bush . . . . Now what else do you want to know?'

Suri's smile was fixed. 'What if I tell Mr Kapoor?'

'You won't tell him,' said Rusty.

'Why not?'

'Because you are the last person he'll believe. And you'll probably get a kick in the pants for the trouble.'

Suri's smile had gone.

'Cheer up,' said Rusty. 'What about the essay, do you want me to correct it?'

*

That afternoon the old car stood beneath the banana trees with an impatient driver tooting on the horn. The dickey and bumpers were piled high with tin trunks and bedding-rolls, as though the Kapoors were going away for a lifetime. Meena wasn't going to let Kapoor drive her all the way to Delhi, and had taken on a professional instead.

Kapoor sat on the steps of the house, wearing his green dressing-gown, and making a throaty noise similar to that of the motor-horn.

'The devil!' he exclaimed, gesticulating towards Meena, who was bustling about indoors. 'The devil of a wife is taking me to Delhi! Ha! The car will never get there.'

'Oh yes, it will,' said Meena, thrusting her head out of the window, 'and it will get there with you in it, whether or not you shave and dress. So you might as well take a seat from now.'

Rusty went into the house, and found Meena locking rooms. She was looking a little tired and irritable.

'You're going sooner than I expected,' said Rusty. 'Has Kishen got the money?'

'No, you must keep it. I'll give it to you in five rupee notes, wait a minute . . . . He'll have to sleep with you, I'm locking the house . . . .'

She opened a drawer and, taking out an envelope, gave it to Rusty.

'The money,' she said. Rusty picked up a small suitcase and followed Meena outside to the car. He waited until she was seated before handing her the case and, when he did, their hands touched. She laced her fingers with his, and gave him a quick smile, and squeezed his fingers.

From the front seat Kapoor beckoned Rusty. He grasped the boy's hand, and slipped a key into it.

'My friend,' he whispered, 'these are the keys of the back door. In the kitchen you will find six bottles of whisky. Keep them safe, until our return.'

Rusty shook Kapoor's hand, the hand of the man he laughed at, but whom he could not help loving as well.

In the confusion Kishen had gone almost unnoticed, but he was there all the time, and now he suffered a light kiss from his mother and a heavy one from his father.

The car belched and, after narrowly missing a banana tree, rattled down the gravel path, bounced over a ditch, and disappeared in a cloud of dust.

Kishen and Rusty were flapping their handkerchiefs for all they were worth. Kishen was not a bit sorry that his parents had gone away, but Rusty felt like crying. He was conscious now of a sense of responsibility, which was a thing he did not like having, and of a sense of loss. But the depression was only momentary.

'Hey!' said Kishen. 'Do you see what I see?'

'I can see a lot of things that you can see, so what do you mean?'

'The clothes! Mummy's washing, it is all on the rose bushes!'

Meena had left without collecting her washing which, as always, had been left to dry on the rose bushes. Mr Kapoor's underwear spread itself over an entire bush, and another tree was decorated with bodices and blouses of all colours.

Rusty said: 'Perhaps she means them to dry by the time she comes back.'

He began to laugh with Kishen, so it was a good thing, Meena's forgetfulness; it softened the pain of parting.

'What if we hadn't noticed?' chuckled Kishen.

'They would have been stolen.'

'Then we must reward ourselves. What about the chaat shop, bhai?'

At the risk of making himself unpopular, Rusty faced Kishen and, with a determination, said: 'No chaat shop. We have got seventy rupees to last a month, and I am not going to write for more once this finishes. We are having our meals with Somi. So, bhai, no chaat shop!'

'You are a swine, Rusty.'

'And the same to you.'

In this endearing mood they collected the clothes from the rose bushes, and marched upstairs to the room on the roof.

*

There was only one bed, and Kishen was a selfish sleeper; twice during the night Rusty found himself on the floor. Eventually he sat in the chair, with his feet on the table, and stared out of the window at the black night. Even if he had been comfortable, he would not have slept; he felt terribly lovesick. He wanted to write a poem, but it was too dark to write; he wanted to write a letter, but she hadn't been away a day; he wanted to run away with Meena, into the hills, into the forests, where no one could find them, and he wanted to be with her for ever and never grow old . . . neither of them must ever grow old . . . .

Chapter XV

I N the morning there was a note from Suri. Rusty wondered how Suri had managed to leave it on the door-step without being seen. It went:

Tomorrow I'm going up to Mussoorie. This is to request the pleasure of Misters Rusty and Kishen to my good-bye party, five o'clock sharp this same evening.

As soon as it became known that Suri was leaving, everyone began to love him. And everyone brought him presents, just so he wouldn't change his mind and stay.

Kishen bought him a pair of cheap binoculars so that he could look at the girls more closely, and the guests sat down at a table and Suri entertained them in grand style; and they tolerated everything he said and were particularly friendly and gave him three cheers, hooray, hooray, hooray, they were so glad he was going.

They drank lemonade and ate cream cakes (specially obtained from the smart restaurant amongst the smart shops) and Kishen said, 'We are so sorry you are leaving, Suri,' and they had more cream cakes and lemonade, and Kishen said, 'You are like a brother to us, Suri dear'; and when the cream cakes had all been finished, Kishen fell on Suri's neck and kissed him.

It was all very moving, those cream cakes and lemonade and Suri going away.

Kishen made himself sick, and Rusty had to help him back to the room. Kishen lay prostrate on the bed, whilst Rusty sat in front of the window, gazing blankly into the branches of the banyan tree.

Presently he said: 'It's drizzling. I think there'll be a storm, I've never seen the sky so black.'

As though to confirm this observation, there was a flash of lightning in the sky. Rusty's eyes lit up with excitement; he liked storms; sometimes they were an expression of his innermost feelings.

'Shut the window,' said Kishen.

'If I shut the window, I will kill the flowers on the creeper.'

Kishen snorted, 'You're a poet, that's what you are!'

'One day I'll write poems.'

'Why not today?'

'Too much is happening today.'

'I don't think so. Nothing ever happens in Dehra. The place is dead. Why don't you start writing now? You're a great writer, I told you so before.'

'I know.'

'One day . . . one day you'll be a king . . . but only in your dreams . . . . Meanwhile, shut the window!'

But Rusty liked the window open, he liked the rain flecking his face, and he liked to watch it pattering on the leaves of the banyan tree.

'They must have reached Delhi now,' he said, half to himself.

'Daddy's drunk,' said Kishen.

'There's nothing for him to drink.'

'Oh, he'll find something. You know, one day he drank up all the hair oil in the house. Hey, didn't he give you the keys of the back door? Let's drink one of the bottles ourselves . . . .'

Rusty didn't reply. The tense sky shuddered. The blanket of black cloud groaned aloud and the air, which had been still and sultry, trembled with electricity. Then the thunder gave a great clap, and all at once the hailstones came clattering down on the corrugated iron roof.

'What a noise!' exclaimed Kishen. 'You'd think a lot of skeletons were having a fight on the roof!'

The hailstones, as big as marbles, bounced in from the doorway, and on the roof they were forming a layer of white ice. Through the window Rusty could see one of the ayahs tearing down the gravel path, the pram bouncing madly over the stones, the end of her head-cloth flapping wildly.

'Will you shut the window!' screamed Kishen.

'Why are you so cruel, bhai?'

'I'm not cruel, I'm *sick*! Do you want me to get sick all over the place?'

As gently as he could, Rusty pushed the creeper out of the window and laid it against the outside wall. Then he closed the window. This shut out the view, because the window was made of plywood and had no glass panes.

'And the door,' moaned Kishen

With the door closed, the room was plunged into darkness.

'What a room,' complained Kishen, 'not even a light. You'll have to live downstairs when they come back.'

'But I like it here.'

The storm continued all night; it made Kishen so nervous that, instead of pushing Rusty off the bed, he put his arms round him for protection.

*

The rain had stopped by morning, but the sky was still overcast and threatening. Rusty and Kishen lay in bed, too bored to bestir themselves. There was some dried fruit in a tin, and they ate the nuts continuously. They could hear the postman making his rounds below, and Rusty suddenly remembered that the postman wouldn't know the Kapoors had left. He leapt out of bed, opened the door, and ran to the edge of the roof.

'Hey postman!' he called. 'Anything for Mr and Mrs Kapoor?'

'Nothing,' said the postman, 'but there is something for you, shall I come up?'

But Rusty was already on his way down, certain that it was a letter from Meena.

It was a telegram. Rusty's fingers trembled as he tore it open, and he had read it before he reached the room. His face was white when he entered the room.

'What's wrong,' said Kishen, 'you look sick. Doesn't Mummy love you any more?'

Rusty sat down on the edge of the bed, his eyes staring emptily at the floor.

'You're to go to Hardwar,' he said at last, 'to stay with your aunty.'

'Well, you can tell Mummy I'm staying here.'

'It's from your aunty.'

'Why couldn't Mummy say so herself?'

'I don't want to tell you.'

'But you have to tell me!' cried Kishen, making an ineffectual grab at the telegram. 'You have to tell me, Rusty, you have to!'

There was panic in Kishen's voice, he was almost hysterical.

'All right,' said Rusty, and his own voice was strained and hollow. 'The car had an accident.'

'And something happened to Daddy?'

'No.'

There was a terrible silence. Kishen looked helplessly at Rusty, his eyes full of tears and bewilderment; and Rusty could stand the strain no longer, and threw his arms round Kishen, and wept uncontrollably.

'Oh, Mummy, Mummy,' cried Kishen, 'Oh, Mummy. . . .'

Chapter XVI

I T was late evening the same day, and the clouds had passed and the whole sky was sprinkled with stars. Rusty sat on the bed, looking out at the stars and waiting for Kishen.

Presently bare feet sounded on the stone floor, and Rusty could make out the sharp lines of Kishen's body against the faint moon in the doorway.

'Why do you creep in like a ghost?' whispered Rusty.

'So's not to wake you.'

'It's still early. Where have you been, I was looking for you.'

'Oh, just walking . . . .'

Kishen sat down beside Rusty, facing the same way, the stars. The moonlight ran over their feet, but their faces were in darkness.

'Rusty,' said Kishen.

'Yes.'

'I don't want to go to Hardwar.'

'I know you don't, bhaiya. But you will not be allowed to stay here. You must go to your relatives. And Hardwar is a beautiful place, and people are kind . . . .'

'I'll stay with you.'

'I can't look after you, Kishen, I haven't got any money, any work . . . you must stay with your aunt. I'll come to see you.'

'You'll never come.'

'I'll try.'

Every night the jackals could be heard howling in the nearby jungle, but tonight their cries sounded nearer, much nearer the house.

Kishen slept. He was exhausted; he had been walking all evening, crying his heart out. Rusty lay awake; his eyes were wide open, brimming with tears; he did not know if the tears were for

87

himself or for Meena or for Kishen, but they were for someone.

Meena is dead, he told himself, Meena is dead; if there is a God, then God look after her; if God is Love, then my love will be with her; she loved me; I can see her so clearly, her face speckled with sun and shadow when we kissed in the forest, the black waterfall of hair, her tired eyes, her feet like jade in the lamplight, she loved me, she was mine . . . .

Rusty was overcome by a feeling of impotence and futility, and of the unimportance of life. Every moment, he told himself, every moment someone is born and someone dies, you can count them one, two, three, a birth and a death for every moment . . . what is this one life in the whole pattern of life, what is this one death but a passing of time . . . . And if I were to die now, suddenly and without cause, what would happen, would it matter . . . we live without knowing why or to what purpose.

The moon bathed the room in a soft, clear light. The howl of the jackals seemed to be coming from the field below, and Rusty thought, 'A jackal is like death, ugly and cowardly and mad . . . .' He heard a faint sniff from the doorway, and lifted his head.

In the doorway, a dark silhouette against the moonlight, stood the lean, craving form of a jackal, its eyes glittering balefully.

Rusty wanted to scream. He wanted to throw everything in the room at the snivelling, cold-blooded beast, or throw himself out of the window instead. But he could do none of these things.

The jackal lifted its head to the sky and emitted a long, blood-curdling howl that ran like an electric current through Rusty's body. Kishen sprang up with a gasp and threw his arms round Rusty.

And then Rusty screamed.

It was half shout, half scream, and it began in the pit of his stomach, was caught by his lungs, and catapulted into the empty night. Everything around him seemed to be shaking, vibrating to the pitch of the scream.

The jackal fled. Kishen whimpered and sprang back from Rusty and dived beneath the bedclothes.

And as the scream and its echo died away, the night closed in again, with a heavy, petrifying stillness; and all that could be heard was Kishen sobbing under the blankets, terrified not so much by the jackal's howl as by Rusty's own terrible scream.

'Oh, Kishen bhai,' cried Rusty, putting his arms around the boy, 'don't cry, please don't cry. You are making me afraid of myself. Don't be afraid, Kishen. Don't make me afraid of myself . . . .'

*

And in the morning their relationship was a little strained.

Kishen's aunt arrived. She had a tonga ready to take Kishen away. She give Rusty a hundred rupees, which she said was from Mr Kapoor; Rusty didn't want to take it, but Kishen swore at him and forced him to accept it.

The tonga pony was restless, pawing the ground and champing at the bit, snorting a little. The driver got down from the carriage and held the reins whilst Kishen and his aunt climbed on to their seats.

Kishen made no effort to conceal his misery.

'I wish you would come, Rusty,' he said.

'I will come and see you one day, be sure of that.'

It was very seldom that Kishen expressed any great depth of feeling; he was always so absorbed with comforts of the flesh that he never had any profound thoughts; but he did have profound feelings, though they were seldom thought or spoken.

He grimaced and prodded his nose.

'Inside of me,' he said, 'I am all lonely . . . .'

The driver cracked his whip, the horse snorted, the wheels creaked, and the tonga moved forward. The carriage bumped up in the ditch, and it looked as though everyone would be thrown out; but it bumped down again without falling apart, and Kishen and his aunt were still in their seats. The driver jingled his bell, and the tonga turned on to the main road that led to the station; the horse's hoofs clip-clopped, and the carriage-wheels squeaked and rattled.

Rusty waved. Kishen sat stiff and upright, clenching the ends of his shirt.

Rusty felt afraid for Kishen, who seemed to be sitting on his own, apart from his aunt, as though he disowned or did not know her: it seemed as though he were being borne away to some strange, friendless world, where no one would know or care for him; and, though Rusty knew Kishen to be wild and independent, he felt afraid for him.

The driver called to the horse, and the tonga went round the bend in the road and was lost to sight.

Rusty stood at the gate, staring down the empty road. He thought: 'I'll go back to my room and time will run on and things will happen but *this* will not happen again . . . there will still be sun and litchees, and there will be other friends, but there will be no Meena and no Kishen, for our lives have drifted apart . . . . Kishen and I have been going down the river together, but I have been caught in the reeds and he has been swept onwards; and if I do catch up with him, it will not be the same, it might be sad . . . . Kishen has gone, and part of my life has gone with him, and inside of me I am all lonely.'

Chapter XVII

IT was a sticky, restless afternoon. The water-carrier passed below the room with his skin bag, spraying water on the dusty path. The toy-seller entered the compound, calling his wares in a high-pitched sing-song voice, and presently there was the chatter of children.

The toy-seller had a long bamboo pole, crossed by two or three shorter bamboos, from which hung all manner of toys—little celluloid drums, tin watches, tiny flutes and whistles, and multi-coloured rag dolls—and when these ran out, they were replaced by others from a large bag, a most mysterious and fascinating bag, one in which no one but the toy-seller was allowed to look. He was a popular person with rich and poor alike, for his toys never cost more than four annas and never lasted longer than a day.

Rusty liked the cheap toys, and was fond of decorating the room with them. He bought a two-anna flute; and walked upstairs, blowing on it.

He removed his shirt and sandals and lay flat on the bed staring up at the ceiling. The lizards scuttled along the rafters, the bald maina hopped along the window-ledge. He was about to fall asleep when Somi came into the room.

Somi looked listless.

'I feel sticky,' he said, 'I don't want to wear any clothes.'

He too pulled off his shirt and deposited it on the table, then stood before the mirror, studying his physique. Then he turned to Rusty.

'You don't look well,' he said, 'there are cobwebs in your hair.'

'I don't care.'

'You must have been very fond of Mrs Kapoor. She was very kind.'

91

'I loved her, didn't you know?'

'No. My own love is the only thing I know. Rusty, best favourite friend, you cannot stay here in this room, you must come back to my house. Besides, this building will soon have new tenants.'

'I'll get out when they come, or when the landlord discovers I'm living here.'

Somi's usually bright face was somewhat morose, and there was a faint agitation showing in his eyes.

'I will go and get a cucumber to eat,' he said, 'then there is something to tell you.'

'I don't want a cucumber,' said Rusty, 'I want a coconut.'

'I want a cucumber.'

Rusty felt irritable. The room was hot, the bed was hot, his blood was hot. Impatiently, he said: 'Go and eat your cucumber, I don't want any . . . .'

Somi looked at him with a pained surprise; then, without a word, picked up his shirt and marched out of the room. Rusty could hear the slap of his slippers on the stairs, and then the bicycle tyres on the gravel path.

'Hey, Somi!' shouted Rusty, leaping off the bed and running out on to the roof. 'Come back!'

But the bicycle jumped over the ditch, and Somi's shirt flapped, and there was nothing Rusty could do but return to bed. He was alarmed at his liverish ill-temper. He lay down again and stared at the ceiling, at the lizards chasing each other across the rafters. On the roof two crows were fighting, knocking each other's feathers out. Everyone was in a temper.

What's wrong? wondered Rusty. I spoke to Somi in fever, not in anger, but my words were angry. Now I am miserable, fed up. Oh, hell . . . .

He closed his eyes and shut out everything.

He opened his eyes to laughter. Somi's face was close, laughing into Rusty's.

'Of what were you dreaming, Rusty, I have never seen you smile so sweetly!'

'Oh, I wasn't dreaming,' said Rusty, sitting up, and feeling better now that Somi had returned. 'I am sorry for being so grumpy, but I'm not feeling. . . .'

'Quiet!' admonished Somi, putting his finger to the other's lips. 'See I have settled the matter. Here is a coconut for you, and here is a cucumber for me!'

They sat cross-legged on the bed, facing each other; Somi with his cucumber, and Rusty with his coconut. The coconut milk trickled down Rusty's chin and on to his chest, giving him a cool, pleasant sensation.

' Rusty said: 'I am afraid for Kishen. I am sure he will give trouble to his relatives, and they are not like his parents. Mr Kapoor will have no say, without Meena.'

Somi was silent. The only sound was the munching of the cucumber and the coconut. He looked at Rusty, an uncertain smile on his lips but none in his eyes; and, in a forced conversational manner, said: 'I'm going to Amritsar for a few months. But I will be back in the spring, Rusty, you will be all right here . . . .'

This news was so unexpected that for some time Rusty could not take it in. The thought had never occurred to him that one day Somi might leave Dehra, just as Ranbir and Suri and Kishen had done. He could not speak. A sickening heaviness clogged his heart and brain.

'Hey, Rusty!' laughed Somi. 'Don't look as though there is poison in the coconut!'

The poison lay in Somi's words. And the poison worked, running through Rusty's veins and beating against his heart and hammering on his brain. The poison worked, wounding him.

He said, 'Somi . . . ' but could go no further.

'Finish the coconut!'

'Somi,' said Rusty again, 'if you are leaving Dehra, Somi, then I am leaving too.'

'Eat the coco . . . what did you say?'

'I am going too.'

'Are you mad?'

'Not at all.'

Serious now, and troubled, Somi put his hand on his friend's wrist; he shook his head, he could not understand.

'Why, Rusty? Where?'

'England.'

'But you haven't money, you silly fool!'

'I can get an assisted passage. The British Government will pay.'

'You are a British subject?'

'I don't know . . . .'

'*Toba!*' Somi slapped his thighs and looked upwards in despair. 'You are neither Indian subject nor British subject, and you think someone is going to pay for your passage! And how are you to get a passport?

'How?' asked Rusty, anxious to find out.

'*Toba!* Have you a birth certificate?'

'Oh, no.'

'Then you are not born,' decreed Somi, with a certain amount of satisfaction. 'You are not alive! You do not happen to be in this world!'

He paused for breath, then waved his finger in the air. 'Rusty, you cannot go!' he said.

Rusty lay down despondently.

'I never really thought I would,' he said, 'I only said I would because I felt like it. Not because I am unhappy—I have never been happier elsewhere—but because I am restless as I have always been. I don't suppose I'll be anywhere for long . . . .'

He spoke the truth. Rusty always spoke the truth. He defined truth as feeling, and when he said what he felt, he said truth. (Only he didn't always speak his feelings.) He never lied. You don't have to lie if you know how to withhold the truth.

'You belong here,' said Somi, trying to reconcile Rusty with circumstance. 'You will get lost in big cities, Rusty, you will break your heart. And when you come back—if you come back—I will be grown-up and you will be grown-up—I mean more than we are now—and we will be like strangers to each other . . . . And besides, there are no chaat shops in England!'

'But I don't belong here, Somi. I don't belong anywhere. Even if I have papers, I don't belong. I'm a half-caste, I know it, and that is as good as not belonging anywhere.'

What am I saying, thought Rusty, why do I make my inheritance a justification for my present bitterness? No one has cast me out . . . of my own free will I run away from India . . . why do I blame inheritance?

'It can also mean that you belong everywhere,' said Somi. 'But you never told me. You are fair like a European.'

'I had not thought much about it.'

'Are you ashamed?'

'No. My guardian was. He kept it to himself, he only told me when I came home after playing Holi. I was happy then. So, when he told me, I was not ashamed, I was proud.'

'And now?'

'Now? Oh, I can't really believe it. Somehow I do not really feel mixed.'

'Then don't blame it for nothing.'

Rusty felt a little ashamed, and they were both silent awhile, then Somi shrugged and said: 'So you are going. You are running away from India.'

'No, not from India.'

'Then you are running away from your friends, from me!'

Rusty felt the irony of this remark, and allowed a tone of sarcasm into his voice.

'*You*, Master Somi, *you* are the one who is going away. I am still here. *You* are going to Amritsar. I only *want* to go. And I'm here alone; everyone has gone. So if I do eventually leave, the only person I'll be running away from will be myself!'

'Ah!' said Somi, nodding his head wisely. 'And by running away from yourself, you will be running away from me and from India! Now come on, let's go and have chaat.'

He pulled Rusty off the bed, and pushed him out of the room. Then, at the top of the steps, he leapt lightly on Rusty's back, kicked him with his heels, and shouted: 'Down the steps, my *tuttoo*, my pony! Fast down the steps!'

So Rusty carried him downstairs and dropped him on the grass. They laughed: but there was no great joy in their laughter, they laughed for the sake of friendship.

'Best favourite friend,' said Somi, throwing a handful of mud in Rusty's face.

Chapter XVIII

N ow everyone had gone from Dehra. Meena would never return; and it seemed unlikely that Kapoor could come back. Kishen's departure was final. Ranbir would be in Mussoorie until the winter months, and this was still summer and it would be even longer before Somi returned. Everyone Rusty knew well had left, and there remained no one he knew well enough to love or hate.

There were, of course, the people at the water-tank—the servants, the ayahs, the babies—but they were busy all day. And when Rusty left them, he had no one but himself and memory for company.

He wanted to forget Meena. If Kishen had been with him, it would have been possible; the two boys would have found comfort in their companionship. But alone, Rusty realized he was not the master of himself.

And Kapoor. For Kapoor, Meena had died perfect. He suspected her of no infidelity. And, in a way, she had died perfect; for she had found a secret freedom. Rusty knew he had judged Kapoor correctly when scorning Suri's threat of blackmail; he knew Kapoor couldn't believe a single disparaging word about Meena.

And Rusty returned to his dreams, that wonderland of his, where he walked in perfection. He spoke to himself quite often, and sometimes he spoke to the lizards.

He was afraid of the lizards, afraid and at the same time fascinated. When they changed their colours, from brown to red to green, in keeping with their immediate surroundings, they fascinated him. But when they lost their grip on the ceiling and fell to the ground with a soft, wet, boneless smack, they repelled him. One night, he reasoned, one of them would most certainly fall on his face . . . .

An idea he conceived one afternoon nearly sparked him into sudden and feverish activity. He thought of making a garden on the roof, beside his room.

The idea took his fancy to such an extent that he spent several hours planning the set-out of the flower-beds, and visualizing the completed picture, with marigolds, zinnias and cosmos blooming everywhere. But there were no tools to be had, mud and bricks would have to be carried upstairs, seeds would have to be obtained; and, who knows, thought Rusty, after all that trouble the roof might cave in, or the rains might spoil everything . . . and anyway, he was going away . . . .

His thoughts turned inwards. Gradually, he returned to the same frame of mind that had made life with his guardian so empty and meaningless; he began to fret, to dream, to lose his grip on reality. The full life of the past few months had suddenly ended, and the present was lonely and depressing; the future became a distorted image, created out of his own brooding fancies.

One evening; sitting on the steps, he found himself fingering a key. It was the key Kapoor had asked him to keep, the key to the back door. Rusty remembered the whisky bottles—'let's drink them ourselves' Kishen had said—and Rusty thought, 'why not, why not . . . a few bottles can't do any harm . . .' and before he could have an argument with himself, the back door was open.

In his room that night he drank the whisky neat. It was the first time he had tasted alcohol, and he didn't find it pleasant; but he wasn't drinking for pleasure, he was drinking with the sole purpose of shutting himself off from the world, and forgetting.

He hadn't drunk much when he observed that the roof had a definite slant; it seemed to slide away from his door to the field below, like a chute. The banyan tree was suddenly swarming with bees. The lizards were turning all colours at once, like pieces of rainbow.

When he had drunk a little more, he began to talk; not to himself any more, but to Meena, who was pressing his head and trying to force him down on the pillows. He struggled against Meena, but she was too powerful, and he began to cry.

Then he drank a little more. And now the floor began to

wobble, and Rusty had a hard time keeping the table from toppling over. The walls of the room were caving in. He swallowed another mouthful of whisky, and held the wall up with his hands. He could deal with anything now. The bed was rocking, the chair was sliding about, the table was slipping, the walls were swaying, but Rusty had everything under control he was everywhere at once, supporting the entire building with his bare hands.

And then he slipped, and everything came down on top of him, and it was black.

In the morning when he awoke, he threw the remaining bottles out of the window, and cursed himself for a fool, and went down to the water-tank to bathe.

*

Days passed, dry and dusty, every day the same. Regularly, Rusty filled his earthen *sohrai* at the water-tank, and soaked the reed mat that hung from the doorway. Sometimes, in the field, the children played cricket, but he couldn't summon up the energy to join them. From his room he could hear the sound of ball and bat, the shouting, the lone voice raised in shrill disagreement with some unfortunate umpire . . . or the thud of a football, or the clash of hockey-sticks . . . but better than these sounds was the jingle of the bells and bangles on the feet of the ayahs, as they busied themselves at the water-tank.

Time passed, but Rusty did not know it was passing. It was like living in a house near a river, and the river was always running past the house, on and away; but to Rusty, living in the house, there was no passing of the river; the water ran on, the river remained.

He longed for something to happen.

Chapter XIX

DUST. It blew up in great clouds, swirling down the road, clutching and clinging to everything it touched; burning, choking, stinging dust.

Then thunder.

The wind dropped suddenly, there was a hushed expectancy in the air. And then, out of the dust, came big black rumbling clouds.

Something was happening.

At first there was a lonely drop of water on the window-sill; then a patter on the roof. Rusty felt a thrill of anticipation, and a mountain of excitement. The rains had come to break the monotony of the summer months; the monsoon had arrived!

The sky shuddered, the clouds groaned, a fork of lightning struck across the sky, and then the sky itself exploded.

The rain poured down, drumming on the corrugated roof. Rusty's vision was reduced to about twenty yards; it was as though the room had been cut off from the rest of the world by an impenetrable wall of water.

The rains had arrived, and Rusty wanted to experience to the full the novelty of that first shower. He threw off his clothes, and ran naked on to the roof, and the wind sprang up and whipped the water across his body so that he writhed in ecstasy. The rain was more intoxicating than the alcohol, and it was with difficulty that he restrained himself from shouting and dancing in mad abandon. The force and freshness of the rain brought tremendous relief, washed away the stagnation that had been settling on him, poisoning mind and body.

The rain swept over the town, cleansing the sky and earth. The trees bent beneath the force of wind and water. The field was a bog, flowers flattened to the ground.

Rusty returned to the room, exhilarated, his body weeping. He was confronted by a flood. The water had come in through the door and the window and the skylight, and the floor was flooded ankle-deep. He took to his bed.

The bed took on the glamour of a deserted island in the middle of the ocean. He dried himself on the sheets, conscious of a warm, sensuous glow. Then he sat on his haunches and gazed out through the window.

The rain thickened, the tempo quickened. There was the banging of a door, the swelling of a gutter, the staccato splutter of the rain rhythmically persistent on the roof. The drain-pipe coughed and choked, the curtain flew to its limit; the lean trees swayed, swayed, bowed with the burden of wind and weather. The road was a rushing torrent, the gravel path inundated with little rivers. The monsoon had arrived!

But the rain stopped as unexpectedly as it had begun.

Suddenly it slackened, dwindled to a shower, petered out. Stillness. The dripping of water from the drain-pipe drilled into the drain. Frogs croaked, hopping around in the slush.

The sun came out with a vengeance. On leaves and petals, drops of water sparkled like silver and gold. A cat emerged from a dry corner of the building, blinking sleepily, unperturbed and unenthusiastic.

The children came running out of their houses.

'*Barsaat, barsaat!*' they shouted. 'The rains have come!'

The rains had come. And the roof became a general bathing-place. The children, the night-watchmen, the dogs, all trouped up the steps to sample the novelty of a fresh-water shower on the roof.

The maidan became alive with footballs. The game was called monsoon football, it was played in slush, in mud that was ankle-deep; and the football was heavy and slippery and difficult to kick with bare feet. The bazaar youths played barefooted because, in the first place, boots were too cumbersome for monsoon football, and in the second place they couldn't be afforded.

But the rains brought Rusty only a momentary elation, just as the first shower had seemed fiercer and fresher than those which followed; for now it rained every day . . . .

Nothing could be more depressing than the dampness, the mildew, and the sunless heat that wrapped itself round the steaming land. Had Somi or Kishen been with Rusty, he might have derived some pleasure from the elements; had Ranbir been with him, he might have found adventure; but alone, he found only boredom.

He spent an idle hour watching the slow dripping from the pipe outside the door: where do I belong, he wondered, what am I doing, what is going to happen to me . . . .

He was determined to break away from the atmosphere of timelessness and resignation that surrounded him, and decided to leave Dehra.

'I must go,' he told himself. 'I do not want to rot like the mangoes at the end of the season, or burn out like the sun at the end of the day. I cannot live like the gardener, the cook and the water-carrier, doing the same task every day of my life. I am not interested in today, I want tomorrow. I cannot live in this same small room all my life, with a family of lizards, living in other people's homes and never having one of my own. I *have* to break away. I want to be either somebody or nobody. I don't want to be anybody.'

He decided to go to Delhi and see the High Commissioner for the United Kingdom, who was sure to give him an assisted passage to England; and he wrote to Somi, telling him of this plan. On his way he would have to pass through Hardwar, and there he would see Kishen, he had the aunt's address.

At night he slept brokenly, thinking and worrying about the future. He would listen to the vibrant song of the frog who wallowed in the drain at the bottom of the steps, and to the unearthly cry of the jackal, and questions would come to him, disturbing questions about loving and leaving and living and dying, questions that crowded out his sleep.

But on the night before he left Dehra, it was not the croaking of the frog or the cry of the jackal that kept him awake, or the persistent questioning; but a premonition of crisis and of an end to something.

Chapter XX

THE postman brought a letter from Somi.

Dear Rusty, best favourite friend,

Do not ever travel in a third-class compartment. All the way to Amritsar I had to sleep standing up, the carriage was so crowded.

I shall be coming back to Dehra in the spring, in time to watch you play Holi with Ranbir. I know you feel like leaving India and running off to England, but wait until you see me again, all right? You are afraid to die without having done something. You are afraid to die, Rusty, but you have hardly begun to live.

I know you are not happy in Dehra, and you must be lonely. But wait a little, be patient, and the bad days will pass. We don't know why we live. It is no use trying to know. But we have to live, Rusty, because we really want to. And as long as we want to, we have got to find something to live for, and even die for it. Mother is keeping well and sends you her greetings. Tell me whatever you need.

Somi

Rusty folded the letter carefully, and put it in his shirt pocket; he meant to keep it for ever. He could not wait for Somi's return; but he knew that their friendship would last a lifetime, and that the beauty of it would always be with him. In and out of Rusty's life, his turban at an angle, Somi would go; his slippers slapping against his heels for ever . . . .

Rusty had no case or bedding-roll to pack, no belongings at

102

all; only the clothes he wore, which were Somi's, and about fifty rupees, for which he had to thank Kishen. He had made no preparations for the journey; he would slip away without fuss or bother; insignificant, unnoticed . . . .

An hour before leaving for the station, he lay down to rest. He gazed up at the ceiling, where the lizards scuttled about: callous creatures, unconcerned with his departure: one human was just the same as any other. And the bald maina, hopping on and off the window-sill, would continue to fight and lose more feathers; and the crows and the squirrels in the mango tree, they would be missed by Rusty, but they would not miss him. It was true, one human was no different to any other—except to a dog or a human . . . .

When Rusty left the room, there was activity at the water-tank; clothes were being beaten on the stone, and the ayah's trinkets were jingling away. Rusty couldn't bear to say goodbye to the people at the water-tank, so he didn't close his door, lest they suspect him of leaving. He descended the steps—twenty-two of them, he counted for the last time—and crossed the drain, and walked slowly down the gravel path until he was out of the compound.

He crossed the maidan, where a group of students were playing cricket, whilst another group wrestled; prams were wheeled in and out of the sporting youths; young girls gossiped away the morning. And Rusty remembered his first night on the maidan, when he had been frightened and wet and lonely; and now, though the maidan was crowded, he felt the same loneliness, the same isolation. In the bazaar, he walked with a heavy heart. From the chaat shop came the familiar smell of spices and the crackle of frying fat. And the children bumped him, and the cows blocked the road; and, though he knew they always did these things, it was only now that he noticed them. They all seemed to be holding him, pulling him back.

But he could not return; he was afraid of what lay ahead, he dreaded the unknown, but it was easier to walk forwards than backwards.

The toy-seller made his way through the crowd, children clustering round him, tearing at his pole. Rusty fingered a two-anna piece, and his eye picked out a little plume of red feathers, that seemed to have no useful purpose, and he was determined to buy it.

But before he could make the purchase, someone plucked at his shirt-sleeve.

'Chotta sahib, Chotta sahib,' said the sweeper boy, Mr Harrison's servant.

Rusty could not mistake the shaved head and the sparkle of white teeth, and wanted to turn away; ignore the sweeper boy, who was linked up with a past that was distant and yet uncomfortably close. But the hand plucked at his sleeve, and Rusty felt ashamed, angry with himself for trying to ignore someone who had never harmed him and who couldn't have been friendlier. Rusty was a sahib no longer, no one was his servant; and he was not an Indian, he had no caste, he could not call another untouchable . . . .

'You are not at work?' asked Rusty.

'No work.' The sweeper boy smiled, a flash of white in the darkness of his face.

'What of Mr Harrison, the sahib?'

'Gone.'

'Gone,' said Rusty, and was surprised at not being surprised. 'Where has he gone?'

'Don't know, but he gone for good. Before he go, I get sack. I drop the bathroom-water on veranda, and the sahib, he hit me on the head with his hand, *put*! . . . I say, Sahib you are cruel, and he say cruelty to animals, no? Then he tell me I get sack, he leaving anyway. I lose two days pay.'

Rusty was filled with both relief and uncertainty, and for the same reason; now there could never be a return; whether he wanted to or not, he could never go back to his old home.

'What about the others?' asked Rusty.

'They still there. Missionary's wife a fine lady, she give me five rupees before I go.'

'And you? You are working now?'

Again the sweeper boy flashed his smile. 'No work . . . .'

Rusty didn't dare offer the boy any money, though it would probably have been accepted; in the sweeper boy he saw nobility, and he could not belittle nobility.

'I will try to get you work,' he said, forgetting that he was on his way to the station to buy a one-way ticket, and telling the sweeper boy where he lived.

Instinctively, the sweeper boy did not believe him; he nodded his head automatically, but his eyes signified disbelief; and when Rusty left him, he was still nodding; and to nobody in particular.

*

On the station platform the coolies pushed and struggled, shouted incomprehensibly, lifted heavy trunks with apparent ease. Merchants cried their wares, trundling barrows up and down the platform: soda-water, oranges, betel-nut, *halwai* sweets . . . . The flies swarmed around the open stalls, clustered on glass-covered sweet boxes; the mongrel dogs, ownerless and unfed, roved the platform and railway-lines, hunting for scraps of food and stealing at every opportunity.

Ignoring Somi's advice, Rusty bought a third class ticket and found an empty compartment. The guard blew his whistle, but nobody took any notice. People continued about their business, certain that the train wouldn't start for another ten minutes: the Hardwar Mail never did start on time.

Rusty was the only person in the compartment until a fat lady, complaining volubly, oozed in through the door and spread herself across an entire bunk; her plan, it seemed, was to discourage other passengers from coming in. She had beady little eyes, set in a big moon face; and they looked at Rusty in curiosity, darting away whenever they met with his.

Others came in, in quick succession now, for the guard had blown his whistle a second time: a young woman with a baby, a soldier in uniform, a boy of about twelve . . . . they were all poor people; except for the fat lady, who travelled third class in order to save money.

The guard's whistle blew again, but the train still refused to start. Being the Hardwar Mail, this was but natural; no one ever expected the Hardwar Mail to start on time, for in all its history, it hadn't done so (not even during the time of the British), and for it to do so now would be a blow to tradition. Everyone was for tradition, and so the Hardwar Mail was not permitted to arrive and depart at the appointed hour; though it was feared that one day some young fool would change the appointed hours. And imagine what would happen if the train did leave on time—the entire railway system would be thrown into confusion for, needless to say, every other train took its time from the Hardwar Mail . . . .

So the guard kept blowing his whistle, and the vendors put their heads in at the windows, selling oranges and newspapers and soda-water . . . .

'Soda-water!' exclaimed the fat lady. 'Who wants soda-water! Why, our farmer here has with him a *sohrai* of pure cool water, and he will share it with us, will he not? Paan-wallah! Call the man, quick, he is not even stopping at the window!

The guard blew his whistle again.

And they were off.

The Hardwar Mail, true to tradition, pulled out of Dehra station half an hour late.

*

Perhaps it was because Rusty was leaving Dehra for ever that he took an unusual interest in everything he saw and heard. Things that would not normally have been noticed by him, now made vivid impressions on his mind: the gesticulations of the coolies as the train drew out of the station, a dog licking a banana skin, a naked child alone amongst a pile of bundles, crying its heart out . . . .

The platform, fruit-stalls, advertisement boards, all slipped away.

The train gathered speed, the carriages groaned and creaked and rocked crazily. But, as they left the town and the station behind, the wheels found their rhythm, beating time with the rails and singing a song.

It was a sad song, persistent and fatalistic.

Another life was finishing.

One morning, months ago, Rusty had heard a drum in the

forest, a single drum-beat, *dhum-tap*; and in the stillness of the morning it had been a call, a message, an irresistible force. He had cut away from his roots: he had been replanted, had sprung to life, new life. But it was too quick a growth, rootless, and he had withered. And now he had run away again. No drum now; instead, the pulsating throb and tremor of the train rushing him away; away from India, from Somi, from the chaat shop and the bazaar; and he did not know why, except that he was lost and lonely and tired and old: nearly seventeen, but old . . . .

The little boy beside him knelt in front of the window, and counted the telegraph-posts as they flashed by; they seemed, after a while, to be hurtling past whilst the train stood stationary. Only the rocking of the carriage could be felt.

The train sang through the forests, and sometimes the child waved his hand excitedly and pointed out a deer, the sturdy sambar or delicate cheetal. Monkeys screamed from tree-tops, or loped beside the train, mothers with their young clinging to their breasts. The jungle was heavy, shutting off the sky, and it was like this for half an hour; then the train came into the open, and the sun struck through the carriage windows. They swung through cultivated land, maize and sugar-cane fields; past squat, mud-hut villages, and teams of bullocks ploughing up the soil; leaving behind only a trail of curling smoke.

Children ran out from the villages—brown, naked children—and waved to the train, crying words of greeting; and the little boy in the compartment waved back and shouted merrily, and then turned to look at his travelling companions, his eyes shining with pleasure.

The child began to chatter about this and that, and the others listened to him good-humouredly; the farmer with simplicity and a genuine interest, the fat lady with a tolerant smile, and the soldier with an air of condescension. The young woman and the baby were both asleep. Rusty felt sleepy himself, and was unable to listen to the small boy; vaguely, he thought of Kishen, and of how surprised and pleased Kishen would be to see him.

Presently he fell asleep.

*

When he awoke, the train was nearing Hardwar; he had slept for almost an hour, but to him it seemed like five minutes.

His throat was dry; and, though his shirt was soaked with perspiration, he shivered a little. His hands trembled, and he had to close his fists to stop the trembling.

At midday the train steamed into Hardwar station, and disgorged its passengers.

The fat lady, who was determined to be the first out of the compartment, jammed the doorway; but Rusty and the soldier outwitted her by climbing out of the window.

Rusty felt better once he was outside the station, but he knew he had a fever. The rocking of the train continued, and the song of the wheels and the rails kept beating in his head. He walked slowly away from the station, comforted by the thought that at Kishen's aunt's house there would be food and rest. At night, he would catch the Delhi train.

Chapter XXI

THE house was on top of a hill, and from the road Rusty could see the river below, and the temples, and hundreds of people moving about on the long graceful steps that sloped down to the water: for the river was holy, and Hardwar sacred, a place of pilgrimage.

He knocked on the door, and presently there was the sound of bare feet on a stone floor. The door was opened by a lady, but she was a stranger to Rusty, and they looked at each other with puzzled, questioning eyes.

'Oh . . . namaste ji,' faltered Rusty. 'Does—does Mr Kapoor or his sister live here.'

The lady of the house did not answer immediately. She looked at the boy with a detached interest, trying to guess at his business and intentions. She was dressed simply and well, she had a look of refinement, and Rusty felt sure that her examination of him was no more than natural curiosity.

'Who are you, please?' she asked.

'I am a friend from Dehra. I am leaving India and I want to see Mr Kapoor and his son before I go. Are they here?'

'Only Mr Kapoor is here,' she said. 'You can come in.'

Rusty wondered where Kishen and his aunt could be, but he did not want to ask this strange lady; he felt ill at ease in her presence; the house seemed to be hers. Coming straight into the front room from bright sunshine, his eyes took a little time to get used to the dark; but after a moment or two he made out the form of Mr Kapoor, sitting in a cushioned armchair.

'Hullo, Mister Rusty,' said Kapoor. 'It is nice to see you.'

There was a glass of whisky on the table, but Kapoor was not drunk; he was shaved and dressed, and looked a good deal younger than when Rusty had last seen him. But something else was missing. His jovial friendliness, his enthusiasm, had gone. This Kapoor was a different man to the Kapoor of the beard and green dressing-gown.

'Hullo, Mister Kapoor,' said Rusty. 'How are you?'

'I am fine, just fine. Sit down, please. Will you have a drink?'

'No thanks. I came to see you and Kishen before leaving for England. I wanted to see you again, you were very kind to me . . . .'

'That's all right, quite all right. I'm very glad to see you, but I'm afraid Kishen isn't here. By the way, the lady who just met you at the door, I haven't introduced you yet—this is my wife, Mister Rusty . . . I—I married again shortly after Meena's death.'

Rusty looked at the new Mrs Kapoor in considerable bewilderment, and greeted her quietly. It was not unusual for a man to marry again soon after his wife's death, and he knew it, but his heart was breaking with a fierce anger. He was revolted by the rapidity of it all; hardly a month had passed, and here was Kapoor with another wife. Rusty remembered that it was for this man Kapoor—this weakling, this drunkard, this self-opinionated, selfish drunkard—that Meena had given her life, all of it, devotedly she had remained by his side when she could have left, when there was no more fight in him and no more love in him and no more pride in him; and, had she left then, she would be alive, and he—*he* would be dead . . . .

Rusty was not interested in the new Mrs Kapoor. For Kapoor, he had only contempt.

'Mister Rusty is a good friend of the family,' Kapoor was saying. 'In Dehra he was a great help to Kishen.'

'How did Meena die?' asked Rusty, determined to hurt Kapoor—if Kapoor could be hurt . . . .

'I thought you knew. We had an accident. Let us not talk of it, Mister Rusty . . . .'

'The driver was driving, of course?'

Kapoor did not answer immediately, but raised his glass and sipped from it.

'Of course,' he said.

'How did it all happen?'

'Please, Mister Rusty, I do not want to describe it. We were going too fast, and the car left the road and hit a tree. I can't describe it, Mister Rusty.'

'No, of course not,' said Rusty. 'Anyway, I am glad nothing happened to you. It is also good that you have mastered your natural grief, and started a new life. I am afraid I am not as strong as you. Meena was wonderful, and I still can't believe she is dead.'

'We have to carry on . . . .'

'Of course. How is Kishen, I would like to see him.'

'He is in Lucknow with his aunt,' said Kapoor. 'He wished to stay with her.'

Mrs Kapoor had been quiet till now.

'Tell him the truth,' she said. 'There is nothing to hide.'

'You tell him then.'

'What do you mean?'

'He ran away from us. As soon as his aunt left, he ran away. We tried to make him come back, but it was useless, so now we don't try. But he is in Hardwar. We are always hearing about him. They say he is the most cunning thief on both sides of the river.'

'Where can I find him?'

'I don't know. He is wanted by the police. He robs for others, and they pay him. It is easier for a young boy to steal than it is for a man, and as he is quite a genius at it, his services are in demand. And I am sure he would not hesitate to rob us too . . . .'

'But you must know where I can find him,' persisted Rusty. 'You must have some idea.'

'He has been seen along the river and in the bazaar. I don't know where he lives. In a tree, perhaps, or in a temple, or in a brothel. He is somewhere in Hardwar, but exactly where I do not know . . . no one knows. He speaks to no one and runs from everyone. What can you want with him?'

'He is my friend,' said Rusty.

'He will rob you too.'

'The money I have is what he gave me.'

He rose to leave; he was tired, but he did not want to stay much longer in this alien house.

'You are tired,' said Mrs Kapoor, 'Will you rest, and have your meal with us?'

'No,' said Rusty, 'there isn't time.'

Chapter XXII

ALL hope left Rusty as he staggered down the hill, weak and exhausted. He could not think clearly; he knew he hadn't eaten since morning, and cursed himself for not accepting Mrs Kapoor's hospitality.

He was hungry, he was thirsty; he was tormented by thoughts of what might have happened to Kishen, of what might happen . . . .

He stumbled down the long steps that led to the water. The sun was strong, striking up from the stone and shimmering against the great white temple that overlooked the river. He crossed the courtyard and came to the water's edge.

Lying on his belly on the river bank, he drank of the holy waters. Then he pulled off his shirt and sandals, and slipped into the water. There were men and women on all sides, praying with their faces to the sun. Great fish swam round them, unafraid and unmolested, safe in the sacred waters of the Ganges.

When he had bathed and refreshed himself, Rusty climbed back on to the stone bank. His sandals and shirt had disappeared.

No one was near except a beggar leaning on a stick, a young man massaging his body with oils, and a cow examining an empty, discarded basket; and, of the three, the cow was the most likely suspect; it had probably eaten the sandals.

But Rusty no longer cared what happened to his things. His money was in the leather purse attached to his belt; and, as long as he had the belt, he had both money and pyjamas.

He rolled the wet pyjamas up to his thighs; then, staring ahead with unseeing eyes, ignoring the bowls that were thrust before him by the beggars, he walked the length of the courtyard that ran parallel to the rising steps.

Children were shouting at each other, priests chanting their

112

prayers; vendors, with baskets on their heads—baskets of fruit and chaat—gave harsh cries; and the cows pushed their way around at will. Steps descended from all parts of the hill; broad, clean steps from the temple, and narrow, winding steps from the bazaars; and a maze of alleyways zigzagged about the hill, through the bazaar, round the temples, along the river, and were lost amongst themselves and found again and lost . . . .

Kishen, barefooted and ragged and thin, but with the same supreme confidence in himself, leant against the wall of an alleyway, and watched Rusty's progress along the river-bank.

He wanted to shout to Rusty, to go to him, to embrace him, but he could not do these things. He did not understand the reason for his friend's presence, he could not reveal himself for fear of a trap. He was sure it was Rusty he watched, for who else was there with the same coloured hair and skin who would walk half-naked in Hardwar. It was Rusty, but why . . . was he in trouble, was he sick? Why, why . . . .

Rusty saw Kishen in the alleyway. He was too weak to shout. He stood in the sun, and looked up the steps at Kishen standing in the alleyway.

Kishen did not know whether to run to Rusty, or run away. He too stood still, at the entrance of the alley.

'Hallo, Rusty,' he called.

And Rusty began to walk up the steps, slowly and painfully, his feet burning, his head reeling, his heart thundering with conflicting emotions.

'Are you alone?' called Kishen. 'Don't come if you are not alone.'

Rusty advanced up the steps, until he was in the alleyway facing Kishen. Despite the haze before his eyes, he noticed Kishen's wild condition; the bones protruded from the boy's skin, his hair was knotted and straggly, his eyes danced, searching the steps for others.

'Why are you here, Rusty?'

'To see you . . . .'

'Why?'

'I am going away.'

'How can you go anywhere? You look sick enough to die.'

'I came to see you, anyway.'

'Why?'

Rusty sat down on a step; his wrists hung loose on his knees, and his head drooped forward.

'I'm hungry,' he said.

Kishen walked into the open, and approached a fruit-vendor. He came back with two large watermelons.

'You have money?' asked Rusty.

'No. Just credit. I bring them profits, they give me credit.'

He sat down beside Rusty, produced a small but wicked-looking knife from the folds of his shirt, and proceeded to slice the melons in half.

'You can't go away,' he said.

'I can't go back.'

'Why not?'

'No money, no job, no friends.'

They put their teeth into the water-melon, and ate at terrific speed. Rusty felt much refreshed; he put his weakness and fever down to an empty stomach.

'I'll be no good as a bandit,' said Rusty. 'I can be recognized at sight, I can't go round robbing people, I don't think it's very nice anyway.'

'I don't rob poor people,' objected Kishen, prodding his nose. 'I only rob those who've got something to be robbed. And I don't do it for myself, that's why I'm never caught. People pay me to do their dirty work. Like that, they are safe because they are somewhere else when everything happens, and I am safe because I don't have what I rob, and haven't got a reason for taking it anyway . . . so it is quite safe. But don't worry, bhai, we will not do it in Dehra, we are too well-known there. Besides, I am tired of running from the police.'

'Then what will we do?'

'Oh we will find someone for you to give English lessons. Not one, but many. And I will start a chaat shop.'

'When do we go?' said Rusty; and England and fame and riches were all forgotten, and would soon be dreams again.

114

'Tomorrow morning, early,' said Kishen. 'There is a boat crossing the river. We must cross the river, on this side I am known, and there are many people who would not like me to leave. If we went by train, I would be caught at the station, for sure. On the other side no one knows me, there is only jungle.'

Rusty was amazed of how competent and practical Kishen had become; Kishen's mind had developed far quicker than his body, and he was a funny cross between an experienced adventurer and a ragged urchin. A month ago he had clung to Rusty for protection; now Rusty looked to Kishen for guidance.

I wonder, thought Rusty, will they notice my absence in Dehra? After all, I have only been away a day, though it seems an age . . . the room on the roof will still be vacant when I return, no one but me could be crazy enough to live in such a room . . . . I will go back to the room as though nothing had happened, and no one will notice that anything has.

*

The afternoon ripened into evening.

As the sun sank, the temple changed from white to gold, from gold to orange, from orange to pink, and from pink to crimson, and all these colours were in turn reflected in the surrounding waters.

The noise subsided gradually, the night came on.

Kishen and Rusty slept in the open, on the temple steps. It was a warm night, the air was close and heavy. In the shadows lay small bundles of humanity, the roofless and the homeless, sleeping only to pass the time of night. Rusty slept in spasms, waking frequently with a nagging pain in his stomach; poor stomach, it couldn't stand the unfamiliar strain of emptiness.

Chapter XXIII

BEFORE the steps and the river-tank came to life, Kishen and Rusty climbed into the ferry-boat. It would be crossing the river all day, carrying pilgrims from temple to temple, charging nothing. And though it was very early, and this the first crossing, a free passage across the river made for a crowded boat.

The people who climbed in were even more diverse than those Rusty had met on the train: women and children, bearded old men and wrinkled women, strong young peasants—not the prosperous or mercantile class, but the poor—who had come miles, mostly on foot, to bathe in the sacred waters of the Ganges.

On shore, the steps began to come to life. The previous day's cries and prayers and rites were resumed with the same monotonous devotion, at the same pitch, in the same spirit of timelessness; and the steps sounded to the tread of many feet, sandalled, slippered and bare.

The boat floated low in the water, it was so heavy, and the oarsmen had to strain upstream in order to avoid being swept down by the current. Their muscles shone and rippled under the grey iron of their weather-beaten skins. The blades of the oars cut through the water, in and out; and between grunts, the oarsmen shouted the time of the stroke.

Kishen and Rusty sat crushed together in the middle of the boat. There was no likelihood of their being separated now, but they held hands.

The people in the boat began to sing.

It was a low hum at first, but someone broke in with a song, and the voice—a young voice, clear and pure—reminded Rusty of Somi; and he comforted himself with the thought that Somi would be back in Dehra in the spring.

They sang in time to the stroke of the oars, in and out, and the

116

grunts and shouts of the oarsmen throbbed their way into the song, becoming part of it.

An old woman, who had white hair and a face lined with deep ruts, said: 'It is beautiful to hear the children sing.'

'Then you too should sing,' said Rusty.

She smiled at him, a sweet, toothless smile.

'What are you my son, are you one of us? I have never, on this river, seen blue eyes and golden hair.'

'I am nothing,' said Rusty. 'I am everything.'

He stated it bluntly, proudly.

'Where is your home, then?'

'I have no home,' he said, and felt proud of that too.

'And who is the boy with you?' asked the old woman, a genuine busybody. 'What is he to you?'

Rusty did not answer; he was asking himself the same question: what was Kishen to him? He was sure of one thing, they were both refugees—refugees from the world . . . . They were each other's shelter, each other's refuge, each other's help. Kishen was a *jungli*, divorced from the rest of mankind, and Rusty was the only one who understood him—because Rusty too was divorced from mankind. And theirs was a tie that would hold, because they were the only people who knew each other and loved each other.

Because of this tie, Rusty had to go back. And it was with relief that he went back. His return was justified.

He let his hand trail over the side of the boat: he wanted to remember the touch of the water as it moved past them, down and away: it would come to the ocean, the ocean that was life.

He could not run away. He could not escape the life he had made, the ocean into which he had floundered the night he left his guardian's house. He had to return to the room; *his* room; he had to go back.

The song died away as the boat came ashore. They disembarked, walking over the smooth pebbles; and the forest rose from the edge of the river, and beckoned them.

Rusty remembered the forest on the day of the picnic, when he had kissed Meena and held her hands, and he remembered the magic of the forest and the magic of Meena.

'One day,' he said, 'we must live in the jungle.'

'One day,' said Kishen, and he laughed. 'But now we walk back. We walk back to the room on the roof! It is our room, we have to go back!'

They had to go back: to bathe at the water-tank and listen to the morning gossip, to sit in the fruit trees and eat in the chaat shop and perhaps make a garden on the roof; to eat and sleep; to work; to live; to die.

Kishen laughed.

'One day you'll be great, Rusty. A writer or an actor or a prime minister or something. Maybe a poet! Why not a poet, Rusty?'

Rusty smiled. He knew he was smiling, because he was smiling at himself.

'Yes,' he said, 'why not a poet?'

So they began to walk.

Ahead of them lay forest and silence—and what was left of time . . . .

Vagrants in the Valley

The Homeless

ON the road to Dehra a boy played on a flute as he drove his flock of sheep down the road. He was barefooted and his clothes were old. A faded red shawl was thrown across his shoulders. It was December and the sun was up, pouring into the banyan tree at the side of the road, where two boys were sitting on the great tree's gnarled, protruding roots.

The flute-player passed the banyan tree and glanced at the boys, but did not stop playing. Presently he was only a speck on the dusty road, and the flute music was thin and distant, subdued by the tinkle of sheep-bells.

The boys left the shelter of the banyan tree and began walking in the direction of the distant hills.

The road stretched ahead, lonely and endless, towards the low ranges of the Siwalik hills. The dust was in their clothes and in their eyes and in their mouths. The sun rose higher in the sky; and, as they walked, the sweat trickled down their armpits, and down their legs.

The older boy, Rusty, was seventeen. He walked with his hands in the pockets of his thin cotton trousers, and he gazed at the ground. His fair hair was matted with dust, and his cheeks and arms were scorched red by the fierce sun. His eyes were blue and thoughtful.

'We will be in Raiwala soon,' he said. 'Would you like to rest, bhaiya?'

Kishen shrugged his thin shoulders. 'We'll rest when we get to Raiwala. If I sit down now, I'll never be able to get up. I suppose we have walked about ten miles this morning.'

He was a slim boy, almost as tall as Rusty though he was two years younger. He had dark, rebellious eyes, and bushy eyebrows and thick black hair. His dusty white pyjamas were rolled up above

121

his ankles, and he wore loose Peshawari chappals. An unbuttoned khaki shirt hung outside his pyjamas.

Like Rusty, he was without a home. Rusty had run away from an indifferent guardian a little over a year ago. Kishen had run away from a drunken father. He possessed distant relatives, but he preferred the risks and pleasures of vagrancy to the security of living with people he did not know. He had been with Rusty for a year, and his home was by his friend's side. He was Punjabi; Rusty was Anglo-Indian.

'From Raiwala we'll take the train,' said Rusty. 'It will cost us about five rupees.'

'Never mind,' said Kishen. 'We've done enough walking. And we've still got twelve rupees. Is there anything in our old rooms in Dehra that we can sell?'

'Let me see . . . . The table, the bed and the chair are not mine. There's an old tiger-skin, a bit eaten by rats, which no one will buy. There are one or two shirts and trousers.'

'Which we will need. These are all torn.'

'And some of my books . . . .'

'Which no one will buy.'

'I would not sell them. Well, those were the only things I got out of my guardian's house, before I ran away.'

'Somi!' interrupted Kishen. 'Somi will be in Dehra—he'll help us! He got you a job once, he can do it again.'

Rusty was silent, remembering his friend Somi, who had won him with a smile, and altered the course of his life. Somi, with his turban at an angle, a song on his lips . . . .

Kishen had left Dehra in a hurry and had been taken to Hardwar, a town on the banks of the sacred Ganges, by his aunt, and Rusty had followed him and his aunt. Only priests, beggars and shopkeepers could make a living in Hardwar, and the boys were soon back on the road to Dehra.

Now a cool breeze came across the plain, blowing down from the hills. In the fields there was a gentle swaying movement as the wind stirred the wheat. Then the breeze hit the road, and the dust began to swirl and eddy about the footpath. The boys moved into the middle of the road, holding their hands to their eyes, and stumbling forward. Out of the dust behind them came the rumbling of bullock-cart wheels.

'Ho, there, out of my way!' shouted the driver of the cart. The bullocks snorted and came lumbering through the dust. The boys moved to the side of the road.

'Are you going to Raiwala?' called Rusty. 'Can you take us with you?'

'Climb up!' said the man, and the boys ran through the dust, and clambered on to the back of the moving cart.

The cart lurched and rattled and bumped, and they had to cling to its sides to avoid falling off. It smelt of dry grass and cow-dung cakes. The driver had a red cloth tied around his head, and wore a tight vest, and a dhoti around his waist. His feet and legs were bare, scorched black by the burning sun over the plains. He was smoking a bidi and shouting to his bullocks, cursing them at times, but sometimes speaking to them in endearing terms. He seemed to have forgotten the presence of the boys at the back, had dismissed them from his mind the moment they had climbed up. Rusty and Kishen were too busy clinging to the lopsided cart to bother about making conversation with the driver.

'I'd rather walk,' complained Kishen. 'Rusty, who suggested that we get into this silly old contraption? I am full of bumps and bruises already.'

'Beggars can't be choosers,' said Rusty.

'Please, we are not beggars—not yet, anyway . . . . And if we were, we'd be much better off financially, I can assure you! As far as the rest of the world is concerned, you are still the son of an English sahib, and I am still the distant relative of a distant maharaja.'

'A prince,' said Rusty derisively, 'and riding in a bullock-cart!'

'Well, not every prince can boast of the experience.'

A little later the bullock-cart rumbled across a canal and became involved in the traffic of Raiwala, a busy little market town. The boys jumped off and walked beside the cart.

'Should we give him something?' asked Rusty. 'We ought to offer him some money.'

'How can we?' said Kishen. 'Why didn't you think of that before we jumped on?'

'All right, we'll just thank him. Thank you, bhaiji!' he called, as the cart moved off. 'Thank you, bhaiji!' shouted Kishen.

But either the driver did not hear or did not bother to look around; he continued smoking his bidi and talking to his animals; and to all appearances had not even noticed that the boys had got down. He drove his bullock-cart away, leaving Rusty and Kishen standing on the road.

'I'm hungry,' said Kishen. 'We haven't eaten since last night.'

'Then we must eat,' said Rusty. 'Come on, bhaiya, we will eat.'

They walked through the narrow Raiwala bazaar, looking in at the tea and sweet shops, until they found a place that looked dirty enough to be cheap. A servant-boy brought them chappatis and dal and Kishen ordered an ounce of butter; this was melted and poured over the dal. The meal cost them a rupee, and for this amount they could eat as much as they liked. The butter was an extra, and cost six annas. They were left with a little over ten rupees.

When they came out, the sun was low in the sky and the day was cooler.

'We can't walk tonight,' said Rusty. 'We'll have to sleep at the railway station. Maybe we can get on the train without a ticket.'

'And if we are caught, we'll spend a month in jail. Free board and lodging.'

'And then the social workers will get you, or they'll put you in a remand home and teach you to make mattresses.'

'I think it's better to buy tickets,' said Kishen.

'I know what we'll do,' said Rusty. 'We won't get the train till past midnight, so let's not buy tickets. We'll get to Harrawala early in the morning. Then it's only about eight miles by road to Dehra.'

Kishen agreed, and they found their way to the railway station, where they made themselves comfortable in a first class waiting-room.

'We don't have tickets,' said Kishen.

'But *we* are first class, aren't we?'

Kishen settled down in an armchair and covered his face with a handkerchief. 'Wake me when the train comes in,' he said drowsily.

Rusty went into the bathroom. He put his head under a tap and allowed cold water to play over his neck. He washed his face, drying it with a handkerchief, before returning to the waiting-room.

A man entered, setting out his belongings on the big table in the centre of the room. Rusty judged him to be in his thirties. The man was white, but he was too restless to be a European. He looked virile, but tired; he had a lean, sallow face, and pouches under the eyes. Rusty sat down on the edge of Kishen's armchair.

'Going to Delhi?' asked the stranger. His accent, though not very pronounced, was American.

'No, the other way,' replied Rusty. 'We live in Dehra.'

'I've often been there,' said the man. 'I've been trying to popularize a new steel plough in northern India, but without much success. Are you a student?'

'Not now. I finished with school two years ago.'

'And your friend?' He inclined his head towards the sleeping boy.

'He's with me,' said Rusty vaguely. 'We're travelling together.'

'Buddies.'

'Yes.'

The American took a flask from his bag and looked enquiringly at Rusty. 'Will you join me in a drink while we're waiting? There's almost an hour left for my train to arrive.'

'Well, I don't drink,' said Rusty, hesitating.

'A small one won't harm you. Just to keep me company.'

He took two small glasses from his bag, wiped them with a clean white handkerchief, and set them down on the table. Then he poured some dark brown stuff from his flask.

'Brandy,' said Rusty, sniffing.

'So you recognize it. Yes, it's brandy.'

Rusty reached across the table and took the glass.

'Here's luck!' said the stranger.

'Thank you,' said Rusty, and gulped down a mouthful of neat liquor. He coughed and the tears came to his eyes. He put his head between his hands, but he was feeling better.

'You've come a long way,' said the American looking at the boy's clothes.

'On foot,' said Rusty. 'From Hardwar. Since morning.'

'Hardwar! That's a long walk. What made you do that?'

Rusty emptied his glass and set it down. The friendly stranger poured out more brandy. This is the way they do things in America, thought Rusty. When you meet a stranger, offer him a drink. He must go there one day.

'What made you walk?' asked the stranger again.

'Tomorrow we'll walk some more,' said Rusty.

'But why?'

'Because we have the time. We have all the time in the world.'

'How come?'

'Because we have no money. You can't have both time and money.'

'Oh, I agree. You are quite a philosopher. But what happened?' asked the American, looking at the sleeping boy. 'What is he to you?'

'He's with me,' said Rusty, ignoring the question. He was beginning to feel sleepy. The friendly stranger seemed to be getting further and further away and his voice came from a great distance.

'Tell me what happened.'

'I'll tell you,' said Rusty, leaning unsteadily across the table to see the other better, and speaking slowly. 'I ran away. I ran away from home, nearly a year ago. I had a guardian, an Englishman—my parents died when I was very small—and I lived in his house, in his own community, and it was a world of our own and I never went outside it. Then one day in the rain I met Somi. I became his friend and he took me to his home, and to the bazaar, and he showed me India and the world and life itself. My guardian beat me when I came back from the bazaar, and he beat me when I played Holi and came home drenched in colour. I returned the beating, though, and ran away.'

Rusty paused in order to finish the drink and to see if the man was interested.

'Go on,' said the stranger.

'Somi was my good friend, he did a lot for me. He found a

boy—Kishen over there—who needed English lessons, and his family took a liking to me and gave me a place to stay. She spent time with me often—I mean the boy's mother—Kishen's mother—and she was sweet and kind to me. She was beautiful. There will never be a woman as beautiful . . . .'

He lapsed into silence for about a minute, gazed into the glass as though he sought something there other than brandy, and continued: 'But then they went away. Somi went away, everyone went away. What could I do, but go away too? What could I do, when Kishen's mother died, but go away? And if it wasn't for Kishen, I would never have come back. I tell you that straight, sir—I would never have come back. I wouldn't be here now, talking to you, if it wasn't for Kishen.

'But I didn't know Kishen was alone. He had run away from his father, who was too drunk to care, and he had been living on his wits for weeks—he is good at that. But when I found him, I had to come back, we both had to come back. We have only got each other, you see.'

'I follow you a little,' said the stranger, and he filled Rusty's glass again. 'What are you going to do in Dehra, both of you? Do you have jobs to go to? I guess not. Well, if ever you find yourself in Delhi, look me up. Here's my card.'

A bell clanged on the station platform, and the stranger looked at his watch and said it was almost time for his train to arrive. He wiped the glasses with his handkerchief and returned them to his bag, then went outside and stood on the platform, waiting for the Delhi train.

Rusty leant against the waiting-room door, staring across the railway tracks. He heard the shriek of the whistle as the front light of an engine played over the rails. The train came in slowly, the hissing engine sending out waves of steam. At the same time the carriage doors opened and people started pouring out.

There was a jam on the platform, while men, women and children pushed and struggled, and it was several minutes before anyone could get in or out of the carriage doors. The American had been swallowed up by the crowd. Bundles of belongings were passed through windows, over the heads of bystanders. Several young men climbed in at the windows, heads first, assisted by pushes from behind. Rusty assumed that there was another religious fair at Hardwar, for the rush was even greater than usual.

When the train had gone, a calm descended on the platform. A few people waiting for the morning train to Dehra still slept near their bundles. Vendors selling soda-water, lemons and curds, cups of tea, pushed their barrows down the platform, still calling their wares in desultory, sleepy voices. A baby cried, and the mother took the child to her bosom, but the baby kept on crying.

Rusty returned to the waiting-room. Kishen was still sound asleep in the armchair.

Rusty went to the light switch and turned it off, but the light from the platform streamed in through the gauze-covered doors. He did not think anyone would be coming in again that night. He sat down beside Kishen.

'Kishen, Kishen,' he whispered, touching the boy's shoulder.

Kishen stirred. 'What is it?' he mumbled drowsily. 'Why is it dark?'

'I put the light off,' said Rusty. 'You can sleep now.'

'I *was* sleeping,' said Kishen. 'But thank you all the same.'

The Forest Road

A T Doiwala next morning they had to leave the train. An inspector came round checking tickets, and Rusty and Kishen slipped out of the carriage from the side facing the jungle.

Doiwala stood just outside the Siwalik range, and already the fields were giving way to jungle. But there were maize-fields stretching away from the bottom of the railway banking, and the boys went in amongst the corn and waited in the field until the train had left. Kishen broke three or four corn-cobs from their stalks, stuffing them into his pockets.

'We might not get anything else to eat,' he said. 'Rusty, have you got matches so that we can light a fire and roast the corn?'

'We'll get some at the station.'

At Doiwala station they bought a box of matches, but they did not roast the corn until they had walked two miles up the road, into the jungle. Kishen collected dry twigs, and when they sat down at the side of the road he made a small fire. Kishen turned the corn-cobs over the fire until they were roasted a dark brown, burnt black in places. They dug their teeth into them, eating with relish.

'I wish we had some salt,' said Kishen.

'That would only make us thirsty, and we have no water. I hope we find a spring soon.'

'How far is Dehra now?' asked Kishen.

'About twelve miles, I think. It's funny how some miles seem longer than others. It depends on what you are thinking about, I suppose. What *you* are thinking and what I am thinking. If our thoughts agree, the miles are not so long. We get on better when we are thinking together than when we are talking together!'

'All right then, stop talking.'

When they had finished eating they threw away the corn-cobs

and began walking. They walked in silence; they had grown used to speaking only when they stopped to rest.

Rusty was thinking: I don't know how, but when we get to Dehra I've got to make a living for both of us. Kishen is too young to look after himself. He'll only get into trouble. I would not like to leave him alone even for a little while. Maybe I can get an English tuition. Or if I can write a story, a really good story, and sell it to a magazine, perhaps an American magazine . . . .

And Kishen was thinking: We will get money somehow. There are many ways of getting money. I don't mind anything as long as we are together. I don't mind anything as long as I am not alone.

Suddenly they heard the sound of rushing water. The road emerged from the jungle of sal trees and ended beside a river. There was a swift stream in the middle of the river-bed, coursing down towards the Ganges. A bridge had crossed this once, but it had been swept away during heavy monsoon rains, and the road ended at the river-bank.

They walked over sand and sharp rocks until they reached the water's edge, and they stood looking at the frothy water as it swirled below them.

'It's not deep,' said Kishen. 'I don't think it's above the waist anywhere.'

'It's not deep, but it's swift,' said Rusty. 'And the stones are slippery.'

'Shall we go back?'

'No, let's carry on—if it's too fast, we can turn back.'

They removed their shoes, tying them together by the laces, and hanging them about their necks, then holding hands for security, they stepped into the water.

The stones were slippery underfoot, and the boys stumbled, hindering rather than helping each other. When they were half-way across, the water was up to their waists. They stopped in midstream, unwilling to go further for fear they would be swept off their feet.

'I can hardly stand,' said Kishen. 'It will be difficult to swim against the current.'

'It won't get deeper now,' said Rusty hopefully.

Just then, Kishen slipped and went over backwards into the water, bringing Rusty down on top of him. Kishen began kicking and threshing about, but eventually—by gripping on to Rusty's right foot—came spluttering out of the water.

When they found they were not being swept away by the current they stopped struggling and cautiously dragged themselves across to the opposite bank. They came out of the water about thirty yards downstream.

The sun beat down on them, as they lay exhausted on the warm sand. Kishen sucked at a cut in his hand, spitting the blood into the stream with a contemptuous gesture.

After some time they were walking again, though Kishen kept on bringing up mouthfuls of water.

'I'm getting hungry now,' he said, when he had emptied himself of water.

'We'll be in Dehra soon,' said Rusty. 'And then never mind the money, we'll eat like pigs.'

'Gourmets!' put in Kishen. 'I suppose there are still eight or ten miles left. Now I'm not even thinking. Are you?'

'I was thinking we should visit that river again one day, when we have plenty of food and nothing to worry about.'

'You won't get me coming here again,' said Kishen.

They shuffled along the forest path, tired and hungry, but quite cheerful. Then they rounded a bend and found themselves face to face with a tiger.

Well, not quite face to face. The tiger was about fifteen yards away from them, occupying the centre of the path. He was as surprised to see the boys as the boys were to see him. He lifted his head, and his tail swished from side to side, but he made no move towards them. The boys stood absolutely still in the middle of the path. They were too astonished to do anything else, which was just as well, because, had they run or shouted or shown fear, the tiger might well have been provoked into attacking them. And, after a moment's hesitation, he crossed the path and disappeared into the forest without so much as a growl.

Still the boys did not move, but they found their voices.

'You didn't tell me there were tigers here,' said Kishen in a hoarse whisper.

'I didn't think about it,' said Rusty.

'Shall we go forwards or backwards?'

'Do you want to cross the stream again? Anyway, the tiger didn't seem to worry about us. Let's go on.'

And they walked on through the forest without seeing the tiger again, though they saw several splendid peacocks and a band of monkeys. It was not until they had left the forest behind and were on an open road with fields and villages on either side that they relaxed and showed their relief by bursting into laughter.

'I think we frightened that tiger more than it frightened us,' said Kishen. 'Why, it didn't even roar!'

'And a good thing it didn't, otherwise we might not have been here.'

They laughed at themselves, and when they laughed they were happy.

Rusty felt more at ease with Kishen than he did with anyone else—probably because Kishen had been one of his first friends, because they had grown swiftly together from childhood into adolescence. Rusty had never been at ease with anyone until he had met Somi and Kishen. His mother had died when he was very young, and his father had not lived much longer. His mother was a shadowy figure, and though he remembered her, she seemed, in his mind, to have less substance than his father. He had hated his guardian, who had looked after him when his father died.

Those early years had been very English, and the only Indians he had known were the servants. When he was five, very proud, he had informed the cook that England was ten times as large as India, and the cook had believed him.

As he grew older, the forbidden India—the real India of bazaars and temples and sprawling villages—was discovered in bits and pieces; it was only when Rusty made Indian friends for the first time that he discovered it completely. His guardian had not liked his friends or his visits to the bazaars, and they had quarrelled, and Rusty had run away, living for a year with Kishen's family.

At first everything had been different; physically different— wearing Indian clothes, eating Indian food, bathing Indian fashion—and then different in another, more subtle way, which had him thinking differently too. For though he was old enough to have already absorbed certain Western values, he was young enough and flexible enough to be able to adapt himself to his new and unfamiliar environment, and to absorb something of Indian values. He was not conscious of any division of loyalties in himself, but rather of a double inheritance.

For one year he had led an almost idyllic life; he had loved, almost worshipped, Kishen's mother, Meena—loved her with all the mute and helpless fervour of a sixteen-year-old—and she had loved him too, but only as a woman loves a homeless child. Then Meena was killed in a car accident, and Kishen's father returned to his whisky bottle and took another wife. Rusty had been on his way to Delhi, to try and leave India, when he had met Kishen in Hardwar.

And together they were returning to Dehra which was their home.

*

The danger they had shared helped to revive their drooping spirits, and they grew light-hearted as they walked into the fertile valley that lay between the Siwaliks and the Himalayan foothills. Spreading over the valley were wheat and maize and sugar-cane fields, tea-gardens and orchards of guava, litchee and mango.

There was a small village on the outskirts of Dehra, and the village lamps were lit when the boys, dusty and dishevelled, walked through with dragging feet. Now that their journey was almost over, they became more aware of their weariness and their aches, and the town which had been their home seemed suddenly strange and heartless, as though it did not recognize them any more.

133

A Place to Sleep

WHEN they got to the Tandoori Fish Shop, Kishen and Rusty were too hungry and tired to think of going any further, so they sat down and ordered a meal. The fish came hot, surrounded by salad and lemon, and when they had finished it, they ate again, fish and salad and lemon, and drank glasses of hot, spiced tea.

'The best thing in life is food,' said Kishen. 'There is nothing to equal it.'

'I agree,' said Rusty. 'Bhaiya, you are absolutely right.'

Afterwards, they walked through the noisy, crowded bazaar, which they knew so well; past the Clock Tower, up the steps of their old room. They were ready to flop down on the string cot and sleep for a week. But when they reached the top of the steps they found the door locked. It was not their lock, but a heavy, unfamiliar padlock, and its presence was ominous.

'Let's smash it!' said Kishen.

'That's no use,' said Rusty. 'The landlord doesn't want us to have the room. He's shut us out at the first opportunity. Well, let's go and see his agent. Perhaps he'll let us have the room back. Anyway, our things are inside.'

Rusty stood at the top of the steps, looking thoughtfully at the grounds—the gravel path, the litchee and mango trees, the grass badminton court, now overgrown with weeds—and half-expected to hear Kishen's mother calling to him from below, calling to him to come and play, while the father, in his green dressing-gown, sat on the steps clutching a bottle. They had gone now, and would never come back. Rusty was not sure that he wanted to stay in the old room.

'Would you like to wait here while I get the key?' he asked.

'No,' said Kishen. 'I'd be afraid to wait here alone.'

'Why?'

'Because,' he looked to Rusty for understanding, 'because this was our house once, and my mother and father lived here, and I'm afraid of the house when they are no longer in it. I'll come with you. I'd like to break the *munshi's* neck, anyway.'

The *munshi* met them at the door of his house. He was a slow, bent and elderly man, dressed in a black coat and white dhoti; a pair of vintage spectacles balanced precariously on his nose. He was in the service of the *seth*, who owned a great deal of property in town; and his duties included the collection of rents, eviction of tenants—this had become increasingly difficult—and seeing to the repair and maintenance of the *seth's* property.

'Your room has been rented out,' explained the *munshi*.

'What do you mean, mister?' said Kishen, bristling.

'Why has it been rented when we haven't given it up?' asked Rusty.

'You were never a tenant,' said the *munshi*, with a shrug that almost unsettled his spectacles. 'Mr Kapoor let you use one of the rooms. Now he has vacated the house. When you went away, I thought you had gone permanently.' The *munshi* made a helpless gesture with his hands, and anticipated the imminent fall of his spectacles by taking them off and wiping them on his shirt.

Finally he said: '*Sethji* ordered me to let the room immediately.'

'But how could I have gone permanently,' argued Rusty, 'when my things are still in the room?'

The *munshi* scratched his head. 'There were not many things, I thought you had no need for them. I thought you were going to England. You can have your things tomorrow. They are in the storeroom, and the key is with the *seth*. But I cannot let you have the room again.'

Uncertain as to what he should do next, Rusty continued to stand in the light thrown from the *munshi's* front room. Kishen stepped forward.

'Give us another room, then,' he said belligerently.

'I cannot do that now,' said the *munshi*. 'It is too late. You will have to come tomorrow, and even then I cannot promise you anything. All our rooms are full. Just now I cannot help you. There must be some place where you can stay . . . .'

'We'll find a place,' said Rusty, tired of the whole business. 'Come on, bhaiya. There's always the railway platform.'

Kishen hesitated, scowling at the *munshi*, before following Rusty out of the gate.

'What now?' he grumbled. 'Where do we go now?'

They stood uncertainly in the middle of the road.

'Let's sit down somewhere,' suggested Rusty. 'Then we can think of something. We can't come to a decision simply by standing stupidly on the road.'

'We'll sit in the tea-shop,' said Kishen. 'We've had enough tea, but let's go there anyway.'

They found the tea-shop at the end of the bazaar, a make-shift wooden affair built over a gully. There were only two tables in the shop, and most of the customers sat outside on a bench, where they could listen to the shopkeeper, a popular storyteller.

Sitting on the ground in front of the shop was a thick-set youth with his head shaved, wearing rags. He was dumb—they called him the Goonga—and the customers often made sport of him, abusing him good-naturedly, and clouting him over the head from time to time. The Goonga did not mind this; he made faces at the others, and chuckled derisively at their remarks. He could say only one word, 'Goo' and he said it often. This kept the customers in fits of laughter.

'Goo!' he said, when he saw Kishen and Rusty enter the shop. He pointed at the boys, chuckled, and said 'Goo!' again. Everyone laughed. Someone got up from the bench and, with the flat of his hand, whacked the Goonga over his naked head. The Goonga sprang at the man, making queer, gurgling noises. Someone tripped him and sent him sprawling on the ground, and there was more laughter.

Rusty and Kishen sat at an inside table. Everyone, except the Goonga, was drinking tea.

'Give the Goonga a glass of tea,' said Kishen to the shopkeeper.

The shopkeeper grinned and made the tea. The Goonga looked at Kishen and Rusty and said, 'Goo!'

'Now how much money is left?' asked Kishen, getting down to business.

'About nine rupees,' said Rusty. 'If we are careful, it will last us a few days.'

'More than a week,' said Kishen. 'We can get enough food for a rupee a day, as long as we don't start eating chicken. But you should find some work in a day or two.'

'Don't be too optimistic about that.'

'Well, it's no use worrying as yet.'

There was an interesting story being told by the shopkeeper, about a jinn who used his abnormally long reach to steal sweets, and the boys forgot about their 'conference' until the story was finished.

'Now it's someone else's turn,' said the shopkeeper.

'The fair boy will tell us one,' said a voice, and everyone turned to look at Rusty.

The person who had made the request was one of the boys who served tea to the customers. He could not have been more than twelve years old, but he had a worldly look about him, in spite of the dimples in his cheeks and the mischievous glint in his eyes. His fair complexion and high cheekbones showed that he came from the hills, from one of the border districts.

'I don't know any stories,' said Rusty.

'That isn't possible,' said the shopkeeper. 'Everyone knows at least one story, even if it is his own.'

'Yes, tell us,' said the hill boy.

'You find us a room for the night,' said Kishen, always ready to bargain in true Punjabi fashion, 'and he'll tell you a story.'

'I don't know of any place,' said the shopkeeper, 'but you are welcome to sleep in my shop. You won't sleep much, because there are people coming and going all night, especially the truck drivers.'

'Don't worry,' said the hill boy. 'I know of many places where you can stay. Now tell us the story.'

So Rusty embarked on a ghost story which held his audience enthralled.

'All right, now tell us,' said Rusty, after his story was over, 'where are we going to sleep tonight? You can't get a hotel room for less than two rupees.'

'It's not too cold,' and Kishen. 'We can sleep on the maidan. There's shelter there.'

Rusty gave a sigh of resignation, and thought: A year ago when I ran away I slept on the maidan, and again I am going to sleep on the maidan. That's called 'Progress'.

He said, 'The last time I slept on the maidan, it rained. I woke up in a pool of mud.'

'But it won't rain today,' said Kishen cheerfully. 'There isn't a cloud in the sky.'

They looked out at the night sky. The moon was almost at the full, robbing the stars of their glory.

*

They left the shop and began walking towards the open grassland of the maidan. The bazaar was almost empty now, the shops closed, lights showing only from upper windows. Rusty became conscious of the sound of soft footfalls behind him, and looking over his shoulder, saw that they were being followed by the Goonga.

'Goo,' said the Goonga, on being noticed.

'Damn!' said Kishen. 'Why did we have to give him tea? He probably thinks we are rich and won't let us out of sight again.'

'He can do no harm,' said Rusty, though he quickened his step. 'He'll change his mind about us when he finds we're sleeping on the maidan.'

'Goo,' said the Goonga from behind, quickening his step.

They turned abruptly down an alleyway, trying to shake the Goonga off, but he padded after them, chuckling ghoulishly to himself. They cut back to the main road, but he was behind them at the Clock Tower.

At the edge of the maidan Rusty turned and said: 'Go away, Goonga. We've got no money, no food, no clothes. We are no better off than you. Go away!'

'Yes, buzz off!' said Kishen, a master of Indo-Anglian slang.

But the youth said, 'Goo!' and took a step forward, and his shaved head glistened in the moonlight. Rusty shrugged, and led Kishen on to the maidan. The Goonga stood at the edge, shaking his head and chuckling. His dry black skin showed through his rags, and his feet were covered with mud. He watched the boys as they walked across the grass, watched them until they lay down; and then he shrugged his shoulders, and said, 'Goo,' and went away.

The Old Church

'LET'S leave our things with the *munshi*,' said Rusty, yawning and stretching his limbs. 'It's no use collecting them until we have somewhere to stay. But I *would* like to change my clothes.'

It had been cold on the maidan until the sun threw its first pink glow over the hills. On the grass lay yesterday's remnants—a damp newspaper, a broken toy, a kite hanging helplessly from the branches of a tree. The boys were sitting on the dew-sodden grass, waiting for the sun to seep through to their skin and drive the chill from their bones. They had not slept much, and their eyes were ringed and heavy. Rusty's hair looked like a small, untidy stack of hay. Kishen's legs were swollen with mosquito bites.

'Why is it that you haven't been bitten as much as I have?' complained Kishen.

'No doubt you taste better,' said Rusty. 'We had better split up now, I suppose.'

'But why?'

'We will get more done that way. You go to the *munshi* and see if you can persuade him to let us have another room. But don't pay anything in advance! Meanwhile, I'll call at the schools to see if I can get any English tuitions.'

'All right, Rusty. Where do we meet?'

'At the Clock Tower. At about twelve o'clock.'

'Then we can eat,' said Kishen with enthusiasm.

Rusty smiled. He had not smiled so brightly for a long time; and seeing the smile on Rusty's face, Kishen felt sure everything would come out all right.

'Eating is something we always agree upon,' said Rusty.

They washed their faces at the public tap at the edge of the maidan, where the wrestlers were usually to be found. The wrestlers had not assembled that morning, and the pit was empty, otherwise Rusty might have encountered a friend of his, called Hathi, who often came there to wrestle and use the weights. Scrubbing his back and shoulders at the tap, he realized that he needed a haircut and, worse still, a shave.

'I will have to get a shave,' he said ruefully. 'You're lucky to have only a little fluff on your cheeks so far. I have to shave at least once a week, do you know that?'

'How extravagant!' exclaimed Kishen. 'Can't you grow a beard? A shave will cost four annas.'

'Nobody will give me a tuition if they see this growth on my face.'

'Oh, all right,' grumbled Kishen, stroking the faint beginning of a moustache. 'You take four annas and have your shave, but I will keep the rest of the money with me in case I have to give the *munshi* something. It will be all right to let him have a rupee or two in advance, if he can give us a room.'

He left Rusty at the tap and went straight to the *munshi's* house, but he had no luck there. The *munshi* asked for an advance of fifteen rupees before he would rent them a room. He was polite but firm: he was only the *seth's* servant, he insisted, and he had to carry out orders. Kishen made a few insulting remarks about the *seth* before leaving.

Disgruntled, but far from depressed (it was not in his nature to be easily depressed), Kishen sauntered off into the alleyways behind the bazaar. There were two hours ahead of him before he could meet Rusty; he was not sure what he should do with himself.

In a courtyard off one of the alleyways, three young men squatted in the sun, playing cards. Kishen watched them for a while, until one of the players beckoned to him, inviting him to join in the game.

Kishen was with the card-players till twelve o'clock.

*

Rusty went to the barber's shop and had his shave for four annas. And the barber, who was a special friend of his, and took great pleasure in running his fingers through Rusty's fair hair, gave him a head massage into the bargain.

It was a wonderful massage and included not only the head, but Rusty's eyes, neck and forehead. The barber was a dark, glistening man, with broad shoulders and a chest like a drum; he wore a fine white Lucknow shirt, through which you could see his hard body. His strong fingers drummed and stroked and pressed; and with the palms and sides of his hands he thumped and patted Rusty's forehead. Rusty felt the blood rush to his temples; and when the massage was finished, he was hardly conscious of having a head, and walked into the street with a peculiar, elated, headless feeling.

He made a somewhat fruitless round of the three principal schools. At each of them he was told that if anything in his line turned up, they would certainly let him know; but they did not ask him where he could be found if he was wanted. The last school asked him to call again in a day or two.

On the outskirts of the town Rusty found the old church of St. Paul's, which had been abandoned for over a year, due to meagre parish resources and a negligible attendance. The Catholics of Dehra had been able to afford the upkeep of their church and convent, but nobody outside Dehra had bothered about St. Paul's, and eventually the padre had locked the building and gone away. Rusty regretted this, not because he had been fond of church-going—he had always disliked large gatherings of people—but because it was old, with historic and personal associations, and he hated to see old things, old people, suffer lonely deaths.

The plaster was crumbling, the paint peeling off the walls, moss growing in every crack. Wild creepers grew over the stained-glass windows. The garden, so well-kept once, was now a jungle of weeds and irrepressible marigolds.

Rusty leaned on the gate and gazed at the church. There had been a time when he hated visiting this place, for it had meant the uncomfortable presence of his guardian, the gossip of middle-aged women, the boredom of an insipid sermon; but now, seeing the neglected church, he felt sorry for it—not only for the people who had been there, but for the place itself, and for those who were buried in the graves that kept each other silent company in the grounds. People he had known lay there, and some of them were

142

people his father had known.

He opened the creaking wooden gate and walked up the overgrown path. The front door was locked. He walked round, trying the side doors, finding them all closed. There was no lock on the vestry door, though it seemed to be bolted from within. Two panes of glass were set in the top of the door. Standing on his toes, Rusty reached up to them, pressing his fingers against the panes to test the thickness of the glass. He stood back from the door, took his handkerchief from his pocket and wrapped it round his hand. Standing on his toes again, he pushed his fist through one of the panes.

There was a tinkle of falling glass. Rusty groped around and found the bolt. Then he stepped back and kicked at the door.

The door opened. The handkerchief had fallen from his hand and one of his knuckles was bleeding. He picked up the handkerchief and wrapped it round the cut; then he stepped into the vestry.

The place was almost empty. A cupboard-door hung open on one hinge and a few old cassocks lay on a shelf in a dusty pile. An untidy heap of prayer books and hymnals was stacked in a packing-case, and a mouse sat on top of a half-eaten hymnal, watching the intruder.

Rusty went through the vestry, into the church hall, where it was lighter. Sunlight poured through a stained-glass window, throwing patches of mellow orange and gold on the pews and on the frayed red carpet that ran down the aisle. The windows were full of cobwebs. As Rusty walked down the aisle, he broke through cordons of cobwebs, sending the frightened spiders scurrying away across the pews.

He left the church by the vestry door, closing it behind him, and, removing the splintered glass from the window, he threw the pieces into the bushes.

*

Kishen could always find plenty to do in the bazaar, apart from gambling with cards. The bazaar was a mile long, stretching from the station to the Clock Tower; little alleys led off the main road, winding towards the stench of the fish market or the wet freshness of the vegetable market.

Another alley led to the junk, or *kabari*, market, which was always interesting. Here you could get anything from valuable antiques and rare books to old footballs, shoes, haversacks, tins and bottles. Most of the *kabaris* were Muslims, who had been either too old or too poor to leave Dehra after the partition of the country. They made up only a small part of the town's very mixed population, which included sturdy little Gurkhas from Nepal, easy-going smiling Garhwalis from the hills, and bustling, Punjabi Hindus and Sikhs.

The Punjabis had brought activity and noise to this once sleepy little town, and small shops and hotels had mushroomed up on all the roads. Skilled tailors and carpenters and businessmen who had lost nearly everything in their flight across the border when the country was divided, had set to work again, to make new livings and new fortunes. Only a Punjabi can make and lose a fortune with both speed and daring, and Kishen (who was Punjabi) could do it too, in his own small way.

He met Rusty at the Clock Tower, and together they went to the chaat shop to have a cheap meal of spiced fruits and vegetables. Kishen had been again to the *munshi*, to get into the storeroom, and now carried a bundle of clothes; he had done this to please Rusty, as the matter of the card-game would be difficult to explain.

'The *munshi* wouldn't give me a room without an advance of fifteen rupees,' he said. 'But I got some clothes, anyway.'

'It doesn't matter about the room. I've found a place to stay.'

'Oh good! What is it like?'

'Wait till you see it. I had no luck at the schools, though there may be something for me in a day or two. How much money did you say was left?'

'Eight rupees,' said Kishen, looking guilty, and stuffing his mouth with potatoes to hide his confusion.

'I thought it was nine rupees,' said Rusty.

'It was nine,' said Kishen. 'But I lost one rupee. I was sure I could win, but those fellows had a trick I didn't know!'

'I see,' said Rusty resignedly. 'From now on I'll keep everything.'

Without any shame Kishen put the notes and coins on the table. Rusty separated the money into two piles, put the notes in his pocket, and pushed six annas across the table to Kishen.

Kishen grinned. 'So you are letting me keep something, after all?'

'That's to pay for the chaat,' said Rusty, and Kishen's grin turned into a grimace.

*

They walked to the church, Kishen grumbling a little, Rusty feeling very cheerful. Sometimes it would be the other way round. They were seldom cheerful together; and they never grumbled together, which was fortunate.

'I want a bath,' said Kishen unreasonably. 'How far is this place where you've got a room?'

'I didn't say anything about a room, and there's no place for a bath. But there's a stream not far away, in the jungle behind the road.'

Kishen looked puzzled and scratched his fuzzy head, but he did not say anything, reserving judgement till later.

'Hey, where are you going, Rusty?' he said, when Rusty turned in at the church gate.

'To the church,' said Rusty.

'What for—to pray?' asked Kishen anxiously. 'I never knew you were religious.'

'I'm not. But we're going to live in the place.'

Kishen slapped his forehead in astonishment, then burst into laughter. 'The places we stay at!' he exclaimed. 'Railway stations. Maidans. And now cathedrals!'

'It's not a cathedral, it's a church.'

'What's the difference? It's the same religion. A mosque can be different from a temple, but how is a cathedral different from a church?'

Rusty did not try to explain, but led Kishen in through the vestry door. Kishen crept cautiously into the quiet church, looking nervously at the dark, spidery corners, at the high windows, the bare altar, the gloom above the rafters.

145

'I can't stay here,' he said. 'There must be a ghost in the place.' He ran his fingers over the top of a pew, leaving tracks in the thick dust.

'We can sleep on the benches or on the carpet,' said Rusty. 'And we can cover ourselves with those old cassocks.'

'Why are they called cassocks?'

'I haven't the slightest idea.'

'Then don't lecture me about cathedrals. If someone finds out we are staying here, there will be trouble.'

'Nobody will find out. Nobody comes here any more. The place is not looked after, as you can see. Those who used to come have all gone away. Only I am left, and I never came here willingly.'

'Up till now,' said Kishen. 'Let some air in.'

Rusty climbed on a bench and opened one of the high windows. Fresh air rushed in, smelling sweet, driving away the mustiness of the closed hall.

'Now let's go to the stream,' said Rusty.

They left the church by the vestry door, passed through the unkempt garden and went into the jungle. A narrow path led through the sal trees, and they followed it for about a quarter of a mile. The path had not been used for a long time, and they had to push their way through thorny bushes and brambles. Then they heard the sound of rushing water.

They had to slide down a rock face into a small ravine, and there they found the stream running over a bed of shingle. Removing their shoes and rolling up their trousers, they crossed the stream. Water trickled down from the hillside, from amongst ferns and grasses and wild flowers; and the hills, rising steeply on either side, kept the ravine in shadow. The rocks were smooth, almost soft, and some of them were grey and some yellow. A small waterfall fell across them, forming a deep, round pool of apple-green water.

They removed their clothes and jumped into the pool. Kishen went too far out, felt the ground slipping away from beneath his feet, and came splashing back into the shallows.

'I didn't know it was so deep,' he said.

Soon they had forgotten the problem of making money, had forgotten the rigours of their journey. They swam and romped about in the cold mountain water. Kishen gathered the clothes together and washed them in the stream, beating them out on the smooth rocks, and spreading them on the grass to dry. When they had bathed, they lay down on the grass, under a warm afternoon sun, talking spasmodically and occasionally falling into a light sleep.

'I am going to write to Somi,' said Rusty, 'but I don't know his address.'

'Isn't his mother still here?' said Kishen

Rusty sat up suddenly. 'I never thought of her. Somi said he was the only one leaving Dehra. She must be here.'

'Then let us go and see her,' said Kishen. 'She might be able to help us.'

'We'll go now,' said Rusty.

They waited until their clothes were dry, and then they dressed and went back along the forest path. The sun was setting when Rusty and Kishen arrived at Somi's house, which was about a mile from the church, in the direction of the station. It was an old yellow bungalow, almost lost amongst litchee and guava trees, and as Rusty passed beneath the trees he remembered a day when Somi, a golden boy singing in the sun, had sat on the limb of a guava tree, had fallen lightly on Rusty's shoulders, ruffling his hair and shouting, 'Run, my pony, my best favourite friend!'

He missed Somi's welcoming laughter as he walked up the veranda steps, but he found Somi's mother busy in the kitchen, while the baby sister crawled about on the floor. Rusty took the child in his arms and lifted her high above his head; and the little girl screamed with delight as he tossed her in the air. Somi's mother, grey-haired, smiling, and dressed in a simple white sari, put her hands to her cheeks.

'Master Rusty!' she exclaimed. 'And Kishen bhaiya! Where have you been all these weeks?'

'Travelling,' said Rusty. 'We have been doing a world tour.'

'On foot,' added Kishen.

They sat in cane chairs on the veranda, and Rusty gave Somi's mother an account of their journey, deliberately omitting to mention that they were without work or money. But she had sensed their predicament.

147

'Are you having any trouble about your room?' she asked.

'We left it,' said Rusty. 'We are staying in a bigger place now.'

'Yes, much bigger,' said Kishen.

'What about that book you were going to write—is it published?'

'No, I'm still writing it,' said Rusty.

'How much have you done?'

'Oh, not much as yet. These things take a long time.'

'And what is it about?'

'Oh, everything I suppose,' said Rusty, feeling guilty and changing the subject, for his novel had not progressed beyond the second chapter. 'I'm starting another tuition soon. If you know of any people who want their children to learn English, please pass them on to me.'

'Of course I will. Somi would not forgive me if I did not do as you asked. But why don't you stay here? There is plenty of room.'

'Oh, we are quite comfortable in our place,' said Rusty.

'Oh, yes, very comfortable,' said Kishen glaring at him.

Somi's mother made them stay for dinner, and they did not take much persuading, for the aroma of rich Punjabi food had been coming to them from the kitchen. They were prepared to sleep in churches and waiting-rooms all their lives, provided there was always good food to be had—rich, fleshy food, for they scorned most vegetables . . . .

Somi's mother gave them a feast of tandoori bread and buffalo's butter, meat cooked with spinach, vegetables with cheese, a sour pickle of turnip and lemon, and a jug of *lassi*. They did full justice to the meal, and Somi's mother watched them with satisfaction—the satisfaction of a mother and a good cook.

'Do you need any money?' she asked, when they had finished.

'Oh, no,' said Rusty, 'we have plenty of that.'

Kishen kicked him under the table.

'Enough for a week, anyway,' said Rusty.

After the meal, he took Somi's Amritsar address, with the intention of writing to him the next day. He also stuffed his pockets with pencils and writing-paper. When they were about to leave, Somi's mother thrust a ten-rupee note into Rusty's hand, and he blushed, unable to refuse the money.

Once on the road, he said: 'We didn't come to borrow money, bhaiya.'

'But you can pay it back in a few days. What's the use of having friends if you can't go to them for help?'

'I would have gone when there was nothing left. Until there is nothing left, I don't want to trouble anyone.'

They walked back to the church, buying two large candles on the way. Rusty lit one candle at the church gate, and led the way down the dark, disused path.

New Encounters

'It's creepy,' said Kishen, keeping close to Rusty. 'It's so quiet here. I think we should go back and stay at Somi's house. There must be something wrong with sleeping in a church.'

'It is no more wrong than sleeping in a tree.'

When they were inside, Rusty placed the burning candle on the altar steps. A bat swooped down from the rafters and Kishen ducked under a pew. 'I would rather sleep in the maidan,' he said.

'It's better here,' said Rusty. He came back from the vestry with a bundle of cassocks, which he dumped on the floor. 'I'll do some writing,' he said, sitting down near the candle and producing pencil and paper from his pocket.

Kishen sat down on a bench and removed his shoes, rubbing his feet and playing with his toes. When he had got used to the bats diving overhead, he stood up and undressed. Long and bony in his vest and underpants, he sat down on the pile of cassocks; and with his elbows resting on his knees, and his chin cupped in the palms of his hands, he watched Rusty write.

He knew better than to interrupt when Rusty was writing or reading, particularly so when he was reading. Once Rusty was absorbed in a book, only something disastrous would get him away from it. He had been a bookworm ever since he had learnt to read, but the final commitment had been made at the age of twelve.

At this ripe and impressionable age he had been taken, by his guardian and several other sportsmen on a shikar expedition into the Terai jungles near Dehra. The prospect of a week in the jungle, as camp-follower to several egotistic adults with guns, filled Rusty with dismay. He knew that many long weary hours would be spent tramping behind tall, professional-looking huntsmen, who spoke in terms of bagging this tiger or that wild elephant, when all they ever got, if they were lucky, was a hare or a partridge. Tigers and excitement, it seemed, came only to Jim Corbett. Rusty had been on several shikar trips and had always been overtaken by ennui.

That particular expedition had been different, but not because the hunters had been more than usually successful. At the end of the week all they had shot were two miserable, underweight wild fowl. But Rusty had contrived, on the second day, to be left behind in the forest rest house; and there he discovered a shelf of books half-hidden in a corner of the old bungalow.

Who had left them there? A literary forest officer? Some memsahib who had been bored with her husband's campfire boasting? Or someone who, pained at the prospect of slaughtering wild animals, insured himself against boredom by bringing his library along. But why leave it behind? For fellow sufferers, perhaps. Or possibly the poor fellow had gone into the jungle one day, as a sort of gesture to his more bloodthirsty companions, and been trampled by an elephant, or gored by a wild boar, or (more likely) accidentally shot by one of the shikaris—and his sorrowing friends had taken his remains away, but left his books behind.

Anyway, there they were—a shelf of some thirty volumes. The shelf was catholic in its contents—and Rusty had soaked up Dickens, Wodehouse, M. R. James, George Eliot, Maugham and Barrie, while the big-game hunters, instead of feasting on roast pig or venison, opened their tins of corned meat.

*

In the early hours of the morning a mouse nibbled at Kishen's toes and the boy woke with a yelp and shook Rusty.

'I've been bitten,' said Kishen urgently, Rusty surfaced from the cassocks, 'I've been bitten by a church mouse.'

'At least it isn't a cathedral rat,' said Rusty. 'I've had one crawling over me all night.' He shook out the cassocks, and, with a squeak, a mouse leapt from the clothes and made a dash for safety.

Kishen put out his hand and touched Rusty's shoulder. The warmth of his friend's body reassured him, and he drew nearer and went to sleep with his arm round Rusty.

They rose before the sun was up, and went straight to the pool.

It was a cold morning. They gasped and cried out from the shock of the ice-cold mountain water. Rusty was brown on his arms and legs, where the sun had burnt him, and the rest of his body was pink from the slap of the water. Kishen had long loose limbs, and he threshed the water vigorously, but with little skill. They both tried diving off a rock, but landed on their bellies every time.

As they swam about, the sun came striking through the sal trees, making emeralds of the dewdrops, and pouring through the clear water till it touched the yellow sand. Rusty felt the sun touch his skin, felt it sink deep into his blood and bones and marrow, and, exulting in it, he hurled himself at Kishen. They tumbled over in the water, going down with a wild kicking of legs, and came spluttering to the surface, gasping and shouting. Then they lay on the rocks till they were dry.

When they left the pool, they walked to the maidan.

Every morning a group of young men wrestled at one end of the maidan, in a pit of soft, newly-dug earth. Hathi was one of the wrestlers. He was like a young bull, with a magnificent chest, and great broad thighs. His light brown hair and eyes were in startling contrast to the rest of his dark body.

Hathi relied more on strength than skill, and with a sweep of his broad hand he could level an opponent to the ground. Rusty had met him when he used to watch the wrestling with Somi and Kishen, and Hathi had always greeted them with a wide smile, inviting them to wrestle.

Kishen and Rusty found him at the tap, washing the mud and oil from his body, pummelling himself with resounding slaps. When he looked up and saw Rusty, he gave a shout of recognition, left the tap running, and gave Rusty an exuberant wet hug, transferring a fair amount of mud and oil on to his friend's already soiled shirt.

'My friend! Where have you been all these weeks? I thought you had forgotten me. And Kishen bhaiya, how are you?'

Kishen received the bear-hug with a grumble: 'I've already had my bath, Hathi.'

But Hathi continued talking, while he put on his shirt and pyjamas. 'You are just in time to see me, as I am going away in a day or two,' he said.

'Where are you going?' asked Rusty.

'To my village in the hills. I have land there, you know—I am going back to look after it. Come and have tea with me—come! I wanted to make both of you wrestlers, but you disappeared, and now it is too late.'

He took them to the tea-shop near the Clock Tower, where he mixed each of them a glass of hot milk, honey and beaten egg. The morning bath had refreshed them and they were feeling quite energetic.

'How do you get to your village?' asked Rusty. 'Is there a motor road?'

'No. The road ends at Lansdowne. From there one has to walk about thirty miles. It is a steep road, and you have to cross two mountains, but it can be done in a day if you start out early enough. Why don't you come with me?' he asked suddenly.

'There you will be able to write many stories. That is what you want to do, isn't it? There will be no noise or worry.'

'I can't come just now,' said Rusty. 'Maybe later, but not now.'

'You come too, Kishen,' pressed Hathi. 'Why not?'

'Kishen would be bored by mountains,' said Rusty.

'How do you know?' said Kishen, looking annoyed.

'Well, if you want to come later,' said Hathi, 'you have only to take the bus to Lansdowne, and then take the north-east road for the village of Manjari. You can come whenever you like. I will be living alone.'

'If we come,' said Rusty, 'we should be of some use to you there.'

'I will make farmers of you!' exclaimed Hathi, slapping himself on the thigh.

'Kishen is too lazy.'

'And Rusty too clumsy.'

'Well, maybe we will come,' said Rusty. 'But first I must see if I can get some sort of work here. I'm going to one of the schools again today. What will you do, Kishen?'

Kishen shrugged. 'I'll wait for you in the bazaar.'

'Stay with me,' said Hathi. 'I have nothing to do except recover money from various people. If I don't get it now, I will never get it.'

*

While Hathi was engaged at the Sindhi Sweet Shop, arguing with a man about a certain amount of money, Kishen wandered off on his own, lounging about in front of the shops. He was standing in front of a cloth shop when he saw an old family friend, Mrs Bhushan, with her vixenish, fifteen-year-old daughter, Aruna, an old playmate of his. They were in the shop, haggling with the shopkeeper over the price of a sari. Mrs Bhushan was in the habit of going from shop to shop, like a bee sampling honey; she would have bales of cloth unfurled for inspection, but she seldom bought anything. Aruna was a dark, thin girl. She had pretty green eyes, and a mischievous smile, and she was not as innocent as she looked. Kishen would have liked to speak to her, but he did not relish the prospect of meeting Mrs Bhushan, who would make things awkward for him, so he turned his back on the shop and looked around for Hathi. He was about to walk away when he felt a heavy hand descend on his shoulder, and, turning, found himself looking into the large, disagreeable eyes of Mrs Bhushan.

Mrs Bhushan was an imposing woman of some thirty-five years and she walked with a heavy determination that kept people, and even bulls, out of her way. Her dogs, her husband, and her servants were all afraid of her and submitted to her dictates without a murmur. A masculine woman, she bullied men and children, and lavished most of her affection on dogs. Her cocker spaniels slept on her bed, and her husband slept in the drawing-room.

'Kishen!' exclaimed Mrs Bhushan, pouncing upon the poor boy. 'What are you doing here?' And at the same time Aruna saw him, and her green eyes brightened, and she cried, 'Kishen! What are you doing here? We thought you were in Hardwar!'

Kishen was confused. To have Mrs Bhushan towering over him was like experiencing an eclipse of the sun. Moreover, he did not know how to explain his presence in Dehra. He contented himself with grinning sheepishly at Aruna.

'Where have you been, boy?' demanded Mrs Bhushan, getting business-like. 'Your clothes are all torn and you're a bundle of bones!'

'Oh, I've been on a walking-tour,' said Kishen unconvincingly.

'A walking-tour! Alone?'

'No, with a friend . . . .'

'You're too young to be wandering about like a vagrant. What do you think relatives are for? Now get into the car and come home with us.'

Kishen had not noticed the pre-War Hillman that stood beneath the tamarind tree. It had once belonged to a British magistrate, who had sold it cheap when he went away after Indian independence. Mrs Bhushan, in her aggressive way, had done her best to shorten the car's life, but it had lasted into the middle of the 1950s.

'What about my friend?' asked Kishen unhappily.

'You can see him later, can't you? Come on, Aruna, get in. There's something fishy about this walking-tour business, and I mean to get to the bottom of it!' And she trod on the accelerator with such ferocity that a lame beggar, who had been dawdling in the middle of the road, suddenly regained the use of both legs and sprang nimbly on to the pavement.

*

When they arrived at Mrs Bhushan's smart white bungalow, Kishen was placed in an armchair and subjected to Mrs Bhushan's own brand of third degree, which consisted of snaps and snarls and snorts of disapproval. The cocker spaniels, disapproving of Kishen's ragged condition, snapped at his long-suffering legs, which had, so far, endured blisters, mosquito bites, and the nibbling of mice.

Before long, Kishen had told them the whole story of his journey from Hardwar with Rusty. Aruna listened to every word, full of admiration for the two boys, but Mrs Bhushan voiced her disapproval in strong terms.

'Well, this is the end of your wanderings, young man,' she said. 'You're staying right here in this house. I won't have you wandering about the country with a lot of loafers.'

Mrs Bhushan, who was given to exaggeration, had visualized Rusty not as one person, but as several, an entire gang of tramps.

'Who would you rather stay with?' she demanded. 'Your father or me?'

'With you,' said Kishen hurriedly, certain that he had no choice.

'Then go and have a bath, while I get some clean clothes ready for you.'

Kishen spent half an hour under a hot shower, luxuriating in its warmth, while steam filled the room and his skin began to glow. It was weeks since he had used soap, and he lathered himself from head to foot, and watched the effect in the bathroom mirror. The water sent the soap scurrying down his legs, across the floor and down the drain and into the garden. He dried himself briskly and, hating the sight of his dusty old clothes, wrapped the towel around his waist and walked barefoot into the drawing-room.

Mrs Bhushan was searching for a pair of her husband's pyjamas to fit Kishen, and Aruna was alone in the room, reclining on the carpet. She pulled Kishen down beside her, and held his hand.

'I wish I had been with you,' she said.

'Have you ever slept with a rat?' said Kishen. 'Because I did last night.'

'What about your friend Rusty? I can ask Mummy to let him stay with us for some time.'

'He won't come.'

'Why not?'

'He just won't come.'

'Is he too proud?'

'No, but you are proud. That's why he won't come.'

Aruna tossed the hair away from her face. 'Then let him stay where he is.'

'But I must go and tell him what has happened. He'll be waiting for me at the Clock Tower.'

'Not today, you won't,' said Mrs Bhushan, marching back into the room with a pink pyjama over her shoulder. 'You can see him tomorrow, when we will drive you over in the car. I'm sure he can look after himself all right. If he had any sense, he'd have taken you home when he found you. The fellow must be an absolute rogue!'

And so, for the rest of the day, Kishen was held prisoner in Mrs Bhushan's comfortable drawing-room where Aruna kept him company, feeding him with chicken curry and soft juicy papayas.

*

The school to which Rusty had been (the visit proved fruitless) stood near the dry river-bed of the Rispana, and on the other side of the river-bed lay mustard fields and tea-gardens. As he had more than an hour left before meeting Kishen, he crossed the sandy river-bed and wandered through the fields. A peacock ran along the path with swift, ungainly strides.

A small canal passed through the tea-gardens, and Rusty followed the canal, counting the horny grey lizards that darted in and out of the stones. He picked a tea leaf from a bush and, holding it to his nose, found the smell sweet and pleasant. When he had walked about a mile, he came to a small clearing. There was a house in the clearing, surrounded by banana and poinsettia trees, the poinsettia leaves hanging down like long red tongues of fire. Bougainvillaea and other creepers covered the front of the house.

Sitting in a cane chair on the veranda was an Englishman. At least, Rusty assumed that the gentleman he saw was an Englishman. He may have been a German or an American or a Russian, but the only Europeans Rusty had known were Englishmen, and he immediately took the white-haired gentleman in the cane chair to be English—and he happened to be right.

The gentleman was elderly, red-faced, dressed in a tweed coat and flannel shorts and thick woollen stockings. Sola-topees had gone out of fashion, otherwise he might have been wearing one. An unlit pipe was held between his teeth, and on his knees lay a copy of *The Times Literary Supplement.*

It was over a year since Rusty had seen an Englishman. The last one had been his guardian, and he had hated his guardian. But the old man in the chair seemed, somehow, bluff and amiable. Rusty advanced cautiously up the veranda steps, then waited for the old man to look up from his paper.

The old man did not look up, but he said, 'Yes, come in, boy. Pull up a chair and sit down.'

'I hope I'm not disturbing you,' said Rusty.

'You are, but it doesn't matter. Don't be so self-effacing.' The old man looked up at Rusty, and his grey eyes softened a little, but he did not smile; it was too much trouble to remove the pipe from his mouth.

Rusty pulled up a chair and sat down awkwardly, twiddling his thumbs. The old man looked him up and down, said, 'Have a drink, I expect you're old enough,' and producing another glass from beneath the table, poured out two fingers of Solan whisky into Rusty's glass. He poured three fingers into his own glass. Then, from under the table, he produced two soda-water bottles and an opener. The bottle-tops flew out of the veranda with loud pops, and the golden liquid rose fuzzily to the top of the glass.

'Cheers,' said the old man, tossing down most of his drink.

'Pettigrew is the name,' said the old man. 'They used to call me Petty, though, down in Bangalore.'

'I'm pleased to meet you, Mr Pettigrew,' said Rusty politely. 'Is this your house?'

'Yes, the house is mine,' said Mr Pettigrew, knocking out his pipe on the table. 'It's about all that is still mine; the house and my library. These gardens were mine, once, but I only have a share in them now. It's third-grade tea, anyway. Only used for mixing.'

'Isn't there anyone to look after you?' asked Rusty, noticing the emptiness of the house.

'Look after me!' exclaimed Pettigrew indignantly. 'Whatever for? Do you think I'm a blooming invalid! I'm seventy, my boy, and I can ride a horse better than you can sit a bicycle!'

'I'm sure you can,' said Rusty hastily. 'And you don't look a year older than sixty. But I suppose you have a servant.'

'Well, I always thought I had one. But where the blighter is half the time, I'd like to know. Running after some wretched woman, I suppose.' A look of reminiscence passed over his face. 'I can remember the time when I did much the same thing. That was in the Kullu valley. There were two things Kullu used to be famous for—apples and pretty women!' He spluttered with laughter, and his face became very red. Rusty was afraid the old man's big blue veins were going to burst.

'Did you ever marry anyone?' he asked

'Marry!' exclaimed Pettigrew. 'Are you off your head, young fellow? What do you think a chap like me would want to marry for? Only invalids get married, so that they can have someone look after them in their old age. No man's likely to be content with one woman in his life.'

He stopped then, and looked at Rusty in a peculiar defiant way, and Rusty gathered that the old man was not really as cynical as he sounded.

'You're Harrison's boy, aren't you?' he asked suddenly.

'He was my guardian,' said Rusty. 'How did you know?'

'Never mind; I know. You ran off on your own a year ago, didn't you? Well, I don't blame you. Never could stand Harrison myself. Awful old bounder. Never bought a man a drink if he could help it. Guzzled òther people's though. Don't blame you for running away. But what made you do it?'

'He was mean and he thrashed me and didn't allow me to make Indian friends. I was fed up. I wanted to live my own life.'

'Naturally. You're a man now. Your father was a fine man, too.'

'Did you know him?'

'Of course I knew him. He managed this estate for me once. I wanted to see you before, but Harrison never gave me the opportunity.'

'It was just chance that brought me this way.'

'I know. That's how everything happens.'

'Tell me about my father,' said Rusty. 'I was too small, when he died, to remember much of him now.'

'Well, he was a good friend of mine, and we saw quite a lot of each other. He was interested in birds and insects and wild flowers—in fact, anything that had to do with natural history. Both of us were great readers and collectors of books, and that was what brought us together. But what I've been wanting to tell you was this. When he died, he had been living with an aunt of yours in the hills—near some village in Garhwal. Well, I may be wrong, but I think that if there was anything of value that your father may have wanted you to have, he'd have left it in the keeping of this aunt of yours. He trusted her—he trusted her a great deal more than he trusted Harrison, your legal guardian.'

'What was her name?' asked Rusty.

'I don't remember. I never saw her myself. But I do know she lived in the hills, where she had some land of her own.'

'Do you think I should look for her?' asked Rusty, surprised at his growing interest and enthusiasm.

'It might be a good idea,' said Mr Pettigrew. 'She must be about forty, now. I think she lived in a small house on the banks of the river, about forty miles from Lansdowne. You'll have to walk much of the way from Lansdowne.'

'I'm used to walking. I have a Garhwali friend; perhaps he can help me.' Rusty was thinking of Hathi. He rose to go, anxious to tell Kishen and Hathi about this new development.

'Don't be in a hurry,' said Mr Pettigrew. 'Have you got any money?'

'A little.'

'Well, if you need any help, remember I'm here. I was your father's friend, you know.'

'Thank you, Mr Pettigrew. I'll see you again before I leave.'

After Rusty had gone, Mr Pettigrew refilled his pipe but did not bother to light it. Idly, he turned the pages of his paper, and when his servant came rushing up the path he forgot to reprimand the boy for being late. He was thinking of Rusty, and of how wonderful it was to be young, and regretting that he was now too old to climb mountains and look for lost friends.

'Damn!' he said in disgust, and threw the empty soda bottle into the bushes.

Prospect of a Journey

RUSTY waited at the Clock Tower for almost an hour, until it was nearly one o'clock. He had been feeling slightly impatient, not because he was anxious about Kishen, but because he wanted to tell him about Mr Pettigrew and the aunt in the hills. He presumed Kishen was loafing somewhere in the bazaar, or spending money at the Sindhi Sweet Shop. This did not worry him, as he had kept most of the money; but one never knew what indiscretions Kishen might indulge in.

Rusty leant against the wall of the Clock Tower, watching the pedlars move lazily about the road, calling their wares in desultory, afternoon voices; the toy-seller, waiting for the schools to close for the day and spill their children out into the streets; the fruit-vendor, with his basket of papayas, oranges, bananas and Kashmiri apples, which he continually sprinkled with water to make them look fresh; a cobbler drowsing in the shade of the tamarind tree, occasionally fanning himself with a strip of uncut leather. Rusty saw them all, without being very conscious of their existence, for his thoughts were far away, visualizing a strange person in the mountains.

A tall Sikh boy, with a tray hanging by a string from his shoulders, approached Rusty. He wore a bright red turban, broad white pyjamas, and black Peshawari chappals which had been left unbuckled. He had long hands and feet, and if he was slim it was because he was still growing and had not had time to fill out. Though he was tall, he was upright, and his light brown eyes were friendly and direct. In the tray hanging from his neck lay an assortment of goods—combs, buttons, key-rings, reels of thread, bottles of cheap perfume, soaps and hair oils. He stopped near Rusty, but did not ask the boy if there was anything he wanted to buy. He stopped only to look at Rusty.

Rusty, feeling the other's gaze upon him, came out of his dreams, and looked at the Sikh. They stared at each other for a minute, with mutual interest; it was the first time they had set eyes on each other, but there was a compelling expression in the stranger's eyes, a haunting, half-sad, half-happy quality, that held Rusty's attention, appealing to some odd quirk in his nature. The atmosphere was charged with this quality of sympathy.

A crow flapped down between them, and the significance of the moment vanished, and the bond of sympathy was broken.

Rusty turned away, and the Sikh boy wandered on down the road.

*

After waiting for another ten minutes, Rusty left the Clock Tower and began walking in the direction of the church, thinking that perhaps Kishen had gone there instead. He had not walked far when he found the Sikh boy sitting in the shade of a mango tree, with his tray beside him and a book in his hands. Rusty paused to take a look at the book. It was Goldsmith's *The Traveller*. That was enough to make Rusty talk.

'Do you like the book?' he asked.

The Sikh looked up with a smile. 'It is in my Intermediate course. My exams begin next month. But I read other books, too,' he added.

'But when do you go to school?' asked Rusty, looking at the tray, which was obviously the boy's means of livelihood.

'In the evenings there are classes. During the day I sell this rubbish. I make enough to eat and to pay for my tuition. My name is Devinder.'

'My name is Rusty.'

Rusty leant against the trunk of the mango tree. 'What about your parents?' he asked. In India, when strangers meet, they must know each other's personal history before they can be friends: Rusty was well versed with the formalities.

'They are dead,' said Devinder. He spoke bluntly. 'They were killed during Partition, in 1947, when we had to leave the Punjab.

162

I was looked after in the refugee camp. But I prefer to be on my own, like this. I am happier this way.'

'And where do you stay?'

'Anywhere,' said Devinder, closing the book and standing up. 'In somebody's kitchen or veranda, or in the maidan. During the summer months it doesn't matter where I sleep, and in the winter people are kind and find some place for me.'

'You can sleep with us,' said Rusty impulsively. 'But I live in a church. I've been there since yesterday. It isn't very comfortable, but it's big.'

'Are you a refugee too?' asked Devinder with a smile.

'Well, I'm a displaced person all right.'

They began walking down the road. They walked at a slow, easy pace, stopping now and then to sit on a wall or lean against a gate. They were not in a hurry to get anywhere. They had everywhere to go, and they could take their own time going there, and there was no one to hurry them on. Kishen would always have one foot in Rusty's world, and the other foot in a world of middle class homes. Devinder had both his feet planted in the greater world, the open world, the world that is both lonely and free. He had been in it even longer than Rusty.

Rusty told Devinder about himself and about Kishen, and when he found that Kishen was not waiting at the church he really began to worry, but there was nothing he could do except wait for him. Devinder left his tray in the church, and went with Rusty to the pool. They bathed and lay in the sun, and they were at the pool for about an hour.

The Goonga must have been following Rusty again, for he was sitting on the vestry steps when they returned to the church. 'Goo,' he said chuckling at his own cunning.

'Now I suppose he'll stay here too,' said Rusty.

*

In the company of Aruna, Kishen managed to forget Rusty for a few hours. They played carom and listened to the radio. Kishen took her hand and, examining her palm, predicted misery; his predictions were made at length, for he enjoyed holding Aruna's hand. Forgetting—or pretending to forget—that they were almost grown-up people, they began wrestling on the white Afghan carpet until Mrs Bhushan, who had been visiting the neighbours to tell them about Kishen, came home and lifted them off the carpet by the scruffs of their necks.

Aruna had to do her school homework, so she got Kishen to help her with arithmetic. They carried a bench and table out under a sweet-smelling pomalo tree.

As Kishen leant over Aruna, explaining sums which he did not understand, he became acutely conscious of the scent of her hair and the proximity of her right ear, and the sum gradually lost its urgency. The right ear, with its soft creamy lobe, was excruciatingly near. Kishen was tempted to bite it.

'You have a nice ear, Aruna,' he said.

Aruna smiled at the sum.

*

But at night, lying in bed, he began to think of Rusty sitting alone in the empty church, waiting for him. It was an intolerable vision.

He was sleeping in a separate room. Mrs Bhushan and Aruna slept together in the big bedroom. (Mr Bhushan was in Delhi, enjoying a week's freedom.) Kishen had only to open his window and slip out into the garden.

He crept quietly out of bed and slipped off Mr Bhushan's pink pyjamas. Soft moonlight came in from the window, playing on his naked legs. He hunted about the room until he found his old pyjamas and then, taking his chappals in his hands, he went slowly to the bedroom door. Opening it slowly, he peered into the other room.

Mrs Bhushan lay flat on her back, her bosom heaving as though it were in the throes of a minor earthquake, her breath making strange, whistling sounds. There was no likelihood of her waking up. But Aruna was wide awake. She sat up in bed, staring at Kishen.

Kishen put a finger to his lips and approached the bed.

'I'm going to see Rusty,' he whispered. 'I will come back before morning.'

164

His fingers found hers and squeezed them, then he left the room, climbing out of the window, and running down the path to the gate. He kept running until he reached the church.

He was about to enter the vestry when he was almost startled out of his wits by a wild, frightening figure that suddenly loomed up before him.

'Goo!' said the Goonga.

'Oh, it's you!' gasped Kishen. 'I might have known it.'

He was even more taken aback to find Rusty sitting on the ground with Devinder, reading from *The Traveller*. The Sikh boy had removed his turban, and his long hair fell over his shoulders, giving him a wild, rather dangerous look.

Rusty looked up from the book as Kishen's shadow fell across the page.

'Where have you been, bhaiya?' he asked. 'You did not tell me you would be so late.'

'I was kidnapped,' said Kishen, sitting down on a bench and looking suspiciously at Devinder.

'He is our new member,' exclaimed Rusty lightly. 'He will be staying here too, from now on.'

Kishen gave Devinder a hostile nod. He was inclined to be possessive in his friendships, and resented anyone else being too close to Rusty.

'Is the Goonga staying here too?' he asked.

'He followed me again. We can use him as a chowkidar. But tell me, what happened to you?'

'I met Mrs Bhushan, an old friend of my mother's. I bluffed her that I was on a walking-tour, but she didn't believe me. I had to go home with her, and it was only when she went to sleep that I managed to get away. But she will be sure to arrive here in the morning. What should I do then?'

'You never trouble to make up your own mind, do you bhaiya?'

'I don't want to live with relatives.'

'But we can't wander about aimlessly for ever.'

'We have stopped wandering now,' said Kishen.

'You have. I think I must go away again. There is a relative of mine living in the hills. Perhaps she can help me.'

'I am definitely going with you!' exclaimed Kishen.

'And if I do not find her, what happens? We will both be stuck on a mountain without anything. If you stay here, you might be able to help me later.'

'Well, when are you going?' asked Kishen impatiently.

'As soon as I collect some money.'

'I will try to get some from Mrs Bhushan, she has plenty, but she is a miser. Will he go with you?' said Kishen, looking at Devinder.

'I cannot go,' said Devinder. 'I have my examinations in a month.'

Kishen kicked off his shoes and made himself comfortable on a pew. Rusty began reading aloud from *The Traveller*, and everyone listened—Kishen, with his feet stuck upon a pew-support; Devinder, with his chin resting on his knees and his eyes on Rusty; and the Goonga (not understanding a word) grinning in the candlelight.

*

Next morning the three boys went down to the pool to bathe. The smell of the neem trees, the sound of the water, the touch of the breeze, intoxicated them, filled them with a zest for living. They ran over the wild wood-sorrel, over the dew-drenched grass, down to the water.

The Goonga, who on principal refused to bathe, sat on top of the rocks and looked on with detached amusement at the others swimming in the pool and wrestling in the shallow water.

Devinder could stand in the deepest part of the pool and still have his head above water. To keep his long hair out of the way, he tied it in a knot, like a bun, on top of his head. His hair was almost auburn in colour, his skin was a burnished gold. He slipped about in the water like a long glistening fish.

Kishen began making balls from loose mud, which he threw at Devinder and Rusty. A mud fight developed. It was like playing snowballs, but more messy. At the height of the battle, the Goonga suddenly appeared on a buffalo.

They took turns mounting the buffalo, but only the Goonga managed to make it move. When Kishen or Rusty sat on it, kicking and shouting, the buffalo refused to budge; at the most, it would roll over on its side in the slush, taking the boys down as well. But it did not matter how muddy they got, because they had only to dive into the pool to be clean again.

They were a long time at the pool. When they returned to the church they found the Hillman parked at the gate, with an impatient and irate Mrs Bhushan sitting at the wheel. She was in a mood to be belligerent, but seeing Kishen accompanied not only by Rusty but by two other dangerous-looking youths, her worst fears were confirmed: Kishen was in the hands of cutthroats, and discretion would be the better part of valour.

'Kishen, my son,' she pleaded, 'we have been worrying about you very much. You should not have left without telling us! Aruna is very unhappy.'

Kishen stood sulkily near his friends.

'You had better go, Kishen,' said Rusty. 'You will be of more help to me if you stay with Mrs Bhushan.'

'But when will I see you?'

'As soon as I come back from the hills.'

Once Kishen was in the car, Rusty confronted Mrs Bhushan and said, 'He won't leave you now. But if he is not happy with you, we will come and take him away.'

'We are his *friends*,' said Mrs Bhushan.

'No, you are like a relative. *We* are his friends.'

Kishen said, 'If you don't come back soon, Rusty, I will start looking for you.' He scowled affectionately at Rusty, and waved to Devinder and the Goonga as the car took him away.

'He might run back again tonight,' said Devinder.

'He will get used to Mrs Bhushan's house,' said Rusty. 'Soon he will be liking it. He will not forget us, but he will remember us only when he is alone. We are only something that happened to him once upon a time. But we have changed him a little. Now he knows there are others in the world besides himself.'

'I could not understand him,' said Devinder. 'But still I liked him.'

'I understood him,' said Rusty, 'and *still* I liked him.'

The Lafunga

'IF you have nothing to do,' and Devinder, 'will you come with me on my rounds?'

'First we will see Hathi. If he has not left yet, I can accompany him to Lansdowne.'

Rusty set out with Devinder in the direction of the bazaar. As it was early morning, the shops were just beginning to open. Vegetable vendors were busy freshening their stock with liberal sprinklings of water, calling their prices and their wares; children dawdled in the road on their way to school, playing hopscotch or marbles. Girls going to college chattered in groups like gay, noisy parrots. Men cycled to work, and bullock-carts came in from the villages, laden with produce. The dust, which had taken all night to settle, rose again like a mist.

Rusty and Devinder stopped at the tea-shop to eat thickly buttered buns and drink strong, sweet tea. Then they looked for Hathi's room, and found it above a cloth shop, lying empty, with its doors open. The string bed leant against the wall. On shelves and window-ledges, in corners and on the floor, lay little coloured toys made of clay—elephants and bulls, horses and peacocks, and images of Krishna and Ganesha; a blue Krishna, with a flute to his lips, a jolly Ganesha with a delightful little trunk. Most of the toys were rough and unfinished, more charming than the completed pieces. Most of the finished products would now be on sale in the bazaar.

It came as a surprise to Rusty to discover that Hathi, the big wrestler, made toys for a living. He had not imagined there would be delicacy and skill in his friend's huge hands. The pleasantness of the discovery offset his disappointment at finding Hathi had gone.

'He has left already,' said Rusty. 'Never mind. I know he will welcome me, even if I arrive unexpectedly.'

He left the bazaar with Devinder, making for the residential part of the town. As he would be leaving Dehra soon, there was no point in his visiting the school again; later, though, he would see Mr Pettigrew.

When they reached the Clock Tower, someone whistled to them from across the street, and a tall young man came striding towards them.

He looked taller than Devinder, mainly because of his long legs. He wore a lose-fitting bush-shirt that hung open in front. His face was long and pale, but he had quick, devilish eyes, and he smiled disarmingly.

'Here comes Sudheer the Lafunga,' whispered Devinder. 'Lafunga means loafer. He probably wants some money. He is the most charming and the most dangerous person in town.' Aloud, he said, 'Sudheer, when are you going to return the twenty rupees you owe me?'

'Don't talk that way, Devinder,' said the Lafunga, looking offended. 'Don't hurt my feelings. You know your money is safer with me than it is in the bank. It will even bring you dividends, mark my words. I have a plan that will come off in a few days, and then you will get back double your money. Please tell me, who is your friend?'

'We stay together,' said Devinder, introducing Rusty. 'And he is bankrupt too, so don't get any ideas.'

'Please don't believe what he says of me,' said the Lafunga with a captivating smile that showed his strong teeth. 'Really I am not very harmful.'

'Well, completely harmless people are usually dull,' said Rusty.

'How I agree with you! I think we have a lot in common.'

'No, he hasn't got anything,' put in Devinder.

'Well then, he must start from the beginning. It is the best way to make a fortune. You will come and see me, won't you, mister Rusty? We could make a terrific combination, I am sure. You are the kind of person people trust! They take only one look at me and then feel their pockets to see if anything is missing!'

Rusty instinctively put his hand to his own pocket, and all three of them laughed.

'Well, I must go,' said Sudheer the Lafunga, now certain that Devinder was not likely to produce any funds. 'I have a small matter to attend to. It may bring me a fee of twenty or thirty rupees.'

'Go,' said Devinder. 'Strike while the iron is hot.'

'Not I,' said the Lafunga, grinning and moving off. 'I make the iron hot by striking.'

*

'Sudheer is not too bad,' said Devinder, as they walked away from the Clock Tower. 'He is a crook, of course—*Shree 420*—but he would not harm people like us. As he is quite well educated, he manages to gain the confidence of some well-to-do people, and acts on their behalf in matters that are not always respectable. But he spends what he makes, and is too generous to be successful.'

They had reached a quiet, tree-lined road, and walked in the shade of neem, mango, jamun and eucalyptus trees. Clumps of tall bamboo grew between the trees. Nowhere, but in Dehra, had Rusty seen so many kinds of trees. Trees that had no names. Tall, straight trees, and broad, shady trees. Trees that slept or brooded in the afternoon stillness. And trees that shimmered and moved and whispered even when the winds were asleep.

Some marigolds grew wild on the footpath, and Devinder picked two of them, giving one to Rusty.

'There is a girl who lives at the bottom of the road,' he said. 'She is a pretty girl. Come with me and see her.'

They walked to the house at the end of the road and, while Rusty stood at the gate, Devinder went up the path. Devinder stood at the bottom of the veranda steps, a little to one side, where he could be seen from a window, and whistled softly.

Presently a girl came out on the veranda. When she saw Devinder she smiled. She had a round, fresh face, and long black hair, and she was not wearing any shoes.

Devinder gave her the marigold. She took it in her hand and, not knowing what to say, ran indoors.

That morning Devinder and Rusty walked about four miles. Devinder's customers ranged from decadent maharanis and the wives of government officials to gardeners and sweeper women. Though his merchandise was cheap, the well-to-do were more finicky about a price than the poor. And there were a few who bought things from Devinder because they knew his circumstances and liked what he was doing.

A small girl with flapping pigtails came skipping down the road. She stopped to stare at Rusty, as though he were something quite out of the ordinary, but not unpleasant.

Rusty took the other marigold from his pocket, and gave it to the girl. It was a long time since he had been able to make anyone a gift.

*

After some time they parted, Devinder going back to the town, while Rusty crossed the river-bed. He walked through the tea-gardens until he found Mr Pettigrew's bungalow.

The old man was not in the veranda, but a young servant salaamed Rusty and asked him to sit down. Apparently Mr Pettigrew was having his bath.

'Does he always bathe in the afternoon?' asked Rusty.

'Yes, the sahib likes his water to be put in the sun to get warm. He does not like cold baths or hot baths. The afternoon sun gives his water the right temperature.'

Rusty walked into the drawing-room and nearly fell over a small table. The room was full of furniture and pictures and bric-à-brac. Tiger-heads, stuffed and mounted, snarled down at him from the walls. On the carpet lay several cheetal skins, a bit worn at the sides. There were several shelves filled with books bound in morocco or calf. Photographs adorned the walls—one of a much younger Mr Pettigrew standing over a supine leopard, another of Mr Pettigrew perched on top of an elephant, with his rifle resting on his knees .... Remembering his own experiences, Rusty wondered how such an active shikari ever found time for reading. While he was gazing at the photographs, Pettigrew himself came in, a large bathrobe wrapped round his thin frame, his grizzly chest looking very raw and red from the scrubbing he had just given it.

'Ah, there you are!' he said. 'The bearer told me you were here. Glad to see you again. Sit down and have a drink.'

Mr Pettigrew found the whisky and poured out two stiff drinks. Then, still in his bathrobe and slippers, he made himself comfortable in an armchair. Rusty said something complimentary about one of the mounted tiger-heads.

'Bagged it in Assam,' he said. 'Back in 1928, that was. I spent three nights on a machan before I got a shot at it.'

'You have a lot of books,' observed Rusty.

'A good collection, mostly flora and fauna. Some of them are extremely rare. By the way,' he said, looking around at the wall, 'did you ever see a picture of your father?'

'Have you got one?' asked Rusty. 'I've only a faint memory of what he looked like.'

'He's in that group photograph over there,' said Mr Pettigrew, pointing to a picture on the wall.

Rusty went over to the picture and saw three men dressed in white shirts and flannels, holding tennis rackets, and looking very self-conscious.

'He's in the middle,' and Pettigrew. 'I'm on his right.'

Rusty saw a young man with fair hair and a fresh face. He was the only player who was smiling. Mr Pettigrew, sporting a fierce moustache, looked as though he was about to tackle a tiger with his racket. The third person was bald and uninteresting.

'Of course, he's very young in that photo,' said Pettigrew. 'It was taken long before you were ever thought of—before your father married.'

Rusty did not reply. He was trying to imagine his father in action on a tennis court, and wondered if he was a better player than Pettigrew.

'Who was the best player among you?' he asked.

'Ah, well, we were both pretty good, you know. Except for poor old Wilkie on the left. He got in the picture by mistake.'

'Did my father talk much?' asked Rusty.

'Well, we all talked a lot, you know, especially after a few drinks. He talked as much as any of us. He could sing, when he wanted to. His rendering of the "Kashmiri Love Song" was always popular at parties, but it wasn't often he sang, because he didn't like parties . . . . Do you remember it? "Pale hands I love, beside the Shalimar . . . . "'

Pettigrew began singing in a cracked, wavering voice, and Rusty was forced to take his eyes off the photograph. Half-way through the melody, Pettigrew forgot the words, so he took another gulp of whisky and began singing "The Rose of Tralee". The sight of the old man singing love songs in his bathrobe, with a glass of whisky in his hand, made Rusty smile.

'Well,' said Pettigrew, breaking off in the middle of the song, 'I don't sing as well as I used to. Never mind. Now tell me, boy, when are you going to Garhwal?'

'Tomorrow, perhaps.'

'Have you any money?'

'Enough to travel with. I have a friend in the hills, with whom I can stay for some time.'

'And what about money?'

'I have enough.'

'Well, I'm lending you twenty rupees,' he said, thrusting an envelope into the boy's hands. 'Come and see me when you return, even if you don't find what you're looking for.'

'I'll do that, Mr Pettigrew.'

The old man looked at the boy for some time, as though summing him up.

'You don't really have to find out much about your father,' he said. 'You're just like him, you know.'

*

Returning to the bazaar, Devinder found Sudheer at a paan shop, his lips red with betel juice. Devinder went straight to the point.

'Sudheer,' he said, 'you owe me twenty rupees. I need it, not for myself, but for Rusty, who has to leave Dehra very urgently. You must get me the money by tonight.'

The Lafunga scratched his head.

'It will be difficult,' he said, 'but perhaps it can be managed. He really needs the money? It is not just a trick to get your own money back?'

'He is going to the hills. There may be money for him there, if he finds the person he is looking for.'

'Well, that's different,' said the Lafunga, brightening up. 'That makes Rusty an investment. Meet me at the Clock Tower at six o'clock, and I will have the money for you. I am glad to find you making useful friends for a change.'

He stuffed another roll of paan into his mouth, and taking leave of Devinder with a bright red smile, strolled leisurely down the bazaar road.

As far as appearances went, he had little to do but loll around in the afternoon sunshine, frequenting tea-shops, and gambling with cards in small back rooms. All this he did very well—but it did not make him a living.

To say that he lived on his wits would be an exaggeration. He lived a great deal on other people's wits. There was the *seth* for instance, Rusty's former landlord, who owned much property and dabbled in many shady transactions, and who was often represented by the Lafunga in affairs of an unsavoury nature.

Sudheer came originally from the Frontier, where little value was placed on human life; and while still a boy, he had wandered, a homeless refugee, over the border into India. A smuggler adopted him, taught him something of the trade, and introduced him to some of the best hands in the profession; but in a border-foray with the police, Sudheer's foster-father was shot dead, and the youth was once again on his own. By this time he was old enough to look after himself. With the help of his foster-father's connections, he soon attained the service and confidence of the *seth*.

Sudheer was no petty criminal. He practised crime as a fine art, and believed that thieves, and even murderers, had to have certain principles. If he stole, then he stole from a rich man, who could afford to be robbed, or from a greedy man, who deserved to be robbed. And if he did not rob poor men, it was not because of any altruistic motive—it was because poor men were not worth robbing.

He was good to those friends, like Devinder, who were good to him. Perhaps his most valuable friends, as sources of both money and information, were the dancing-girls who followed their profession in an almost inaccessible little road in the heart of the bazaar. His best friends were Hastini and Mrinalini. He borrowed money from them very freely, and seldom paid back more than half of it.

Hastini could twang the sitar, and dance—with a rather heavy tread—among various other accomplishments.

Mrinalini, a much smaller woman, had grown up in the profession. She was looked after by her mother, a former entertainer, who kept most of the money that Mrinalini made.

Sudheer woke Hastini in the middle of her afternoon siesta by tickling her under the chin with a feather.

'And who were you with last night, little brother?' she asked running her fingers through his thick brown hair. 'You are smelling of some horrible perfume.'

'You know I do not spend my nights with anyone,' said Sudheer. 'The perfume is from yesterday.'

'Someone new?'

'No, my butterfly. I have known her for a week.'

'Too long a time,' said Hastini petulantly. 'A dangerously long time. How much have you spent on her?'

'Nothing so far. But that is not why I came to see you. Have you got twenty rupees?'

'Villain!' cried Hastini. 'Why do you always borrow from me when you want to entertain some stupid young thing? Are you so heartless?'

'My little lotus flower!' protested Sudheer, pinching her rosy cheeks. 'I am not borrowing for any such reason. A friend of mine has to leave Dehra urgently, and I must get the money for his train fare. I owe it to him.'

'Since when did you have a friend?'

'Never mind that. I have one. And I come to you for help because I love you more than any one. Would you prefer that I borrow the money from Mrinalini?'

'You dare not,' said Hastini. 'I will kill you if you do.'

Between Hastini, of the broad hips, and Mrinalini, who was small and slender, there existed a healthy rivalry for the affections of Sudheer. Perhaps it was the great difference in their proportions that animated the rivalry. Mrinalini envied the luxuriousness of Hastini's soft body, while Hastini envied Mrinalini's delicacy, poise, slenderness of foot, and graceful walk. Mrinalini was the colour of milk and honey; she had the daintiness of a deer, while Hastini possessed the elegance of an elephant.

Sudheer could appreciate both these qualities.

He stood up, looking young even for his twenty-two years, and smiled a crooked smile. He might have looked effeminate had it not been for his hands—they were big, long-fingered, strong hands.

'Where is the money?' he asked.

'You are so impatient! Sit down, sit down. I have it here beneath the mattress.'

Sudheer's hand made its way beneath the mattress and probed about in search of the money.

'Ah, here it is! You have a fortune stacked away here. Yes, ten rupees, fifteen, twenty—and one for luck . . . . Now give me a kiss!'

*

About an hour later Sudheer was in the street again, whistling cheerfully to himself. He walked with a long, loping stride, his shirt hanging open. Warm sunshine filled one side of the narrow street, and crept up the walls of shops and houses.

Sudheer passed a fruit stand, where the owner was busy talking to a customer, and helped himself to a choice red Kashmiri apple. He continued on his way down the bazaar road, munching the apple.

The bazaar continued for a mile, from the Clock Tower to the railway station, and Sudheer could hear the whistle of a train. He turned off at a little alley, throwing his half-eaten apple to a stray dog. Then he climbed a flight of stairs—wooden stairs that were loose and rickety, liable to collapse at any moment . . . .

Mrinalini's half-deaf mother was squatting on the kitchen floor, making a fire in an earthen brazier. Sudheer poked his head round the door and shouted: 'Good morning, Mother, I hope you are making me some tea. You look fine today!' And then, in a lower tone, so that she could not hear: 'You look like a dried-up mango.'

'So it's you again,' grumbled the old woman. 'What do you want now?'

'Your most respectable daughter is what I want,' said Sudheer.

'What's that?' She cupped her hand to her ear and leaned forward.

'Where's Mrinalini?' shouted Sudheer.

'Don't shout like that! She is not here.'

'That's all I wanted to know,' said Sudheer, and he walked through the kitchen, through the living-room, and on to the veranda balcony, where he found Mrinalini sitting in the sun, combing out her long silken hair.

'Let me do it for you,' said Sudheer, and he took the comb from her hand and ran it through the silky black hair. 'For one so little, so much hair. You could conceal yourself in it, and not be seen, except for your dainty little feet.'

'What are you after, Sudheer? You are so full of compliments this morning. And watch out for Mother—if she sees you combing my hair, she will have a fit!'

'And I hope it kills her.'

'Sudheer!'

'Don't be so sentimental about your mother. You are her little gold mine, and she treats you as such—soon I will be having to fill in application forms before I can see you! It is time you kept your earnings for yourself.'

'So that it will be easier for you to help yourself?'

'Well, it would be more convenient. By the way, I have come to you for twenty rupees.'

Mrinalini laughed delightedly, and took the comb from Sudheer. 'What were you saying about my little feet?' she asked slyly.

'I said they were the feet of a princess, and I would be very happy to kiss them.'

'Kiss them, then.'

She held one delicate golden foot in the air, and Sudheer took it in his hands (which were as large as her feet) and kissed her ankle.

'That will be twenty rupees,' he said.

She pushed him away with her foot. 'But, Sudheer, I gave you fifteen rupees only three days ago. What have you done with it?'

'I haven't the slightest idea. I only know that I must have more. It is most urgent, you can be sure of that. But if you cannot help me, I must try elsewhere.'

'Do that, Sudheer. And may I ask, whom do you propose to try?'

'Well, I was thinking of Hastini.'

'*Who?*'

'You know, Hastini, the girl with the wonderful figure . . . . '

'I should think I do! Sudheer, if you so much as dare to take a rupee from her, I'll never speak to you again!'

'Well then, what shall I do?'

Mrinalini beat the arms of the chair with her little fists, and cursed Sudheer under her breath. Then she got up and went into the kitchen. A great deal of shouting went on in the kitchen before Mrinalini came back with flushed cheeks and fifteen rupees.

'You don't know the trouble I had getting it,' she said. 'Now don't come asking for more until at least a week has passed.'

'After a week, I will be able to supply you with funds. I am engaged tonight on a mission of some importance. In a few days I will place golden bangles on your golden feet.'

'What mission?' asked Mrinalini, looking at him with an anxious frown. 'If it is anything to do with the *seth*, please leave it alone. You know what happened to Satish Dayal. He was smuggling opium for the *seth*, and now he is sitting in jail, while the *seth* continues as always.'

'Don't worry about me. I can deal with the *seth*.'

'Then be off! I have to entertain a foreign delegation this evening. You can come tomorrow morning, if you are free.'

'I may come. Meanwhile, goodbye!'

He walked backwards into the living-room, pivoted into the kitchen and, bending over the old woman, kissed her on the forehead.

'You dried-up old mango,' he said. And went away, whistling.

To the Hills

IN the church, on the night of his departure, Rusty felt the sadness of one leaving a familiar home and familiar faces. Up till now he had been with friends, people who had given him help and comradeship; but now he would be on his own, without Kishen or Devinder. That was the way it had always turned out.

He gave his spare clothes to the Goonga, because he did not feel like carrying them with him. He left his books with Devinder.

'Stay here, Devinder,' he said. 'Stay here until I come back. I want to find you in Dehra.'

A breeze from the open window made the candles flutter, and the shadows on the walls leapt and gesticulated; but Devinder stood still, the candle-light playing softly on his face.

'I'm always here, Rusty,' he said.

*

The northern-bound train was not crowded, because in December few people went to the hills. Rusty had no difficulty in finding an empty compartment.

It was a small compartment with only two lower berths. Lying down on one of them, he stared out of the far window, at the lights across the railway tracks. He fell asleep, and woke only when the train jerked into motion.

Looking out of the window, he saw the station platform slipping away, while the shouts of the coolies and vendors grew fainter, until they were lost in the sound of the wheels and the rocking of the carriage. The town lights twinkled, grew distant, were swallowed up by the trees. The engine went panting through the jungle, its red sparks floating towards the stars.

There were four small stations between Dehra and Hardwar, and the train stopped for five or ten minutes at each station. At Doiwala he was woken from a light sleep by a tap at the window. It was dark outside, and he could not make out the face that was pressed against the glass. When he opened the door, a familiar, long-legged youth stepped into the carriage, swiftly shutting the door behind him. Before sitting down, he dropped all the shutters on the side facing the platform.

'We meet again,' said the youth, sitting down opposite Rusty, as the train began to move. 'Don't you remember me? I'm Sudheer. I met you at the Clock Tower with Devinder.'

Rusty did not know that the money Devinder had given him had come through Sudheer, but it did not take him long to recognize the Lafunga.

'Of course, I remember you,' he said. 'When I saw you just now, appearing suddenly out of the dark, I had the feeling you were someone I had seen seldom but knew quite well. But what are you doing on this train?'

'I'm going to Hardwar,' said Sudheer, a smile playing about the corners of his mouth. 'On business. Don't ask me for details.'

'Why didn't you get on the train at Dehra?'

'Because I have to use strategy, my friend.' He kicked off his shoes, and put his feet on the opposite bunk. 'And where are you going now?'

'I'm going to the hills, to see a friend.' Rusty was not sure if he should confide his plans to Sudheer, but if Devinder could trust him, why not?

'And when you come back? I suppose you will come back.'

'I'm not sure what I'll do. I want to give myself a chance to be a writer, because I may succeed. It is the only kind of work I really want to do—if you can call it work.'

'Yes, it is work. Real work is what you want to do. It is only when you work for yourself that you really work. I use my eyes and my fingers and my wits. I have no morals and no scruples . . . .'

'But you have principles, I think.'

'I don't know about that.'

'You have feelings?'

'Yes, but I pay no attention to them.'

'I cannot do that.'

'You are too noble! Why don't you join me? I can guarantee money, excitement, friendship—my friendship, anyway . . . . '

Sudheer leant forward and took Rusty's hand. There was earnestness in his manner, and also a challenge.

'Come on. Be with me. The day I met you, I wanted you to be with me. I'm a crook, and I don't have any real friends. I don't ask you to be a crook. I ask you to be my friend.'

'I will be your friend,' said Rusty, taking a sudden liking to Sudheer; he almost said, 'I will be a crook, too,' but thought better of it.

'Why not get down at Hardwar?'

'Why not come with me to Lansdowne?'

'I have work in Hardwar.'

'And I in the hills.'

'That is why friends are so difficult to keep.' Sudheer smiled and leant back in the seat. 'All right, then. We will join up later. I will meet you in the hills. Wait for me, remember me, don't put me out of your mind.'

*

When the train drew into Hardwar, Sudheer got up and stood near the door.

'I have to go quickly,' he said. 'I will see you again.'

As the engine slowed down, and the station lights became brighter, Sudheer opened the carriage door and jumped down to the railway banking.

Alarmed, Rusty ran to the open door and shouted, 'Are you all right, Sudheer?'

'Just worry about yourself!' called Sudheer, his voice growing faint and distant. 'Good luck!'

He was hidden from view by a signal box, and then the train drew into the brightly-lit, crowded station, and pilgrims began climbing into the compartments.

Two policemen came down the platform, looking in at carriage windows and asking questions. They stopped at Rusty's window, and asked him if he had had a companion during the journey, and gave him an unmistakable description of Sudheer.

'He got off the train long ago,' lied Rusty. 'At Doiwala, I think. Why, what do you want him for?'

'He has stolen one thousand rupees from a *seth* in Dehra,' said the policemen. 'If you see him again, please pull the alarm cord.'

*

Two days later, Rusty was in Hathi's house, sitting on a string cot out in the courtyard. There was snow on the tiled roof and in the fields, but the sun was quite warm. The mountains stretched away, disappearing into sky and cloud. Rusty felt he belonged there, to the hills and the pine and deodar forests, and the clear mountain streams.

There were about thirty families in the village. There were not many men about, and the few that could be found were either old or inactive. Most young men joined the army or took jobs in the plains, for the village economy was poor. The women remained behind to do the work. They fetched water, kept the houses clean, cooked meals, and would soon be ploughing the fields. The old men just sat around and smoked hookahs and gossiped the morning away.

It had been a long, lonely walk from the bus terminus at Lansdowne to Hathi's village. Rusty had walked fast, because there had been no one to talk to, and no food to be had on the way. But he had met a farmer, coming from the opposite direction, and had shared the man's meal. All the farmer had were some onions and a few chappatis; but Rusty was hungry and he enjoyed the meal. When he had finished, he said goodbye, and they went their different ways.

At first he walked along a smooth slippery carpet of pine-needles; then the pine trees gave way to oak and rhododendron. It was cool and shady; but after Rusty had done about fifteen miles, the forest ended, the hills became bare and rocky, and the earth the colour of copper. He was thirsty, but there was nothing to drink.

His tongue felt thick and furry and he could barely move his lips. All he could do was walk on mechanically, hardly conscious of his surroundings or even of walking.

When the sun went down, a cool breeze came whispering across the dry grass. And then, as he climbed higher, the grass grew greener, there were trees, water burst from the hillsides in small springs, and birds swooped across the path—bright green parrots, tree-pies, and paradise flycatchers. He was walking beside a river, above the turbulent water rushing down a narrow gorge. It was a steep climb to Hathi's village; and as it grew dark, he had to pick his way carefully along the narrow path.

As he approached Hathi's house, on the outskirts of the village, he was knocked down by a huge Tibetan mastiff. He got up, and Hathi came out of the house and ran to greet Rusty and knocked him over again. Then he was in the house, drinking hot milk. And later he lay on a soft quilt, and a star was winking at him from the skylight.

The house was solid, built of yellow granite, and it had a black-tiled roof. There was an orange tree in the courtyard, and though there were no oranges on it at that time of the year, the young leaves smelt sweet. When Rusty looked around, he saw mountains, blue and white-capped, with dark clouds drifting down the valleys. Pale blue woodsmoke climbed the hill from the houses below, and people drifted about in the warm winter sunshine.

When Rusty and Hathi walked in the hills they sometimes went barefoot. Once they walked a few miles upstream, and found a waterfall dashing itself down on to smooth rocks fifty feet below. Here the forest was dark and damp, and at night bears and leopards roamed the hillsides. When the leopards were hungry, they did not hesitate to enter villages and carry off stray dogs.

Once Rusty heard the hunting-cry of a leopard on the prowl. It was evening, and he was close to the village, when he heard the harsh, saw-like cry, something between a grunt and a cough. Then the leopard appeared to his right, slinking through the trees, crouching low, a swift black shadow . . . .

There was only one shop in the village, and that was also the post office; it sold soap and shoes and the barest necessities. When Rusty passed it, he was hailed by the shopkeeper, who was brandishing a postcard. Rusty was surprised that there should be a letter for him.

He was even more surprised when he discovered that the card was from Sudheer, the Lafunga.

It said: 'Join me at Landsdowne. I have news of your aunt. We will travel together. I have money for both of us, as I consider you a good investment.'

Rum and Curry

S UDHEER and Rusty left Lansdowne early one morning, and by the time they reached the oak and deodar forests of Kotli they were shivering with the cold.

'I am not used to this sort of travel,' complained Sudheer. 'If this is a wild goose chase, I will curse you, Rusty. At least we should have mules to sit on.'

'We are sure to find a village soon,' said Rusty. 'We can spend a night there. As for it being a wild goose chase, it was you who told me that my aunt lived somewhere here. If she is not in this direction, it is all your fault, Lafunga.'

There was little light in the Kotli forest, for the tall, crowded deodars and oaks kept out the moonlight. The road was damp and covered with snails.

They were relieved to find a few small huts clustered together in an open clearing. A light showed from only one of the houses. Rusty rapped on the hard oak door, and called out: 'Is anyone there? We want a place to spend the night.'

'Who is it?' asked a nervous, irritable voice.

'Travellers,' said Sudheer. 'Tired, hungry and poor.'

'This is not a *dharamsala*,' grumbled the man inside. 'This is no place for pilgrims.'

'We are not pilgrims,' said Sudheer, trying a different approach. 'We are road inspectors, servants of the government—so open up, my friend!'

They heard much ill-natured muttering before the door opened, revealing an old and dirty man, who had stubble on his chin, warts on his feet, and grease on his old clothes.

'Where do you come from?' he asked suspiciously.

'Lansdowne,' said Rusty. 'We have walked twenty miles since morning. Can we sleep in your house?'

'How do I know you are not thieves?' asked the old man, who did not look very honest himself.

'If we were thieves,' said Sudheer impatiently, 'we would not stand here, talking to you. We would have cut your throat and thrown you to the vultures, and carried off your beautiful daughter.'

'I have no daughter here.'

'What a pity! Never mind. My friend and I will sleep in your house tonight. We are not going to sleep in the forest.'

Sudheer strode into the lighted room, but backed out almost immediately, holding his fingers to his nose.

'What dead animal are you keeping here?' he cried.

'They are sheepskins, for curing,' said the old man. 'What is wrong?'

'Nothing, nothing,' said Sudheer, not wishing to hurt their host's feelings so soon; but in an aside to Rusty, he whispered, 'There is such a stink, I doubt if we will wake up in the morning.'

They stumbled into the room, and Rusty dumped his bundle on the ground. The room was bare, except for dilapidated sheep and deer skins hanging on the walls. There was a small fire in a corner of the room. Sudheer and Rusty got as close to it as they could, stamping their feet and chafing their hands. The old man sat down on his haunches and glared suspiciously at the intruders. Sudheer looked at him, and then at Rusty, and shrugged eloquently.

'May we know your name?' asked Rusty.

'It is Ram Singh,' said the old man grudgingly.

'Well, Ram Singh, my host,' said Sudheer solicitously, 'have you had your meal as yet?'

'I take it in the morning,' said Ram Singh.

'And in the evening?' Sudheer's voice held a note of hope.

'It is not necessary to eat more than once a day.'

'For a rusty old fellow like you, perhaps,' said Sudheer, 'but we have got blood in our veins. Is there nothing here to eat? Surely you have some bread, some vegetables?'

'I have nothing,' said the old man.

'Well, we will have to wait till morning,' said Sudheer. 'Rusty, take out the blanket and the bottle of rum.'

Rusty took the blanket from their bag, and a flask of rum slipped out from the folds. Ram Singh showed unmistakable signs of coming to life.

'Is that medicine you have?' asked the old man. 'I have been suffering from headaches for the last month.'

'Well, this will give you a worse headache,' said Sudheer, gulping down a mouthful of rum and licking his lips. 'Besides, for people who eat only once a day, it is dangerous stuff.'

'We could get something to eat,' said the old man eagerly.

'You said you had nothing,' said Rusty, taking the bottle from Sudheer and putting it to his lips.

'There are some pumpkins on the roof,' said the old man. 'And I have a few potatoes and some spices. Shall I make a curry?'

And an hour later, warmed by rum and curry, they sat round the fire in a most convivial fashion. Rusty and Sudheer had gathered their only blanket about their shoulders, and Ram Singh had covered himself in sheepskins. He had been asking them questions about life in the cities—a life that was utterly foreign to him.

'You are men of the world,' said Ram Singh. 'You have been in most of the cities of India, you have known all kinds of men and women. I have never travelled beyond Lansdowne, nor have I seen the trains and ships which I hear so much about. I am seventy and I have not seen these things, though I have sons who have been away many years, and one who has even been out of India with his regiment. I would like to ask your advice. It is lonely living alone, and though I have had three wives, they are all dead.'

'If you have had three wives,' said Sudheer, 'you are a man of the world!'

He had his back to the wall, his feet stuck out towards the fire. Rusty was half-asleep, his head resting on Sudheer's shoulder.

'My daughters are all married,' continued Ram Singh. 'I would like to get married again, but tell me, how should I go about it?'

Sudheer laughed out loud. The old man in his youth must have been as crafty a devil as the Lafunga himself.

'Well, you would have to pay for her, of course,' said Sudheer.

'Tell me of a suitable woman. She should be young, of course. Her nose—what kind of nose should she have?'

'A flat nose,' said Sudheer, without the ghost of a smile. 'The nostrils should not be turned up.'

'Ah! And the shape of her body?'

'Not too manly. She should not be crooked. Do not expect too much, old man!'

'Her head?' asked the old man eagerly. 'What should her head be like?'

Sudheer gave this a moment's consideration. 'The head should not be bald,' he said.

'Ram Singh nodded his approval; his opinion of Sudheer was going up by leaps and bounds.

'And her colour, should it be white?'

'No, not very white.'

'Black?'

'Not too black. But she would have to be evil-smelling, otherwise she would not stay with you.'

*

A bear kept them awake during the early part of the night. It clambered up on the roof and made a meal of the old man's store of pumpkins.

'Can it get in?' asked Rusty.

'It comes every night,' said Ram Singh. 'But it is a vegetarian and eats only the pumpkins.'

There was a thud as a pumpkin rolled off the roof and landed on the ground. Then the bear climbed down from the roof and shambled off into the forest.

The fire was glowing feebly, but Sudheer and Rusty were warm beneath their blanket and, being very tired, were soon asleep, despite the efforts of an army of bugs to keep them awake. But at about midnight they were woken by a loud cry and , starting up, found the lantern lit, and the old man throwing a fit.

Ram Singh was leaping about the room, waving his arms, going into contortions, and bringing up gurgling sounds from the back of his throat.

'What is the matter?' shouted Rusty, from under the blanket. 'Have you gone mad?'

For reply, the old man gurgled and shrieked, and continued his frenzied dance.

'A demon!' he shouted. 'A demon has entered me!'

Sudheer leapt to his feet. He had heard of the superstitions of some hill-people, of their belief in spirits, but he had never expected to witness such a performance.

'It's the medicine you gave me!' cried Ram Singh. 'The medicine was evil, it is all your doing!' And he continued dancing about the room.

'Should I throw the medicine away?' asked Sudheer.

'No, don't do that!' shouted Ram Singh, appearing normal for a moment. 'Throw yourself on the ground!'

Sudheer threw himself on the ground.

'On your back!' gasped the old man.

Sudheer turned over on to his back. Rusty had lifted a corner of the blanket, and was watching, fascinated.

'Raise your left foot,' said the old man. 'Take it in your mouth. That will charm the demon away.'

'I will not put my foot in my mouth,' said Sudheer, getting to his feet, having lost faith in the genuineness of the old man's fit. 'I don't think there is any demon in you. It is probably your curry. Have something more to drink, and you will be all right.'

He produced the all but empty flask of rum, made the old man open his mouth, and poured the rest of the spirit down his throat.

Ram Singh choked, shook his head violently, and grinned at Sudheer. 'The demon has gone now,' he said.

'I am glad to know it,' said Sudheer. 'But you have emptied the bottle. Now let us try to sleep again.'

The cold had come in through the blanket, and Rusty found sleep difficult. Instead, he began to think of the purpose of his journey, and wondered if it would not have been wiser to stay in Dehra. Outside, the air was still; the wind had stopped whistling through the pines. Only a jackal howled in the distance. The old man was tossing and turning on his sheepskins.

'Ram Singh,' whispered Rusty. 'Are you awake?'

Ram Singh groaned softly.

'Tell me,' said Rusty. 'Have you heard of a woman living alone in these parts?'

'There are many old women here.'

'No, I mean a well-to-do woman. She must be about forty. At one time she was married to a white sahib.'

'Ah, I have heard of such a woman . . . . She was beautiful when she was young, they tell me.'

Rusty was silent. He was afraid to ask any further questions; afraid to know too much; afraid of finding out too soon that there was nothing for him and nowhere to go.

'Ram Singh,' he whispered. 'Where does this woman live?'

'She had her house on the road to Rishikesh . . . . '

'And the woman, where is she? Is she dead?'

'I do not know, I have not heard of her recently,' said Ram Singh. 'Why do you ask of her? Are you related to the sahib?'

'No,' said Rusty. 'I have heard of her, that's all.'

Silence. The old man grumbled to himself, muttering quietly, and then began to snore. The jackal was silent, the wind was up again; the moon was lost in the clouds. Rusty felt Sudheer's hand slip into his own, and press his fingers. He was surprised to find him awake.

'Forget it,' whispered Sudheer. 'Forget the dead, forget the past. Trouble your heart no longer. I have enough for both of us, so let us live on it till it is finished, and let us be happy, Rusty, my friend, let us be happy . . . . '

Rusty did not reply, but he held the Lafunga's hand and returned the pressure of his fingers to let him know that he was listening.

'This is only the beginning,' said Sudheer. 'The world is waiting for us.'

*

Rusty woke first, scratching and rubbing his legs. Looking up at the skylight, he saw the first glimmer of dawn. He slipped on his clothes and torn socks and, without waking Sudheer or the old man, unlatched the door and stepped outside.

Before him lay a world of white.

It had snowed in the early hours of the morning, while they

had been sleeping. The snow lay thick on the ground, carpeting the hillside. There was not a breath of wind; the pine trees stood blanched and still, and a deep silence hung over the forest and the hills.

Rusty did not immediately wake the others. He wanted this all to himself—the snow and the silence and the coming of the sun . . . .

Towards the horizon, the sky was red; and then the sun came over the hills and struck the snow; and Rusty ran to the top of the hill and stood in the dazzling sunlight, shading his eyes from the glare, taking in the range of mountains and the valley and the stream that cut its way through the snow like a dark trickle of oil. He ran down the hill and into the house.

'Wake up!' he shouted, shaking Sudheer. 'Get up, and come outside!'

'Why—have you found your treasure?' complained Sudheer sleepily. 'Or has the old man had another fit?'

'More than that—it has snowed!'

'Then I shall definitely not come outside,' said Sudheer. And turning over, he went to sleep again.

Lady with a Hookah

RUSTY glimpsed the house as they came through the trees, and he knew at once that it was the place they had been looking for. It had obviously been built by an Englishman, with its wide veranda and sloping corrugated roof, like the house in Dehra where he had lived with his guardian. It stood in the knoll of a hill, surrounded by an orchard of apple and plum trees.

'This must be the place,' said Sudheer. 'Shall we just walk in?'

'Well, the gate is open,' said Rusty.

They had barely entered the gate when a huge black Tibetan mastiff appeared on the front veranda. It did not bark, but a low growl rumbled in its throat, and this was a more dangerous portent. The dog bounded down the steps and made for the gate, and Sudheer and Rusty scrambled back up the hillside, showing no signs of their weariness. The dog remained at the gate, growling as before.

A servant-boy appeared on the veranda and called out, 'Who is it? What do you want?'

'We wish to see the lady who lives here,' replied Sudheer.

'She is resting,' said the boy. 'She cannot see anyone now.'

'We have come all the way from Dehra,' said Sudheer. 'My friend is a relative of hers. Tell her that, and she will see him.'

'She isn't going to believe that,' Rusty whispered fiercely.

The boy, with a doubtful glance at both of them, went indoors, and was gone for some five minutes. When he reappeared on the veranda, he called the dog inside and chained it to the railing. Then he beckoned to Rusty and Sudheer to follow him. They went in cautiously at the gate.

He was a fair, lynx-eyed boy, and he stared appraisingly at them for a few moments, before saying, 'She is at the back. Come with me.'

They went round the house, along a paved path, and on to another veranda which looked out on the mountains. Rusty looked first at the view, and took his eyes away from the hills only when Sudheer tugged at his sleeve; then he looked into the veranda, but he could see nothing at first because of a difference in light. Only when he stepped into the shade was he able to make out someone—a woman reclining, barefooted and wearing a white sari, on a string cot. An elaborate hookah was set before her, and its long, pliable stem rose well above the level of the bed, so that she could manœuvre it with comfort.

She looked surprisingly young. Rusty had expected to find an older woman. His aunt did not look over thirty-five; she was, in fact, forty. Having met an aged contemporary of his father's in Mr Pettigrew, he had expected his aunt to be an old woman; but now he remembered that she had been the wife of his father's younger brother. She came from a village in the higher ranges; and this accounted for her good colour, her long black hair—and her hookah. She looked physically strong, and her face, though lacking femininity, was strikingly handsome.

'Please sit down,' she said; and Sudheer and Rusty, finding that chairs had materialized from behind while they stood staring at the lady, sank into them. The boy pattered away into the interior of the house.

'You have come a long way to see me,' she said. 'It must be important.' And she looked from Rusty to Sudheer, and back to Rusty, curious to know which of them concerned her. Her eyes rested on Rusty, on his eyes, and she said, 'You are *angrez*, aren't you?'

'Partly,' he said. 'I came to see you, because—because you knew my father—and I was told—I was told you would see me . . . .' Rusty did not quite know what he should say, or how to say it.

'Your father?' she said encouraging him, and he noticed a flicker of interest in her eyes. 'Who is your father?'

'He died when I was very young,' said Rusty. And when he told her his father's name, she thrust the hookah aside and leaned forward to look closely at the boy. 'You *are* his son, then . . . .'

Rusty nodded.

'Yes, you are his son. You have his eyes and nose and forehead. I would have known it without your telling me if it had not been so dark in here.' With an agility that was another surprise to Rusty, she sprang off the cot, and pulled aside the curtains that covered one side of the veranda. Sunlight streamed in, bringing out the richness of her colouring.

'So you are only a boy,' she said, smiling at him indulgently. 'You must be sixteen—seventeen—I remember you only as a child, being taken up and down the Mall, in Mussoorie. Fourteen, fifteen years ago . . . .' She put her hands to her cheeks, as though she would feel the lines of advancing age; but her cheeks were still smooth, her youth was still with her. It came of living in the hills; of not having had children, perhaps; of having just enough of everything and not too much.

'I came to you because you knew my father well.'

They were sitting again, and Sudheer's long legs stretched across the width of the veranda. Rusty sat beside his aunt's cot.

'I wish there was something of your father's which I could give you,' she said. 'He did not leave much money. I would have offered to look after you, but I was told you had a guardian, one of your father's relatives. You must have been in good hands. Later, after my husband's death, I tried to get news of you; but I lived far from any town and was out of touch with what was happening elsewhere. I am alone now. But I don't mind. Your uncle left me this house and the land around it. I have my dog.' She stroked the huge mastiff who sat devotedly beside her. 'And I have the boy. He is a good boy and looks after me well. You are welcome to stay with us, Rusty.'

'No, I did not come for that,' said Rusty. 'You are very generous, but I do not want to be a burden on anyone.'

'You will be no burden. And if you are, it doesn't matter.' She shook her head sadly. 'How was he to know? He was well and strong one day, dying the next. But let us not depress ourselves. Come, tell me about your tall friend, and what you propose to do, and where you are going from here. It is late, and you must take your meal with us and stay the night. You will need an entire day

if you are going to Rishikesh. I have rooms and beds sufficient for
several large families.'

*

They sat together in the twilight, and Rusty told his aunt about his
quarrel with his guardian, of his friendship with Kishen and
Devinder and Sudheer the Lafunga. When it was dark, his aunt
drew a shawl around her shoulders and took them indoors; and
Bisnu, the boy, brought them food on brass *thalis*, from which they
ate sitting on the ground. Afterwards, they remained talking for
about an hour, and the Lafunga expressed his admiration for a
woman who could live alone in the hills without giving way to
loneliness or despair. Rusty tried smoking the hookah, but it gave
him a splitting headache, and when eventually he went to bed he
could not sleep. Sudheer set up a rhythmic snoring, each snore
gaining in tone and vibrancy, reminding Rusty of the brain-fever
bird he often heard in Dehra.

He left his bed and walked out on the veranda. The moon
showed through the trees, and he walked down the garden path
where fallen apples lay rotting in the moonlight. When he turned
at the gate to walk back towards the house, he saw someone
standing in the veranda. Could it be a ghost? No, it was his aunt
in her white sari, watching him.

'What is wrong, Rusty?' she asked, as he approached. 'Why
are you wandering about at this time? I thought you were a
ghost—and I was frightened, because I haven't seen one in years.'

'I've never seen one at all,' said Rusty. 'What are ghosts really
like?'

'Oh, they are usually the spirits of immoral women, and they
have their feet facing backwards. They are called *churels*. There are
other kinds, too. But why are you out here?'

'I have a headache. I couldn't sleep.'

'All right. Come and talk to me.' And taking Rusty by the
hand, she led him into her large moonlit room, and made him lie
down. Then she took his head in her hands, and with her strong
cool fingers pressed his forehead and massaged his temples; and

she began telling him a story, but her fingers were more persuasive than her tongue, and Rusty fell asleep before the tale could be finished.

Next morning, while Sudheer slept late, she took Rusty round the house and grounds.

'I have some of your books,' she said, when they came indoors. 'You are probably too old for some of them now, but your father asked me to keep them for you. Especially *Alice in Wonderland*. He was particular about that one, I don't know why.'

She brought the books out, and the sight of their covers brought back the whole world of his childhood—lazy afternoons in the shade of a jackfruit tree, a book in his hand, while squirrels and magpies chattered in the branches above. The book-shelf in his grandfather's study; the books had not been touched for years when Rusty first discovered them. *Alice* had been there, and *Treasure Island*, and *Mister Midshipman Easy*—they had been Rusty's grandfather's, then his father's and finally his own. He had read them by the time he was eight; but he had been in boarding-school when his father died, and he did not see the books again after going to live in his guardian's house.

Now, after ten years, they had turned up once more, in the possession of this strange aunt who lived alone in the mountains.

He decided to take the books, because they had once been part of his life. They were the only link between him and his father—they were his only legacy.

'Must you go back to Dehra?' asked his aunt.

'I promised my friends I would return. Later, I will decide what I should do and where I should go. During these last few months I have been a vagrant. And I used to dream of becoming a writer!'

'You can write here,' she said. 'And you can be a farmer, too.'

'Oh no, I will just be a nuisance. And anyway, I must stand on my own feet. I'm too old to be looked after by others.'

'You are old enough to look after me,' she said putting her hand on his. 'Let us be burdens on each other. I am lonely, sometimes. I know you have friends, but they cannot care for you if you are sick or in trouble. You have no parents. I have no children. It is as simple as that.'

She looked up as a shadow fell across the doorway. Sudheer was standing there in his pyjamas, grinning sheepishly at them.

'I'm hungry,' he said. 'Aunty, will you feed us before we reluctantly leave your house?'

The Road to Rishikesh

SUDHEER and Rusty set out on foot for Rishikesh, that small town straddling the banks of the Ganges where the great river emerges from the hills to stretch itself across the wide plains of northern India. In this town of saints and mendicants and pilgrims, Sudheer proposed to set up headquarters. Dehra was no longer safe, with the police and the *seth* still looking for him. He had already spent a considerable sum from the money he had appropriated; and he hoped that in Rishikesh, where all manner of men congregated, there would be scope for lucrative projects. And from Rishikesh, Rusty could take a bus to Dehra whenever he felt like returning. He had no immediate plan in mind, but was content to be on the road again with the Lafunga, as he had been with Kishen. He knew that he would soon tire of this aimless wandering, and wondered if he should return to his aunt. But for the time being he was content to wander; and with the Lafunga beside him, he felt carefree and reckless, ready for almost anything.

At noon, they arrived at a small village on the Rishikesh road. From here a bus went twice daily to Rishikesh, and they were just in time to catch the last one.

Though there was no snow, there had been rain. The road was full of slush and heaps of rubble that had fallen from the hillside. The bus carried very few passengers. Sacks of flour and potatoes took up most of the space.

The driver—unshaven, smoking a bidi—did not inspire confidence. Throughout the journey he kept up a heated political discussion with a passenger seated directly behind him. With one hand on the steering-wheel, he used the other hand to make his point, gesticulating, and shouting in order to be heard above the rattle of the bus.

Nevertheless, Sudheer and Rusty enjoyed the ride. Rusty laughed whenever Sudheer's head hit the roof, and Sudheer sought comfort from the other passengers' discomfiture.

A stalwart, good-looking young farmer sitting opposite Sudheer, said, 'I would feel safer if this was a government bus. Then, if we were killed, there would be some compensation for our families—or for us, if we were not dead!'

'Yes, let us be cheerful about these things,' said Sudheer. 'Take our driver, for instance. Do you think he is troubled at the thought of being reborn as a snake tomorrow? Not he!'

'Why should he be a snake?' asked the farmer. 'Why not a rat?'

'Well, he could be a rat,' said Sudheer. 'He's a political person, as you can see.'

They gazed out of the window, down a sheer two-hundred-foot cliff that fell to a boulder-strewn stream. The road was so narrow that they could not see the edge. Trees stood out perpendicularly from the cliff-face. A waterfall came gushing down from the hillside and sprayed the top of the bus, splashing in at the windows. The wheels of the bus turned up stones and sent them rolling downhill; they mounted the rubble of a landslip and went churning through a stretch of muddy water.

The driver was so immersed in his discussion that when he saw a boulder right in the middle of the road he did not have time to apply the brakes. It must be said to his credit that he did not take the bus over the cliff; instead, he rammed it into the hillside, and there it stuck. Being quite used to accidents of this nature, the driver sighed, re-lit his bidi, and returned to his argument.

As there were only eight miles left for Rishikesh, the passengers decided to walk.

Sudheer once more got into conversation with the farmer, whose name he now knew to be Ganpat. Most of the produce in the bus was Ganpat's; no doubt the bus would take an extra day to arrive in Rishikesh, and that would give him an excuse for prolonging his stay in town and enjoying himself out of sight of his family.

'Is there any place in Rishikesh where we can spend the night?' asked Sudheer.

'There are many *dharamsalas* for pilgrims,' said Ganpat.

Finding some purpose to their enforced trek, they set out with even longer and more vigorous strides. Ganpat had a fine sun-darkened body, a strong neck set on broad shoulders, and a heavy, almost military, moustache. He wore his dhoti well; his strong ankles and broad feet were burnished by the sun, hardened by years of walking barefoot through the fields.

Soon he and the Lafunga had discovered something in common—they were both connoisseurs of beautiful women.

'I like them tall and straight,' said Ganpat, twirling his moustache. 'They must not be too fussy, and not too talkative. How does one please them?'

'Have you heard of the great sage Vatsayana? He had three wives. One he pleased with secret confidences, the other with secret respect, and the third with secret flattery.'

'You are a strange fellow,' said Ganpat.

*

Rusty had hurried on ahead of the others. Feeling fresh and exhilarated, he had an urge to reach the river before anyone else. He wanted to be waiting for Sudheer at Rishikesh; and he wanted to be alone for a while.

A thickly forested mountain hid the river, but Rusty knew it was there and where it was and what it looked like. He had heard, from Hathi, of the fish in its waters, of its rocks and currents, and it only remained for him to touch the water and know it personally.

The path dropped steeply into a valley, then rose and went round a big mountain. Rusty passed a woodcutter and asked him how far it was to the river. The woodcutter was a short stocky man, with a creased and weathered face.

'Seven miles,' he said, fairly accurately. 'Why do you want to know?'

'I am going to Rishikesh,' said Rusty.

'Alone?'

'The others are following, but I cannot wait for them. You will meet them on the way. When you see the Lafunga, the tall one, tell him I will be waiting at the river.'

'I will tell him,' said the woodcutter, and took his leave.

The path descended steeply, and Rusty had to run a little. It was a dizzy, winding path; he slipped once or twice. The hillside was covered with lush green ferns, and, in the trees, unseen birds sang loudly. Soon he was in the valley, and the path straightened out. A girl was coming from the opposite direction. She held a long, curved knife, with which she had been cutting grass and fodder. There were rings in her nose and ears, and her arms were covered with heavy bangles. She smiled innocently at Rusty—no girl in the plains had ever done that; the bangles made music when she moved her hands—it was as though her hands spoke a language of their own.

'How far is it to the river?' asked Rusty.

The girl had probably never been near the river, or she may have been thinking of another one, for she replied, 'Twenty miles,' without any hesitation.

Rusty laughed and ran down the path. A parrot screeched suddenly, flew low over his head, a flash of blue and green. It took the course of the path, and Rusty followed its dipping flight, running until the path rose and the bird disappeared in the trees. He loved these hills, which offered him their freedom, their own individual strength, allowing the boy to be himself, Rusty. Yes, he would want to come back to them . . . .

A trickle of water came out of the hillside, and Rusty stopped to drink. The water was cold and sharp and very refreshing. He had walked alone for nearly an hour. Presently he saw another boy ahead of him, driving a few goats down the path.

'How far is the river?' asked Rusty, when he had caught up with the boy.

The village boy said, 'Oh, not far, just round the next hill and then straight down.'

Rusty, feeling hungry, produced some dry bread from his pocket and, breaking it in two, offered one half to the boy. They sat on the hillside and ate in silence. When they had finished, they walked on together and began talking; and talking, Rusty did not notice the smarting of his feet or the distance he had covered. But after some time his companion had to diverge along another path, and Rusty was once more on his own.

He missed the village boy; he looked up and down the path, but could see no one, no sign of Sudheer, and the river was not in sight either. He began to feel discouraged; he felt tired and isolated. But he walked on, along the dusty, stony path; past terraced fields and huts, until there were no more fields, only forest and sun and silence.

The silence was impressive and a little frightening; different from the silence of a room or an empty street. There was not much movement either, except for the bending of grass beneath his feet, and the circling of a hawk high above the pine trees.

And then, as he rounded a sharp bend, the silence broke into sound.

The sound of the river.

Far down in the valley, the river stretched and opened into broad, beautiful motion, and Rusty gasped and began to run. He slipped and stumbled, but still he ran. Then he was ankle-deep in the cold mountain water.

And the water was blue and white and wonderful.

End of a Journey

I T was the Festival of the Full Moon. The temples at Rishikesh
lay bathed in a soft clear light. The broad, slow-moving Ganges
caught the moonlight and held it, to become a river of liquid
silver. Along the shore, devotees floated little lights downstream.
The wicks were placed in earthen vessels, where they burned for a
few minutes, a red-gold glow. Rusty lay on the sand and watched
them float by, one by one, until they went out or were caught
amongst rocks and shingle.

Sudheer and Ganpat had gone into the town to seek
amusement, but Rusty preferred to stay by the river, at a little
distance from the embankment where hundreds of pilgrims had
gathered.

Had it been summer, he could have slept on the sand, but it
was cold, and his blanket was no protection against the icy wind
that blew down from the mountains. He went into a lighted
dharamsala, and settled down in a corner of the crowded room.
Rolling himself into his blanket, he closed his eyes, listening to the
desultory talk of pilgrims sheltering in the building.

The full moon does strange things to some people. In the hills,
it is inclined to touch off a little madness; and its effect on those
who are already a little mad—like Sudheer—is to make them
madder.

When the moon is at the full, some converse with spirits, others
lose all their inhibitions and dance in frenzied abandon; some love
more ardently, and a few kill more readily. 'Do not sleep in the light
of a full moon,' warn the pundits, 'it will bewitch you, and turn
you to beautiful but evil thoughts.'

The moon made Sudheer the Lafunga a little drunk. But the
moon not being enough, he consumed a bottle of country-made

liquor with Ganpat. The drink had confused Ganpat and affected his judgement—was he dreaming, or did he really see Sudheer hopping about in the middle of the street, slapping himself on the buttocks?

'Sudheer,' he said, steadying himself. 'Are you dancing in the road, or am I drunk?'

'You are drunk,' said Sudheer. 'But it is true that I am dancing in the road.'

'Why do you do it?' asked Ganpat.

'Because I feel happy,' said Sudheer.

'Then I must try it,' said Ganpat. And he, too, began hopping about on the road, and slapping himself on the buttocks.

*

Rishikesh comes to life at an early hour. The priests, sanyasis and their disciples rise at three, as soon as there is a little light in the sky, and begin their ablutions and meditation. From about five o'clock, pilgrims start coming down to the river to bathe. Along the bathing-steps walk saffron-robed sadhus and wandering mendicants, whilst the older and senior men sit on small edifices beneath shady trees, where they receive money and gifts from pilgrims, and dispense blessings in return.

Rusty had bathed early, leaving Sudheer and Ganpat asleep in the *dharamsala*. These two revellers had come in at two o'clock in the morning, disturbing others in the shelter. They did not get up until the sun had risen. Then Ganpat crossed the river in a ferry boat, in order to visit the temples on the other side, there to propitiate the gods with offerings of his own. Sudheer made his way outside to try and acquire a suitable disguise, as he had to visit Dehra for a few days. Dressed as he was, he would soon be spotted by the *seth's* informers. Later, he met Rusty at the bus-stand.

'I will be back tomorrow,' said Sudheer. 'I do not take you with me, because in Dehra my company would be dangerous for you.'

'Why must you be going to Dehra, then?' asked Rusty.

'Well, there are one or two people who owe me money,' he said. 'And though, as you know, we have plenty to go on with, these people are not loved by me, so why should they keep my money? And another thing. There are two beautiful women in Dehra—one is Hastini and the other Mrinalini—and I must return the money I borrowed from them.'

'And why did you borrow money from them?' asked Rusty.

'Because I owed a debt to Devinder,' said Sudheer, with a wide smile. 'And he wanted the money for you! Isn't life complicated?'

When the bus moved off in a cloud of dust, Rusty turned away. He sauntered through the bazaar, going from one sweet shop to another, assessing the quality of their different wares. Eventually he bought eight annas worth of hot, fresh, golden jalebis and, carrying them in a large plate made of banana leaves, went down to the river.

At the river-side grew a banyan tree, and Rusty sat in its shade and ate his sweets. The tree was full of birds—parrots and bulbuls and rosy pastors—feeding on the ripe red figs of the banyan. Rusty enjoyed leaning back against the trunk of the tree, listening to the chatter of the birds, studying their plumage.

When the sweets were finished, he rose and wandered along the banks of the river. On a stretch of sand two boys were wrestling. They were on their knees, arms interlocked, pressing forward like mad bulls, each striving to throw the other. The taller boy had the advantage at first; the smaller boy, who was dark and pock-marked, appeared to be yielding; but then there was a sudden flurry of arms and legs, and the small boy sat victorious across his opponent's chest.

When they saw Rusty watching them, the boys asked him if he would like to wrestle. But Rusty declined the invitation. He had eaten too many jalebis and felt sick.

He walked until the sickness had passed and he was hungry again (the trek to Rishikesh had increased his already healthy appetite), and returning to the bazaar, he feasted on puris and a well-spiced vegetable curry.

Well-stuffed with puris, he returned to the banyan tree, and slept right through the afternoon.

*

At midnight, in Dehra, Sudheer was paying a clandestine visit to Mrinalini. Knowing that he would have to stay away for some time, he wished to see her just once again, in order to make her a gift and a promise of his fidelity.

It took him a few seconds to climb the treacherous flight of stairs that led to Mrinalini's rooms. Every time he climbed those stairs, they swayed and plunged about more heavily.

Mrinalini was preparing herself for a visitor; she sat in front of a cracked, discoloured mirror which distorted her fine features into hideous dimensions. Whenever she looked into the distorting mirror, and saw the bloated face, the crooked eyes, the smear of paint, she thought: One day I will look like that; one day, not long from now, I will be as ugly as that reflection . . . . And when she looked in the mirror again, it was always the reflection of her mother that she saw.

By contrast, Sudheer's reflection, when it appeared beside her in the mirror, reminded her of a horse—a horse with a rather long and silly face. And seeing it there, she laughed.

'What are you laughing at?' said Sudheer.

'At you, of course! You look so stupid in the mirror!'

'I did not know that,' said Sudheer, his vanity a little hurt. 'Hastini does not think so.'

'Hastini is a fool. She liked you because she thinks you are handsome. I like you because you have a face like a horse.'

'Well, your horse is going to be away from Dehra for some time. I hope you will not miss him.'

'You are always coming and going, but never staying.'

'That's life.'

'Doesn't it make you lonely?'

Mrinalini had stood up from the mirror, and now she went over to the bed, where she made herself comfortable against a pillow.

'When I am lonely, I do something,' said Sudheer, standing over her, looking very tall. 'I go out and do something foolish or dangerous. When I am not doing things, I am lonely. But I was not made for loneliness.'

'I am lonely sometimes.'

'You! With your mother? She never leaves you alone. And you have visitors nearly every day, and many new faces.'

'Yes. The more people I see, the lonelier I get. You must have some companion, someone to talk to and quarrel with, if you are not to be lonely. You can find such a companion. But who can I find? My mother is old and deaf and heartless.'

'One day I will come and take you away from here. I have some money now, Mrinalini. As soon as I have started a business in another town, I will call you there. Meanwhile, why not stay with Hastini?'

'I hate her.'

'You do not know her yet. When you know her, you will love her!'

'*You* love her.'

'I love her because she is so comfortable. I love you because you are so sweet. Can I help it if I love you both?'

'You are strange,' said Mrinalini with one of her rare smiles. 'Go now. Someone will be coming.'

'Then keep this for me,' said Sudheer.

He took a thin gold ring from his finger, and slipped it on to the third finger of Mrinalini's right hand.

'Keep it for me till I return,' he said. 'And if I do not return, then keep it for ever. Sell it only if you are in need. All right?'

Mrinalini stared at the ring for some time, turning it about on her finger, so that the light fell on it in different places. She slipped it off her finger and hid it in her blouse.

'If I keep it on my hand, my mother will be sure to take it.'

Sudheer said, 'If only you would allow me, I'd finish off your mother for you.'

'Don't talk like that! She has not long to live . . . . '

'She is doing her best to outlive all of us. I would not be violent, I promise you. I would not even touch her. I would simply frighten her to death. I could pounce on her from a dark alley, or let off a firecracker . . . . '

'Sudheer!' cried Mrinalini. 'How can you be so cruel?'

'It would be a kindness.'

'Go now! Stay away from Dehra as long as you can.'

*

It was a wonderful morning in Rishikesh. There was a hint of spring in the air. Birds flashed across the water, and monkeys chased each other over the rooftops. Rusty lay on a stretch of sand, drinking in the crisp morning air, letting the sun sink into his body.

He had risen early, and had gone down to the river to bathe. Even before the *pujaris* had risen, he had run into the river, gasping with the shock of the cold water, threshing and embracing it, until the sluggishness left his body, and he felt clean and fresh and happy.

The touch of the water brought memories of his own secret pool that lay in the forest behind the church. Perhaps Devinder would be there now; perhaps Kishen, too, had joined him for the morning dip; and the Goonga would be sitting on a buffalo.

Rusty sat on the sand, nostalgically thinking of his friends; but there was another pull now, from the house in the hills; and he was certain that his future did not lie in Dehra. He decided he would leave Rishikesh immediately as soon as the Lafunga returned. After all, Sudheer was experienced in the ways of the world, and was never lacking in friends. Devinder and Kishen were of Rusty's age. He could understand and love them; and they could join him later. He could only love the Lafunga; he could not understand him.

Rusty lay on the white sand until the voices of distant bathers reached him, and the sun came hurrying over the hills. Slipping on his shirt and trousers, he went to the bazaar, where he found a little tea-shop; and there he drank a glass of hot, sweet, milky tea, and ate six eggs, to the amazement of the shopkeeper.

When he had finished eating, he strolled down to the bus-stand to see if Sudheer had returned. The second bus from Dehra had arrived, but Sudheer was not to be seen anywhere. Rusty was about to go back when, turning, he found himself looking into the eyes of a distinguished-looking young sadhu, who had three vermilion stripes across his forehead, an orange robe wound about his thighs and shoulders, and an extremely unsaintly grin on his face. The disguise might have deceived Rusty, but not the grin.

'So now you have become a sadhu,' said Rusty. 'And for whose benefit is this?'

'It was for some business in Dehra,' said Sudheer. 'I did not wish to be seen by the *seth* or his servants. Let us find a quiet place where we can talk. And let us get some fruit, I am hungry.'

Rusty bought six apples from a stall, and took Sudheer to the banyan tree. They sat on the ground, talking and munching apples.

'Did you see your friends?' asked Rusty.

'Yes, I went to them first. The bus had made me tired and angry, and there is no one like Hastini for soothing and refreshing one. Then I went to Mrinalini and asked her to come to Rishikesh, but she is still waiting for her mother to die. In life, people do nothing but wait for other people to die.'

Sudheer was already making new plans. 'Do I look all right?' he asked.

'You look as handsome as ever.'

'I know that. But do I look like a sadhu?'

'Yes, a very handsome sadhu.'

'All the better. Come, let us go.'

'Where do we go?' asked Rusty.

'To took for disciples, of course. A sadhu, such as I, must have disciples, and they should be rich disciples. There must be many fat, rich men in the world, who are unhappy about their consciences. Come, we will be their consciences! We will be respectable, Rusty. There is more money to be made that way. Yes, we will be respectable—what an adventure that will be!'

They began walking towards the bazaar.

'Wait!' said Rusty. 'I cannot come with you, Sudheer!'

Sudheer came to an abrupt halt. He turned and faced Rusty, a puzzled and disturbed expression on his face.

'What do you mean, you cannot come with me?'

'I must return to Dehra. I may come this way again, if I want to live with my aunt.'

'But why? You have just left her. You came to the hills for money, didn't you? And she didn't have any money.'

'I wanted to see her, too. I wanted to know what she was like. It isn't just a matter of money.'

'Well, you saw her. And there is no future for you with her, or in Dehra. What's the use of returning?'

'I don't know, Sudheer. What's the use of anything, for that matter? What would be the use of staying with you? I want to give some direction to my life. I want to work, I want to be free, I want to be able to write. I can't wander about the hills and plains with you for ever.'

'Why not? There is nothing to stop you, if you like to wander. India has always been the home of wanderers.'

'I might join you again, if I fail at everything else.'

Sudheer looked sullen and downcast.

'You do not realize . . . . ' he began; but stopped, groping for the right words; he had seldom been at a loss for words. 'I have got used to you, that is all,' he said.

'And I have got used to you, Sudheer. I don't think anyone else has ever done that.'

'That's why I don't want to lose you. But I cannot stop you from going.'

'I shall come to see you, I will, really . . . . '

Sudheer brightened up a little. 'Do you promise? Or do you say that just to please me?'

'Both.'

Sudheer was his old self again, smiling, and digging his fingers into Rusty's arms. 'I'll be waiting for you,' he said. 'Whenever you want to look for treasure, come to me! Whenever you are looking for fun, come to me!'

Then he was silent again, and a shadow passed across his face. Did he, after all, know the meaning of loneliness? Perhaps Mrinalini had been right when she had said, 'You must have some companion, someone to talk to and quarrel with, if you are not to be lonely . . . . '

'Let us part now,' said Sudheer. 'Let us not prolong it. You go down the street, to the bus-stand, and I'll go the other way.'

He held out his hand to Rusty. 'Your hand is not enough,' he said, and he put his arms round Rusty, and embraced him.

People stopped to stare; not because two youths were demonstrating their affection for each other—that was common enough—but because a sadhu in a saffron robe was behaving out of character.

When Sudheer realized this, he grinned at the passers-by; and they, embarrassed by his grin, and made nervous by his height, hurried on down the street.

Sudheer turned and walked away.

Rusty watched him for some time. The Lafunga stood out distinctly from the crowd of people in the bazaar, tall and handsome in his flowing robe.

First and Last Impressions

B ECAUSE he had told no one of his return, there was no one to meet Rusty at Dehra station when he stepped down from a third class compartment. But on his way through the bazaar he met one of the tea-shop boys, who told him that Devinder might be found near the Clock Tower. And so he went to the Clock Tower, but he could not find his friend. Another familiar, a shoeshine boy, said he had last seen Devinder near the Courts, where business was brisk that day.

Rusty, feeling tired and dirty after his journey, decided he would look for Devinder later, and made his way to the church compound where he left his bag. Then he went through the jungle to the pool.

The Goonga was already there, bathing in the shallows, gesticulating and shouting incomprehensibles at a band of langur monkeys who were watching him from the sal trees. When the Goonga saw Rusty, he chortled with delight, and rushed out of the water to give his friend and protector a hug.

'And how are you?' asked Rusty.

'Goo,' said the Goonga.

He was evidently very well. Devinder had been feeding him, and he no longer had need to prowl around tea-shops and receive kicks and insults in exchange for a glass of tea or a stale bun.

Rusty took off his clothes and leapt into the cold, sweet, delicious water of the pool. He floated languidly on the water, gazing up through the branches of an overhanging sal, through a pattern of broad tree leaves, into a blind-blue sky. The Goonga sat on a rock and grinned at the monkeys, making encouraging sounds. Looking from the Goonga to the monkeys and back to the hairy, long-armed youth, Rusty wondered how anyone could doubt Darwin's theories.

'And quite obviously. I belong to the same species,' he thought, joining the Goonga on the rock and making noises of his own. 'Oh, to be a langur, without a care in the world. Acorns and green leaves to feed on, lots of friends, and no romantic complications. But no books either. I suppose being human has its advantages. Not that it would make any difference to the Goonga.'

He was soon dry. He lay on his tummy, flat against the warm smooth rock surface. He wanted to sink deep into that beautiful rock.

'Goo,' said the Goonga, as though he approved.

Then the sun was in the pool and the pool was in the sky and the rock had swallowed Rusty up, and when he woke he thought the Goonga was still beside him; but when he raised his head and looked, he saw that Devinder sat there—Devinder looking cool and clean in a white shirt and pyjamas, his tray lying on the ground a little way off.

'How long have you been here?' asked Rusty.

'I just came. It is good to see you. I was afraid you had left for good.'

'I'm hungry,' said Rusty.

'I'm glad you haven't lost your appetite. I have brought you something to eat.' He produced a paper bag filled with hot bazaar food, and a couple of oranges.

While Rusty ate, he told Devinder of his journey. Devinder was disappointed.

'So there was nothing for you, except a few books. I know money isn't everything, but it's time you had some of it, Rusty. How long can you carry on like this? You can't sell combs and buttons like me. You wouldn't know how to; you're a dreamer, a kind of poet, and you can't live on dreams. You don't have rich friends and relatives, like Kishen, to provide intervals of luxury. You're not like Sudheer, able to live on your wits. There's only this aunt of yours in the hills—and you can't spend the rest of your life lost in the mountains like a hermit. It will take you years to become a successful writer. Look at Goldsmith—borrowing money all the time! And you haven't even started yet.'

'I know, Devinder. You don't have to tell me. Tomorrow I'll

go and see Mr Pettigrew. Perhaps he can help me in some way—perhaps he can find me a job.'

They were silent, gazing disconsolately into the pool.

'Have you seen Kishen?' asked Rusty.

'Once, in the bazaar. He was with that girl, his cousin. They were on bicycles. I think they were going to the cinema. Kishen seemed happy enough. He stopped and spoke to me and asked me when you would be back. They will soon be sending him back to school. That's good, isn't it? He'll never be able to manage without a proper education. Degrees and things.'

'Well, Sudheer has managed well enough without one. You might call him self-educated. And Kishen is worldly enough. Also, he's a Punjabi. No one is likely to get the better of him. All the same, you're right. A couple of degrees behind your name could make all the difference, even if you can't put them down in the right order!'

Already the dream was fading. That's life, thought Rusty; you can't run away from it and survive. You can't be a vagrant for ever. You're getting nowhere, so you've got to stop somewhere. Kishen has stopped; he's thrown in his lot with the settled incomes; he had to. Even Mowgli left the wolf-pack to return to his own people. And India was changing. This great formless mass was taking some sort of shape at last. He had to stop now, and find a place for himself, or go forward to disaster.

'I'll see him tomorrow,' said Rusty. 'I'll see Kishen and say goodbye.'

*

Rusty decided he would leave his books with Mr Pettigrew instead of in the church vestry, a transient abode; so he put them in his bag and, after tea with Devinder near the Clock Tower, set out for the tea-gardens.

He crossed the dry river-bed and the yellow mustard fields which stretched away to the foothills, and found Mr Pettigrew sitting on his veranda as though he had not moved from his cane chair since Rusty had last visited him. Pettigrew gazed out across

214

the flat tea bushes. He seemed to look through Rusty, and at first the boy thought he had not been recognized. Perhaps the old man had forgotten him!

'Good morning,' said Rusty. 'I'm back.'

'The poinsettia leaves have turned red,' said Pettigrew. 'Another winter is passing.'

'Yes.'

'Full sixty hot summers have besieged my brow. I'm growing old so *slowly*. I wish there could be some action to make the process more interesting. Not that I feel very active, but I'd like to have something happening around me. A jolly old riot would be just the thing. You know what I mean, of course?'

'I think so,' said Rusty.

It was loneliness again. In a week Rusty had found two lonely people—his aunt, and this elderly gentleman, moving slowly through the autumn of their lives. It was beginning to affect him. He looked at Mr Pettigrew and wondered if he would be like that one day—alone, not very strong, living in the past, with a bottle of whisky to sustain him through the still, lonely evenings. Rusty had friends—but so had Pettigrew, in his youth. Rusty had books to read, and books to write—but Pettigrew had books, too; did they make much difference? Weren't there any permanent flesh and blood companions to be found outside the conventions of marriage and business?

Pettigrew seemed suddenly to realize that Rusty was standing beside him. A spark of interest showed in his eyes. It flickered and grew into comprehension.

'Drinking in the mornings. that's my trouble. You've returned very soon. Sit down, my boy, sit down. Tell me—did you find the lady? Did she know you? Was it any good?'

Rusty sat down on a step, for there was no chair on the veranda apart from Mr Pettigrew's.

'Yes, she knew me. She was very kind and wanted to help me. But she had nothing of mine, except some old books which my father had left with her.'

'Books! Is that all? You've brought them with you, I see.'

'I thought perhaps you'd keep them for me until I'm properly settled somewhere.'

Mr Pettigrew took the books from Rusty and thumbed through them.

'Stevenson, Ballantyne, Marryat, and some early P. G. Wodehouse. I expect you've read them. And here's *Alice in Wonderland*. "How doth the little crocodile . . . ." Tenniel's drawings. It's a first edition, methinks! It couldn't be—or *could* it?'

Mr Pettigrew fell silent. He studied the title page and the back of the title-leaf with growing interest and solicitude and then with something approaching reverence; for he knew something about books and printing and the value of the first edition. And a first edition of *Alice* would be a rare find.

'It could be, at that,' said Pettigrew, almost to himself, and Rusty was bewildered by the transformation on the old man's face. Ennui had given place to enthusiasm.

'Could be what, sir?'

'A first edition.'

'It was once my grandfather's book. His name is on the fly-leaf.'

'It *must* be a first. No wonder your father treasured it.'

'Is being a first edition very important?'

'Yes, from the book-collector's point of view. In England, on the Continent, and in America, there are people who collect rare works of literature—manuscripts, and the first editions of books that have since become famous. The value of a book depends on its literary worth, its scarcity, and its condition.'

'Well, *Alice* is a famous book. And this is a good copy. Is a first edition of it rare?'

'It certainly is. There are only two or three known copies.'

'And do you think this is one?'

'Well, I'm not an expert, but I do know something about books. This is the first printing. And it's in good condition, except for a few stains on the fly-leaf.'

'Let's rub them off.'

'No, don't touch a thing—don't tamper with its condition. I'll write to a bookseller friend of mine in London for his advice. I think this should be worth a good sum of money to you—several hundred pounds.'

'Hundreds!' exclaimed Rusty disbelievingly.

'Five or six hundred, maybe more. Your father must have known the book was valuable and meant you to have it one day. Perhaps this was his legacy.'

Rusty was silent, taking in the import of what Mr Pettigrew had told him. He had never had much money in his life. A few hundred pounds would take him anywhere he wanted to go. It was also, he knew, quite easy to go through a sum of money, no matter how large the amount.

Pettigrew was glancing through the other books. 'None of these are first, except the Wodehouse novels, and you'll have to wait some time with those. But *Alice* is the real thing. My friend will arrange its sale.'

'It would be nice to keep it,' said Rusty.

Mr Pettigrew looked up in surprise. 'In other circumstances, my boy, I'd say keep it. Become a book-collector yourself. But when you're down on your beam-ends, you can't afford to be sentimental. Now leave this business in my hands, and let me advance you some money. Furthermore, this calls for a celebration!'

He poured himself a stiff whisky and offered Rusty a drink.

'I don't mind if I do,' said Rusty, bestowing his rare smile on the old man.

Later, after lunching with Mr Pettigrew, Rusty sat out on the veranda with the old man and discussed his future.

'I think you should go to England,' said Mr Pettigrew.

'I've thought of that before,' said Rusty, 'but I've always felt that India is my home.'

'But can you make a living here? After all, even Indians go abroad at the first opportunity. And you want to be a writer. You can't become one overnight, certainly not in India. It will take years of hard work, and even then—even if you're good—you may not make the reputation that means all the difference between failure and success. In the meantime, you've got to make a living at something. And what can you do in India? Let's face it, my boy, you've only just finished school. There are graduates who can't get jobs. Only last week a young man with a degree in the Arts came to me and asked my help in getting him a job as a petty clerk in the tea-estate manager's office. A clerk! Is that why he went to college—to become a clerk?'

Rusty did not argue the point. He knew that it was only people with certain skills who stood a chance. It was an age of specialization. And he did not have any skills, apart from some skill with words.

'You can always come back,' said Mr Pettigrew. 'If you are successful, you'll be free to go wherever you please. And if you aren't successful, well then, you can make a go of something else—if not in England, then in some other English-speaking country, America or Australia or Canada or the Cook Islands!'

'Why didn't you leave India, Mr Pettigrew?'

'For reasons similar to yours. Because I'd lived many years in India and had grown to love the country. But unlike you, I'm at the fag-end of my life. And it's easier to fade away in the hot sun than in the cold winds of Blighty.'

He looked out rather wistfully at his garden, at the tall marigolds and bright clumps of petunia and the splurge of bougainvillaea against the wall.

'My journeyings are over,' he said. 'And yours have just begun.'

*

It was dark when Rusty slipped over a wall and moved silently round the porch of Mrs Bhushan's house. There was a light showing in the front room and Rusty crept up to the window and looked in, pressing his face against the glass. He felt the music in the room even before he heard it. It came vibrating through the glass with a pulsating rhythm. Kishen and Aruna, both barefooted, were gyrating on the floor in a frenzy of hip-shivering movement. Their faces were blank. They did not sing. All expression was confined to their plunging torsos.

Rusty decided it was not a propitious moment for calling on his old friend. And this was confirmed a few minutes later by the throaty blare of a horn and the glare of a car's headlights.

Mrs Bhushan's Hillman was turning in at the gate. The music came to a sudden stop. Rusty dodged behind a rose-bush, stung his hands on nettle, and remained hidden until Mrs Bhushan had alighted from her car. He was moving cautiously through the shrubbery when one of the dogs started barking. Others took up the chorus.

Rusty was soon clambering over the wall, with two or three cockers snapping at his feet and trousers. He ran down the road until he found the entrance to a dark lane, down which he disappeared.

He slowed to a walk as he approached the crowded bazaar area. He was annoyed and a little depressed at not having been able to see Kishen, but he had to admit that Kishen appeared to be quite happy in Mrs Bhushan's house. Aruna had made all the difference; for Kishen was beginning to grow up.

Perhaps, thought Rusty, I'd better not see him at all.

Start of a Journey

EVENTS moved swiftly—as they usually do, once a specific plan is set in motion—and within a few weeks Rusty was in possession of a passport, a rail ticket to Bombay, his boat ticket, an income tax clearance certificate (this had been the most difficult to obtain, in spite of the fact that he had no income), a smallpox vaccination certificate, various other bits and pieces of paper, and about fifty rupees in cash advanced by Mr Pettigrew. The money for *Alice* would not be realized for several months, and could be drawn upon in London.

He was late for his train. The tonga he had hired turned out to be the most ancient of Dehra's dwindling fleet of pony-drawn carriages. The pony was old, slow and dyspeptic. It stopped every now and then to pass quantities of wind. The tonga-driver turned out to be a bhang-addict who had not quite woken up from his last excursion into dreamland. The carriage itself was a thing of shreds and patches. It lay at an angle, and rolled from side to side. This motion seemed designed to suit the condition of the driver, who dozed off every now and then.

'If it hadn't been for your luggage,' said Devinder, 'we would have done better to walk.'

At their feet was a new suitcase and a spacious hold-all given to Rusty by Mr Pettigrew. Devinder, Rusty and the tonga-driver were the only occupants of the carriage.

'Please hurry,' begged Rusty of the tonga-driver. 'I'll miss the train.'

'Miss the train?' mumbled the tonga-driver, coming out of his coma. 'No one ever misses the train—not when *I* take them to the station!'

'Why, does the train wait for you to arrive?' asked Devinder.

'Oh, no,' said the driver. 'But it waits.'

'Well, it should have left at seven,' said Rusty. 'And it's five past seven now. Even if it leaves on time, which means ten minutes late, we won't catch it at this speed.'

'You will be there in ten minutes, sahib.' And the man called out an endearment to his pony.

Neither Rusty nor Devinder could make out what the tonga-driver said, but it did wonders to the pony. The beast came to life as though it had been injected with a new wonder hormone. Rusty and Devinder were jerked upright in their seats. The pony kicked up its hind legs and plunged forward, and cyclists and pedestrians scattered for safety. They raced through the town, followed by oaths and abuse from a vegetable-seller whose merchandise had been spilled on the road. Only at the station entrance did the pony slow down and then, as suddenly and unaccountably as it had come to life, it returned to its former dispirited plod.

Paying off the man, Rusty and Devinder grabbed hold of the luggage and tumbled on to the railway platform. Here they barged into Kishen who, having heard of Rusty's departure (from the barber, who had got it from an egg-vendor, who had got it from Devinder), had come to see him off.

'You didn't tell me anything,' said Kishen with an injured look. 'You seem to have forgotten me altogether.'

'I hadn't forgotten you, bhaiya. I did come to see you once—but I couldn't bring myself to say goodbye. It seems so final, saying goodbye. I wanted to slip away quietly, that's all.'

'How selfish you are!' said Kishen.

A last-minute quarrel with Kishen was the last thing Rusty wanted.

'We must hurry,' said Devinder urgently. 'The train is about to leave.'

The guard was blowing his whistle, and there was a final scramble among the passengers. If sardines could take a look at the situation in a third class railway compartment, they would not have anything to complain about. It is a perfect example of the individual being swallowed up by the mass, of a large number of identities merging into one corporate whole. Your leg, you discover, is not yours but your neighbour's; the growth of hair on your shoulder is someone's beard; and the cold wind whistling down your neck is his asthmatic breath, a baby materializes in your lap and is reclaimed only after it has wet your trousers; and the corner of a seat which you had happily thought was your own green spot on this earth is suddenly usurped by a huge Sikh with a sword dangling at his side. Rusty knew from experience in third class compartments that if he did not get into one of them immediately, his way would be permanently barred.

'There's no room anywhere,' said Kishen cheerfully. 'You'd better go tomorrow.'

'The boat sails in three days,' said Rusty.

'Then come on, let's squeeze you in somewhere.'

Managing the luggage themselves, and ignoring the protests of the station coolies, they hurried down the length of the platform looking for a compartment less crowded than most. They discovered an open door and a space within, and bundled Rusty and his worldly goods into it.

'It's empty!' said Rusty in delight. 'There's no one in it.'

'Of course not,' said Kishen. 'It's a first class compartment.'

But the train was already in motion and there was no time to get out.

'You can shift into another compartment after Hardwar,' said Kishen. 'The train won't be so crowded, then.'

Rusty closed the door and stuck his head out of the window. Perhaps this mad, confusing departure was the best thing that could have happened. It was impossible to say goodbye in dignified solemnity. And Rusty would have hated a solemn, tearful departure. Devinder and Kishen had time only to look relieved—relieved at having been able to get Rusty into the train. They would not realize, till later, that he was going forever out of their lives.

He waved to them from the window, and they waved back, smiling and wishing him luck. They were not dismayed at his departure. Rather, they were pleased that Rusty's life had taken a new direction; they were impressed by his good fortune, and they took it for granted that he would come back some day, with money and honours. Such is the optimism of youth.

Rusty waved until his friends were lost in the milling throng on the platform, until the station lights were a distant glow. And then the train was thundering through the swift-falling darkness of India. He looked in the glass of the window and saw his own face dimly reflected. And he wondered if he would ever come back.

There was someone else's reflection in the glass, and he realized that he was not alone in the compartment. Someone had just come out of the washroom and was staring at Rusty in some surprise. A familiar face, a foreigner. The man Rusty had met at the Raiwala waiting-room, when he had been travelling with Kishen to Dehra in different circumstances.

'We meet again,' said the American. 'Remember me?'

'Yes,' said Rusty. 'We seem to share a fondness for trains.'

'Well, I have to make this journey every week.'

'How is your work?'

'Much the same. I'm trying, but with little success, to convince farmers that a steel plough will pay greater dividends than a wooden plough.'

'And they aren't convinced?'

'Oh, they're quite prepared to be convinced. Trouble is, they find it cheaper and easier to *repair* a wooden plough. You see how complicated everything is? It's a question of parts. For want of a bolt, the plough was lost, for want of a plough the crop was lost, for want of a crop . . . . And where are *you* going, friend? I see you're alone this time.'

'Yes, I'm going away. I'm leaving India.'

'Where are you going? England?'

Rusty nodded. He looked out of the window in time to see a shooting-star skid across the heavens and vanish. A bad omen; but he was defiant of omens.

'I'm going to England,' he said. 'I'm going to Europe and America and Japan and Timbuctoo. I'm going everywhere, and no one can stop me!'

READ MORE IN PENGUIN

In every corner of the world, on every subject under the sun, Penguin represents quality and variety—the very best in publishing today.

For complete information about books available from Penguin—including Puffins, Penguin Classics and Arkana—and how to order them, write to us at the appropriate address below. Please note that for copyright reasons the selection of books varies from country to country.

In India: Please write to *Penguin Books India Pvt. Ltd. 11 Community Centre, Panchsheel Park, New Delhi 110017*

In the United Kingdom: Please write to *Dept JC, Penguin Books Ltd. Bath Road, Harmondsworth, West Drayton. Middlesex, UB7 ODA. UK*

In the United States: Please write to *Penguin Putnam Inc., 375 Hudson Street, New York, NY 10014*

In Canada: Please write to *Penguin Books Canada Ltd. 10 Alcorn Avenue, Suite 300, Toronto, Ontario M4V 3B2*

In Australia: Please write to *Penguin Books Australia Ltd. 487, Maroondah Highway, Ring Wood, Victoria 3134*

In New Zealand: Please write to *Penguin Books (NZ) Ltd. Private Bag, Takapuna, Auckland 9*

In the Netherlands: Please write to *Penguin Books Netherlands B.V., Keizersgracht 231 NL-1016 DV Amsterdom*

In Germany : Please write to *Penguin Books Deutschland GmbH, Metzlerstrasse 26, 60595 Frankfurt am Main, Germany*

In Spain: Please write to *Penguin Books S.A., Bravo Murillo, 19-1'B, E-28015 Madrid, Spain*

In Italy: Please write to *Penguin Italia s.r.l., Via Felice Casati 20, I-20104 Milano*

In France: Please write to *Penguin France S.A., 17 rue Lejeune, F-31000 Toulouse*

In Japan: Please write to *Penguin Books Japan. Ishikiribashi Building, 2-5-4, Suido, Tokyo 112*

In Greece: Please write to *Penguin Hellas Ltd, dimocritou 3, GR-106 71 Athens*

In South Africa: Please write to *Longman Penguin Books Southern Africa (Pty) Ltd, Private Bag X08, Bertsham 2013*

S/EAS/3730/08/05